VALLEY COMMUNITY LIBRARY
739 RIVER STREET
PECKVILLE, PA 18452
 (570) 489-1765
www.lclshome.org

The Hooded Hawke

AN ELIZABETH I MYSTERY

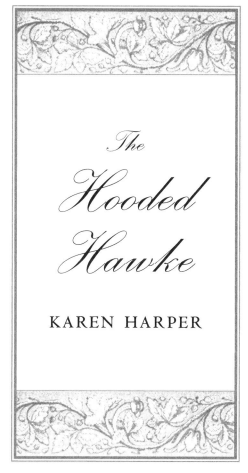

The

Hooded

Hawke

KAREN HARPER

THOMAS DUNNE BOOKS
ST. MARTIN'S MINOTAUR ✻ NEW YORK

This is a work of fiction. All of the characters, organizations, and events portrayed in this novel are either products of the author's imagination or are used fictitiously.

THOMAS DUNNE BOOKS.
An imprint of St. Martin's Press.

www.thomasdunnebooks.com
www.minotaurbooks.com

Map and Timeline by Paul J. Pugliese

Library of Congress Cataloging-in-Publication Data

Harper, Karen (Karen S.)
    The hooded hawke : an Elizabeth I mystery / Karen Harper.—1st ed.
      p. cm.
    ISBN-13: 978-0-312-33887-9
    ISBN-10: 0-312-33887-2
    1. Elizabeth I, Queen of England, 1533–1603—Fiction. 2. Falconry—Fiction.
3. Queens—Fiction. 4. Great Britain—History—Elizabeth, 1558–1603—Fiction.

PS3558.A624792 H66 2005
813'.54—dc22

                                                          2006050561

First Edition: February 2007

10 9 8 7 6 5 4 3 2 1

I started to write this ninth novel in the series, which begins in Elizabethan London, on the very morning terrorists bombed modern London, July 7, 2005. Ironically, this novel is about early terrorism in the queen's realm.

London and Londoners have been through many dangers and deadly assaults, but like their current Queen Elizabeth—and the brilliant and bold first Queen Elizabeth—the English not only survive but thrive.

The names of several of the sites bombed, such as Aldgate and King's Cross, would have been familiar to the English of the Tudor age, such is the living history in that place.

I love London, where my husband and I have often visited, and dedicate this book to the people of that vital city, beloved also of Her Majesty Elizabeth I, who may be my amateur sleuth but who, during her long reign, was a very professional queen.

—Karen Harper

Earlier Events Affecting Elizabeth

1533   Henry VIII marries Anne Boleyn, January 25. Elizabeth born at Greenwich Palace, September 7.

1536   Anne Boleyn executed in Tower of London. Elizabeth disinherited from crown. Henry marries Jane Seymour.

1537   Prince Edward born. Queen Jane dies of childbed fever.

1538 or 1539   Francis Drake born in Tavistock, England.

1542   Execution of Katherine Howard, Henry's fifth queen. Birth in Scotland of Mary Stuart, who becomes Queen of Scots as an infant at death of James V of Scotland this year.

1544   Act of Succession and Henry's will establish Mary Tudor and Elizabeth in line to throne.

1547   Henry VIII dies. Edward VI crowned.

1553   Queen Mary (Tudor) I crowned. She tries to force England back to Catholicism. Weds Philip of Spain.

1558   Queen Mary dies; Elizabeth succeeds to throne. Elizabeth appoints William Cecil principal secretary of state; Robert Dudley made master of the queen's horse.

1560   Death of Francis II of France makes his young wife, Mary Stuart, a widow. Mary soon returns home to Scotland.

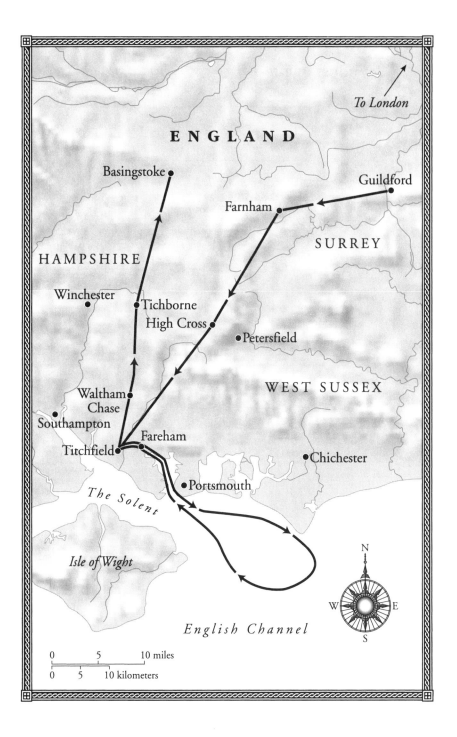

HOUSE OF TUDOR

```
        ┌──────────────────────────────────┬──────────────────────────────────┐
  Arthur (d 1502)                                    Henry VIII (d 1547)
  m Catherine of Aragon                                     m
```

(1)	(2)	(3)	(4)
Catherine of Aragon	Anne Boleyn	Jane Seymour	Anne of Cleves
(d 1536)	(x 1536)	(d 1537)	(d 1557)
Mary I	Elizabeth I	Edward VI	
(d 1558)	(d 1603)	(d 1553)	
m Philip II of Spain			

HOUSE OF HOWARD

John Howard,
1st Duke of Norfolk (d 1485)
m Catherine Moleyns

Thomas, 2nd Duke of Norfolk (d 1524
m

(1)
Elizabeth Tilney

Thomas, 3rd Duke of Norfolk
(d 1554)
m

Lady Elizabeth Stafford
(d 1558)

Henry, Earl of Surrey (x 1547)   Mary
m Lady Frances Vere   m Henry Fitzroy, Duke of Richmond,
                                              illegitimate son of Henry VIII
Thomas, 4th Duke of Norfolk   (d 1536)
(x 1572)

(Issue)

Henry VII (d 1509)
m Elizabeth of York (d 1503)

Margaret (d 1541)   Mary (d 1533) Issue
m

(5)   (6)   (1)   (2)
atherine   Catherine Parr   James IV of Scotland   Archibald,
Ioward   (d 1548)   (d 1513)   Earl of Angus (d 1557)
‹ 1542)   m (2) Thomas
                 Seymour   James V (d 1542)   Margaret Douglas
                                m Mary of Guise   (d 1578)
                                   (d 1560)   m Matthew Stewart,
                                                      Earl of Lennox (d 1571)

                           Mary, Queen of Scots m (2) Henry Stuart,
                                   (x 1587)   Lord Darnley
                                                          (d 1567)

                                               James I (VI of Scotland)

                                               HOUSE OF STUART

                    Elizabeth   other children
                m Thomas Boleyn

        Mary   Anne Boleyn   George, Viscount Rochford (x 1536)
    m William Carey   (x 1536)   m Jane Parker (x 1542)
                           Henry VIII

        (Issue)   Elizabeth I

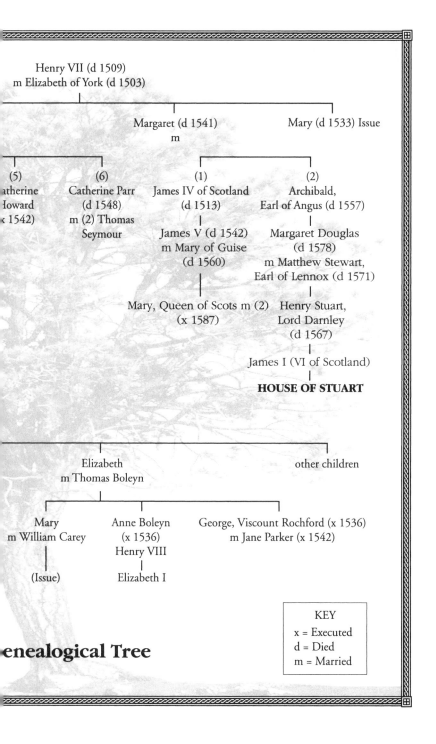

KEY
x = Executed
d = Died
m = Married

enealogical Tree

For look! The wicked bend their bow,
They make ready their arrow on the string,
That they may shoot secretly at the upright in heart.
—PSALM 11:2

Every heart with thought disloyal
Will I dislodge from my court royal;
The bad will find no welcome here,
And no good cheer.

My eyes will be most sharp to find
Dwellers on earth of faithful mind
To me; for he who has true sight
Will serve me right.

He who takes pains to use deceit
Within my house will find no seat;
Never from me will liar or babbler
Get gift or favor.

—FROM A POEM BY CLÉMENT MAROT,
QUOTED BY ELIZABETH TUDOR
IN HER JOURNAL, 1569

The Hooded Hawke

Prologue

ST. JAMES'S PARK, LONDON
MONDAY, AUGUST 1, 1569

 THOUGH SHE WAS RIDING SIDESADDLE WITH BUT ONE hand holding the reins, Elizabeth Tudor spurred her horse to a faster gait, forcing the others to keep up with her. Her crimson hair spilled loose from her snood, her skirt flapped, and the hooded hawk perched on her leather-gauntleted hand spread her great gray wings as if to fly.

The queen was desperate to escape the palace, where problems proliferated like rabbits, or rather, she thought, like rats—perhaps even the sort that leave a leaking ship. She heaved a huge sigh.

"Your Grace, what's amiss?" her dear friend Robert Dudley, Earl of Leicester, who alone kept pace beside her, asked. "Do you feel well enough to test the new hawk?"

"Of course I do! I've led you a merry chase this far today."

Even her longtime court favorite's fervid attentions hardly helped her disposition, however dashing he looked ahorse. He was attired much too grandly for riding and flying her new gerfalcon, the breed fit for a king. Robert, whom she had called Robin all the years they had known each other, had given her the hawk as an early birthday gift. 'S blood, she was nearly thirty-six, she realized, and shook her head, which tumbled more tresses free.

With the excuse of testing the prowess of the bird, the queen had brought a small entourage on a morning's robust ride. She could not wait for her summer progress through Surrey and Hampshire that she had just decided on last night. Though she'd chosen hosts for the journey who needed testing themselves, it always heartened her to be out among the common folk of England.

"This looks to be a good spot with a bit of open ground," she announced as she reined in. "We shall fly Swift here."

Being watchful to keep the bird facing the wind so she wouldn't beat the air with her huge wings, the queen dismounted with Robin's steady hand on her free arm and her loyal guard Jenks holding her horse. The queen's handsome, young falconer, Fenton Layne, four other guards, and two of her ladies-in-waiting hastened to follow their sovereign's lead.

St. James's Park had most often been used by the Tudors to hunt deer; by ordering the surrounding marshes drained, her father, King Henry VIII, had created access to it near his country retreat of St. James's Palace. Elizabeth seldom used the old redbrick edifice, but she loved the crooked, wooded lanes and ragged bits of open meadow. It was but a half hour's ride from her main London palace of Whitehall, though she seldom managed a visit.

For each time she snagged a few hours for herself, more couriers came with news of Mary, Queen of Scots's plotting, though Mary was now England's "guarded guest" in the north of England. Or messengers rode in with word of Spanish hostilities on the seas. Worse, couriers conveyed rumors of possible rebellion in England, a future uprising led by her own northern lords, men who were entirely too close to Elizabeth's Catholic cousin Mary in more ways than one. And almost every time William Cecil, her trusted chief secretary of state, called on her, it boded only bad news and dire dangers.

"The sun and wind feel good," she told Robin. "I pray this mild weather continues as the court moves south next week. We'll go first to Oatlands, then to Guildford and Farnham, even to the River Meon and clear to the south Channel. I seldom see the sea with its vast waters, fresh and free."

"You've made a little sonnet upon it. Our queen is a poet and doesn't know it," he teased, obviously trying to lighten her mood, though, since she'd declared she would not wed him, Robin had moped about a great deal himself.

"I need diversion, it's true," she admitted quietly, so the others would not hear. "With all this wretched talk of attacks on our meager navy by those Spanish bullies who think they own the seas, I look forward to hearing from Captain Francis Drake. I shall send word he is to meet us at one of our destinations on the progress."

"Rough, untutored sea dogs, all those captains from the west country," Robin muttered, his tone taut. "Drake and his cousin John Hawkins—they're all pirates at heart, so beware you do not trust or heed Drake overmuch."

"Robin," she said, as she stroked the gerfalcon's gray back to calm her, "I swear, but you sound jealous—or envious." She sighed again. "But I am envious, too. To be land-bound, England-bound, as I shall ever be, is right for a queen, but I would like not only to see the sea but go to sea."

He hooted a laugh but stopped in midyelp when she glared at him. He quickly sobered. "It's a hard life, Elizabeth," he whispered, using her first name as he did only in their moments of privacy.

" 'S blood and bones, everyone thinks I am coddled and spoiled, but I know much of a hard life, and you'll not tease or gainsay me on that."

She turned away from the others pressing close and put her hand to the feathered and tufted green felt hood that covered the hawk's head. Instantly, her falconer, Fenton, broad-shouldered, blond, and blue-eyed, stepped forward to be ready to take it from her when she freed the bird to fly.

But before she snatched off the hood, she heard something that made her pause. Thunder on this clear day? No, hoofbeats, distant ones but coming closer. Swift sidestepped on her hand, still blinded by the hood and snared by the leather jesses that tethered the bird's ankles to her fist. The small bells on the jesses jingled as the foot-and-a-half-tall bird of prey tensed in anticipation.

The queen frowned into the sun to see who approached. When she was young and exiled from her father's court for being Anne Boleyn's daughter, she had learned to fear a quick, unheralded approach by anyone, for it usually boded ill. Queen she might be, but some things still haunted her heart.

Robin, too, turned in the direction of the hoofbeats and covered his eyes to squint across the little meadow. Four riders burst from the line of trees. Behind her, Elizabeth heard Jenks and several others scrape their swords from their scabbards.

"It's Cecil and his men," she called to them, but her pulse did not stop pounding. "He must have news that could not wait."

Still holding the hawk, Elizabeth strode to meet her chief advisor as he reined in several yards away. She recognized those with him, all Cecil's underlings, a scrivener, two guards, and his favorite courier, Justin Keenan, a handsome man, who often rode back and forth with important documents between Cecil and the court when he was elsewhere on queen's business.

"Bad news, my lord?" she called to him.

Though only forty-eight years of age, the man was out of breath, but then Cecil's strength was in his intellect and loyalty, not his body. He was thin with a shovel-shaped brown beard, which was turning as silvery as frost.

"Only the news that you yourself created, Your Grace, in your suddenly ordering the court to prepare for a progress," he got out in one ragged burst, bowing briefly before rising to face her eye to eye. "Before word reaches those I hear will be your hosts, I need to speak to you about the wisdom of it all."

"Cecil, I am indeed going on my annual progress. I refuse to let either Englishman or foreigner think that threats to my kingdom rile me in the slightest, nor will my concerns about Queen Mary of Scots stop me. *She* is under my control, although I warrant she hardly realizes that yet, even if her dangerous allies mayhap do."

"But to be out of the capital with the threat of the northern rebellion possibly exploding in support of a Catholic queen to replace you on the throne—"

"I am heading south, not north, dear Cecil. Granted, you must needs stay behind in London at least for some of the time, to keep an eye on that serpent of a new Spanish ambassador de Spes. And I am taking along my second-least favorite cousin, Thomas Howard—the great and grand and glorious Duke of Norfolk, at least in his own eyes. That way he can't get into mischief with Mary or the fomenting rebellion, for I'll have him tied to me like this," she added, and lifted her wrist with the bird to show it was firmly tethered by the straps she held.

"But your plans to stay at both Loseley and Titchfield, hosted by Catholic hosts of highly questionable loyalty..." He cleared his throat, then lowered his voice even more. "I realize you have ever had a policy of keeping your friends close and your enemies closer, but with the Spanish so on edge far too near our borders here or even in the New World—"

"I planned to explain it all to you when I returned after flying my new falcon. Look you, Cecil," she said as she whipped the hood from the bird and, loosing the jesses, cast her skyward. Swift's great wings spread as she leaped free, beating the air, circling to climb to a great, soaring height from which she would see and strike her prey.

The queen could tell Cecil still felt thwarted and overthrown. "Yes, Your Majesty," he said, his voice hardly audible over the cheers of the others. "Not only do all your enemies make a fatal error if they believe you are off on a mere jaunt of summer diversions, but—" He stopped and hacked into his fist.

"But what?" she asked, as she watched the gerfalcon swoop like a shot toward some feckless prey they could not yet see.

"I was just thinking that, though that gauntlet is still on your hand, this supposedly carefree royal progress you propose is indeed throwing a gauntlet down in the face of all your enemies, be they English, Scottish, or Spanish."

"And so, as ever, we understand, trust, and support each other perfectly, my Cecil."

Pointing up at the diving hawk, she turned and shouted to everyone, "Look, Swift has already flushed something!" Lifting her skirts, with the others in pursuit, she set off at a run toward where the bird had plunged to earth for its kill.

Chapter the First

 TEN DAYS LATER, THE QUEEN'S SUMMER PROGRESS left Oatlands Palace, where everything had been assembled; the parade of wagons, horses, and people stretched into Surrey for nearly four miles. They stopped and ate outside for midday meal, then went on.

Led by green-clad harbingers and nearly four hundred laden baggage and provision carts, each pulled by six horses, the middle of the entourage consisted of a military escort, then scarlet-attired yeomen guards with their ceremonial halberds gleaming in the sun. After that, in the heart of the procession, came the queen herself, not riding ahorse for the last few miles toward the town of Guildford but ensconced in a ceremonial gilt and ostrich-feathered coach-and-six.

Pulled by matching white horses with manes and tails dyed orange, the conveyance was open-sided with crimson cloth and gold lace upholstery. Its leather curtains were drawn back to show England's queen, decked in a golden gown, waving, nodding, and smiling to acknowledge the cheers. Riding behind her came the court, nearly thirteen hundred people, everyone from councilors to lords and ladies to grooms and pages.

"Uncap, knaves!" The cry went out to rude rural fellows standing along country lanes, agape at the grandeur.

They hastily snatched off their caps and shouted, "God save our queen! Good save our good queen!"

Milkmaids cried and shepherds huzzahed. Parents held children up or sat them on their shoulders to see the monarch who loved the common folk, for they adored her as a glorious goddess in return. Despite her worries and the cursed bouncing of the coach into ruts and potholes, Elizabeth's spirits soared to be among her people.

Suddenly, a big-shouldered lout pushed his way through the crowd, dragging two little girls behind him. He snatched a straw hat from his head. Four yeomen guards instantly crossed their halberds to keep him back, but the queen caught the awed look on the man's face. He seemed almost entranced, and she hoped he was not drunk.

"Hold!" she shouted. "Hold here!"

Her coachman Boonen jerked in the horses, and those behind reined in. It was the queen's custom along the way to hear petitions or speak with local folk, though usually during a respite on a shady village green.

"Let him approach," she called to the guards, who stood aside. "My good man, what business, then?"

Though his garments were soiled, his face looked freshly washed; his hair was wet, where he had probably doused sweat or grime away in a trough or stream. When he opened his mouth, no sound came at first, and then a stutter before he knelt in the road, pulling the two small girls down with him—ages six and eight, the queen guessed.

"Ju-just wanted them to see you close so b-bad," he got out.

"Rise, man, and bring them forward. At what task do you make your livelihood?"

"Thatcher—roof thatcher—c-climbing ladders with reeds, Majesty."

"I have well noted how fine some of the cottage thatching is in this area. And the girls' names?"

"Anne and Jane, Majesty."

Both girls were wide-eyed and tongue-tied. Elizabeth pulled off her perfumed, gold-threaded gloves and leaned out of the coach to touch the children on their shoulders as they rose awkwardly to their feet.

"God bless you, master thatcher, and may our good God in heaven keep your family and all of us safe," she said loudly enough so the others, now hushed, could hear. "On, Boonen!" she shouted, before the stunned thatcher realized she'd given each girl one of her gloves.

As the procession picked up again, Elizabeth's cousin, Thomas Howard, Duke of Norfolk, rode up on her other side. Though he was but thirty-one, he now headed the powerful House of Howard, royal relatives through her mother's sprawling Boleyn family. To everyone's amazement, the wily Howards had managed to survive the downfalls of both beheaded queens, Anne Boleyn and Catherine Howard.

Norfolk was England's sole duke and the queen's hereditary marshal, who, unfortunately, was a widower for the third time and fancied, though supposedly in secret, that he might wed Elizabeth's rival, Mary, Queen of Scots. Norfolk was such an uncompromising Catholic that he almost made the queen regret she allowed her subjects freedom of conscience, if they worshipped circumspectly. Norfolk was more than circumspect; he was covert and crafty.

She had to admit, though, the man kept in fine physical form; his long face was framed by a nut-brown beard and thick eyebrows under his fringe of hair. He had a hawklike nose, chiseled cheeks, and thin lips, all of which made him look older than he was. He seldom smiled, and when he did, it looked forced, flitting across his face without lifting the corners of his narrow chestnut eyes. Frowns were more his *forte*—and stealthy behavior of late, which Cecil's spies tried to ferret out.

"Should word of your generous gesture to those two roadside urchins be noised about, Your Grace," Norfolk said, speaking out of the side of his mouth as he was wont to do, "you'll soon be out of gloves or missing your entire vast wardrobe if the mobs keep coming forward with flattery and open hands."

"Then perhaps you will purchase me new garb with all your money, my lord, that is, unless you are buying pretty gifts for someone else these days."

"No one, Your Grace."

Norfolk always called her that, rather than Your Majesty, though both forms of address were entirely proper. She and Cecil weren't certain whether he did it intentionally or without realizing it, though Norfolk's brazen flaunting of his lofty rank to one of far loftier did boggle her mind. It seemed she and the duke were ever verbally fencing or wrestling in some silent sport.

"As first peer of the realm, cousin," he went on, "I am sore grieved that you undervalue my influence and all I could do for you in the way of advice and counsel. For instance, the breakneck elevation of new names within your court— Cecil, for instance, and I hear you've sent for that baseborn seaman Francis Drake to inform you. That is perhaps why such bootlickers as that laborer back there think they can approach you."

"Norfolk, the common people of my realm believe they

can approach me because they *can* approach me. And I shall continue to elevate men of merit and not only those of rank."

Robin suddenly appeared on the other side of the coach as if she had sent for him. "Enough," she said, raising her voice because of the increasing din from up ahead. "Whatever is that caterwauling about? Can either of you see?"

"I shall ride ahead to look," Robin offered.

"No, let Norfolk. He is eager to be of aid."

Obviously seething at her subtle snubs, the duke spurred his huge horse ahead.

"He's livid you made him come along at all," Robin said.

"I'm doing him a favor, for I'll not have him all cozy with the northern lords or sending secret marriage proposals to Queen Mary. I am trying to save his hide, and I shall tell him that plainly again, so you need not put in your pennysworth to him, my lord."

"Not I," he said with that flash of white smile that stood out so in a face so handsome it made her heart flutter. "For I am along on this jaunt only to please the woman I adore— as well as the queen I honor."

Not wanting Robin to know he could still make her blush, she was almost grateful when Norfolk came flying back along the edge of the progress. "It's just some dirty, drunken louts having a brawl of a football game," he reported, as he reined in between Robin and her coach. Robin glowered at being cut off. Now both men looked like thunderclouds, and she knew she'd have to stop at least their impending brawl—no, she'd stop two brawls. For football oft turned bloody with bones broken; even bystanders had been hurt. More than once, a player had died, so the state had passed an edict against such violent matches, however much few heeded it.

"Stand down, you two!" she said quietly, glaring at each in turn. Then she shouted again to Boonen. "Hold! Halt here!"

"Your Grace," Norfolk said, as Robin edged out his horse to leap down and help her alight, "the local sheriff gave everyone the day off from labors, and they probably don't realize, with all their own noise, that your procession has arrived. I suggest you send some grooms or guards to break it up if you must, but stay put."

That did it. She was getting to the point with this man where she couldn't abide him and didn't trust him. As soon as the footman smacked down the coach's wooden steps, she took Robin's hand and alighted.

She did not have to ask for directions to the football game, for the noise and dust gave the spot away. When she lifted her hems and strode across the road to look at the raucous game in the adjoining field, her guards and then the common folk parted as the Red Sea had for Moses.

Both teams were so intent on driving a leather-covered bladder ball between their opponents' goalposts that no one so much as noted her. Men kicked, tripped, and punched each other to get to the ball. In a knot of at least four men, fists flew. One lout lay on the ground, holding an obviously broken leg and cursing at the top of his voice, while more than one oaf looked beaten and bloody.

"Your Majesty," Robin said beside her, "let me—" But she strode out onto the long, narrow field. One man, another, then the rest saw her with her guards trailing and Robin and Norfolk hustling to flank her.

The closest fellow, sporting a bloody nose and two black eyes, gasped and fell to both knees. The sudden silence was deafening across the field and behind her on the road as man after man turned her way. They went still as statues before going down to their knees like ninepins, all except the one with the broken leg and two who groveled facedown.

"You—each man jack of you," her clarion voice rang out, as she leveled a finger at each in turn, "are attacking those whom your queen might require to defend this realm! I do not deny you games of sport, but I will not have fellows who may be needed as archers if our enemies attack being bloodied and beaten by each other! Have you not heard of the ruling that each Englishman must be able to pull a bow in defense of queen and country? My lord Leicester, I believe you were in council when the edict outlawing rough sport and promoting the protection of our realm was passed shortly after I became queen. Tell them, then."

"Ah, yes," he said, clearing his throat, then raising his voice. "Male subjects between ages seven and fifty—"

"Sixty," she corrected.

"And sixty are to possess bows and arrows and to be able to shoot them. This entails weekly practice at the butts, and should there be some national need, all must stand ablebodied and ready to serve."

"Exactly," she said. "Is there anyone here who does not understand why we must not maim and harm our fellow countrymen when the greedy Spanish would like to gobble up our kingdom for themselves and force us back to the foolish faith of a pope who threatens to excommunicate your queen?"

Beside her, Norfolk visibly startled, but she ignored him. The sweating, dirty lot of rural men hardly breathed. She could hear nothing but a screeching jay somewhere in the distant trees and the snorts of impatient horses from her retinue behind her.

"Excellent. Good day to you all, defenders of queen and country," she said, and turned away with a wave and a smile that left everyone—but for Norfolk, whom she could see grinding his teeth— with mouths agape, just the way she liked to see all people regard her when she passed.

Meg Milligrew, the queen's herbalist and strewing herb mistress of the privy chamber, slumped in a corner of the royal rooms at Loseley House, a fine gray-stone mansion where the huge entourage would spend several nights near Guildford, Surrey, as the guests of Sir William More.

It didn't matter to Meg where she was. She stared at the rush-strewn floor in the corner of the royal withdrawing chamber and not out the nearby, sun-struck window. The voices of the ladies-in-waiting and that of Her Majesty blurred with the buzz of a fly. Nothing mattered but that, two months ago today, Edward, her and Ned's year-old son, had died of the croup.

". . . she's going out hawking with Sir William, and we're to go along . . . *al fresco* supper in the meadow . . . a sea captain newly arrived, Francis something . . . a fine fantasy of a play tonight with Ned Topside acting . . ."

My Ned acting, Meg thought, trying to seize on the women's words, to make them mean something—Edward Thompson, alias Ned Topside, the queen's principal player and master of revels whom Meg had loved for so long and had wed nearly three years ago, dear handsome, volatile, green-eyed Ned. Since Meg had lost the babe they'd named after Ned—she'd tried every herbal cure she knew to save him, and the queen's doctor had tried, too—she could not make herself feel anything or want to do anything. The queen had insisted she come along, said the change of scene would do her good . . . but nothing seemed good anymore . . .

"I said, good, there you are," the queen's voice pierced the babble of the others. "Come along, Meg. I am certain there are herbs to be had outside, and the fresh air and activity will help."

Meg nodded listlessly and stood up straight. How proud she had once been that she was more than a servant to the queen. Her Majesty had chosen to have her tutored by Ned, because Meg resembled the queen and could stand in for her when there was some dire need. Elizabeth Tudor had even included Meg with Ned, Jenks, and several other servants in solving certain crimes right along with Secretary Cecil and others of rank.

"Meg, *now!*" the queen repeated, as she swept by and her women made neatly matched pairs to depart the chamber.

Meg dragged herself after them, putting one foot ahead of the other, from the privy chamber into the presence chamber, where most courtiers attending the queen awaited, but in the corridor, she fell back again and leaned against the wainscoted wall as everyone's footsteps faded down the stairs. After all, she'd forgotten the large, curved knife she used to cut herbs. Thick patches of yarrow bobbed in the breeze near the spot the court was going hawking; she'd seen that much when they rode in yesterday.

Meg went down a crooked back staircase to a small, windowless room near the kitchens. Both courtiers and servants were packed in cheek by jowl on a royal progress. Certainly, no host could spare a room for wedded servants; sometimes not even married courtiers bedded together. Ned was staying with their friend Jenks and with Fenton, the queen's falconer, in the east wing while Meg was housed with several tiring girls and Jenks's wife, the royal laundress, Ursala, who had a child—fourteen-month-old Bessie—she'd brought along and kept with her all the time.

No one was within now, though, so Meg grabbed the knife from the basket of drying herbs and forced herself to go outside. At first the sunlight staggered her, but she meandered across the front lawn and down the lane where the queen, her elderly host, and many courtiers were flying falcons in a meadow edged with yarrow.

The lord of Loseley House, Sir William More, was a Catholic sympathizer, one with a big family. Most of his children and grandchildren were here to meet the queen. The sea captain must be that new man standing near Her Majesty. He sported a reddish beard trimmed to a sharp point, and the queen was half a head taller. Meg had heard he was newly wed, so he'd probably have babes soon, a whole boatload of them, however much he went to sea.

Meg gazed down at the knife, shaped like, though smaller than, a scythe, and was surprised to find she gripped its bone handle so hard her knuckles had turned white. She flexed her fingers, then cradled the curved blade in her arms as if she could cuddle it to her, however sharp, just like her memories.

Laughter and shouts floated to her. Meg began to hack at the long green necks of tall yarrow.

The queen had liked Francis Drake from the moment she met him. Though he was a bit blustery and rough-hewn among her clever courtiers, his bluff speech and lack of politician's skill meant to her he cared not for prevarication or pride. Like her, he was red-haired as well as ambitious and driven by duty and discipline. Besides, it was obvious he hated the Spanish, perhaps almost as much as she did.

"Later I shall have you tell me privily all that happened on that dreadful day our ships were bested on your fateful voyage," she told him, "and I shall ask that you share your opinions of our future seafaring and navy."

She sensed how deflated Robin and Norfolk were that she would not request that recital before them all. Both had edged closer to Drake with ears flapping to hear of his tales and exploits. But enough of business—public business—for she intended to fly all four of her hawks Fenton Layne had brought along on this progress.

"I'll send word back to my ship, then," Drake said, "that I shall remain at your disposal at least until you reach your southernmost staying point." He'd explained how he had sailed the tattered *Judith* from Plymouth westward through the Channel and had come up the River Meon to lease a horse to ride to her. The fact he'd been newly wed but a month had given her a moment's pause, but a seaman's wife, even a new bride, must become accustomed to having her helpmeet away.

"That will be fine," she told him, as Fenton placed Swift on her gauntlet. When she nodded toward her guest, Fenton placed a gauntlet, then another hawk, a fine sacret, fit for a knight, on Drake's arm. "Indeed, I would like to see that ship," she went on. "We will need many privately owned ones like yours and mine to bolster our defenses against the Spanish should they be foolish enough to defy England's might in any way, isn't that true, Norfolk?"

"Of course, Your Grace," he clipped out. He wiped his damp brow, then swept his red velvet cap off in a circle at a fly or gnat she didn't see.

"Fenton," the queen said, "a hawk for the duke, too. Bring Autumn, I think, so he doesn't have time to wish he were elsewhere."

She forced a laugh as Norfolk frowned at her and moved

back toward the crowd. He could have come up on this little elevation with them, but she was just as glad he had not. With her courtiers milling about in the shade, she stood next to Drake, ready to launch Swift. As commanded, Fenton put Autumn, a bastard hawk, fit for a baron two ranks below the breed a duke should fly, on Norfolk's arm.

To be ready to take the hawks' hoods from her and Drake when they plucked them off, Fenton hied himself to stand between them, perhaps before Norfolk could cuff him. With a flourish, the queen unhooded Swift and cast the bird aloft. She laughed at the sheer joy of the bird's strength as she soared skyward. Fenton, she thought, shouted a laugh, too, as she turned to hand the hood to him.

But the delight in her falconer's eyes turned to shock, then fright. Drake was ready to cast his bird, but he, too, saw her falconer's plight and didn't release the jesses.

Drake reached for Fenton as he toppled but couldn't hold him one-handed as the man crumpled to the ground. The wings of Drake's bird beat the air above the queen's head as she fell to her knees beside the stricken falconer.

Someone screamed. Was it she?

Fenton Layne, his face contorted in pain, lay writhing at her feet. Bright blood bloomed from the arrow piercing his chest.

Drake cast his hawk and cradled Fenton's shoulders. First the queen's guard Jenks, coming at a dead run, then Robin grabbed her and dragged her flat onto the ground. She lay between the big men as Robin shouted, "Cover! Everyone, take cover! Someone's shooting arrows!"

Chapter the Second

SCREAMS AND SHRIEKS JOLTED MEG FROM HER butchery of the yarrow herbs. She stood and shaded her eyes, then ran in the direction of the tumult. The cries of women, the shouts of men: It was like the day they lost the baby—her own shrill voice and Ned, talking incessantly, insisting that it wasn't her fault.

"What is it?" she asked the first servant who ran past her.

"The queen's falconer's been shot. We're to take cover."

"I didn't hear a firearm."

"An arrow in his chest."

"Is he dead?" Meg cried, but the woman didn't turn back to answer.

For the first time in weeks, Meg marveled, she could feel something, care about something. "Is the queen or anyone else hurt?" she demanded of the next person, but her question was lost in the flood tide of courtiers and servants alike, fleeing the meadow and crossing the open lawn toward the gray-stone manor house.

Meg stooped to grab a handful of cut yarrow. She'd failed to save her own son. Mayhap she could save someone else's. After all, yarrow's other name was wound wort, and apothecaries used to pack it in the bleeding wounds of jousters or knights lying on the battlefield.

Her knife in one hand and the long-stemmed snow white yarrow in the other, Meg ran through the line of chestnut trees edging the meadow. Some courtiers crouched behind tree trunks; guards, with Jenks leading them, ran headlong away, evidently in the direction from which the attack had come.

On a slight rise in the lea, the queen, the Earl of Leicester, and the sea captain were bending over a prone figure while six standing yeomen guards surrounded them.

"Your Majesty, is he bad hurt?" Meg asked, peeking past a guard's shoulder. "I have wound wort here."

"Oh, Meg," the queen cried, looking up. She was holding the falconer's hand. "We've sent for Dr. Huicke, but I gave him leave to go to town. Here, see if you can help."

Meg knelt beside the queen; the earl shifted away to give her room. "If this herb is to stop the bleeding," Meg told them, "the shaft of the arrow will have to come out—straight out, even if it pains him more. I know this just looks like flowers, but they used to pack the wounds of soldiers with it, fresh cut like this. Maybe it's a godsend—to save him."

"Yes, all right," the queen said. "We can't just let him bleed to death like this."

"I'll help pull the arrow out," the red-bearded sea captain said. "By my faith, I've done it oft afore."

Though he'd lived through a terrible, bloody battle with the cursed Spanish, this simple scene in the meadow shook Francis Drake to his very boot soles. It brought it all back—

the horrid memories he'd tried to bury this last year by going home to Plymouth, by wedding and bedding.

They carefully sat the poor man up and steadied the tip of the arrow, which had gone right through him to emerge barely an inch out his back, between his shoulder blades. While the Earl of Leicester cut his surcote away, then held the arrow firm, the maid named Meg sawed the point of it off with her knife so the shaft could be pulled out the front of the falconer's chest.

The earl made a motion to throw the arrowhead away, but the queen, her voice taut, commanded, "No. Keep everything. We will need it to discover who did this, should my men not catch the culprit."

Meg quickly decapitated the large-headed flowers and pressed two of the downy blooms against the wound where the arrow had tried to exit. When the others turned the man face up again and held him down, Drake put both hands on the arrow shaft. Not a quick jerk out, he recalled the ship's leech had said, but a strong pull with a steady hand. His hands had hardly been steady since they'd lost so many, not since he'd been accused of deserting his duty and his cousin and commander.

Though the falconer had been fading, the slightest pull on the arrow shot him wide awake. Drake froze, his hand on the slippery shaft.

"The falcons . . ." the poor wretch whispered, his voice a wheeze. "I must recall the falcons."

"Do not fear," the queen told him, still gripping his right hand. "We will fetch them back. Now, be brave, Fenton, for we must help you." Though it didn't quite calm the injured man, her steady voice comforted Drake.

Do not fear . . . Be brave, her words echoed in his head. That dreadful day at San Juan d'Ulua on the Gulf of Mexico when their ships had been fired on by the surrounding Spanish, many sailors had died from crossbow bolts. It was his first battle, after all those early years serving as ship's apprentice, then an officer on his cousin's vessels on the English Channel and the North Sea. Being so secure with local tides, currents, shoals, and winds was quite unlike sailing months away into deadly danger in the unknown, not sure he'd come home, not sure he'd live, but loving the danger in his destiny.

As he withdrew the arrow in a steady pull, the falconer gave a cry, shuddered, and fainted. A new gush of the man's lifeblood spurted, but the maid's quick, sure hands packed the wound with the fluffy flower heads.

She was obviously someone the queen trusted. He noted almost a family resemblance, but of course that could not be. Though the maid Meg also blinked back tears, unlike the queen, she looked haunted, just the way he felt, and his heart went out to her.

As Drake sat back on his haunches with the shaft still in his hands, he saw the queen's skirts were bloodied. For her to be bold enough to stay here in the open to tend this man—he'd heard she was brave, and he knew her subjects loved her. Now he could begin to grasp why. She was as shrewd as they said, too, for she looked straight at him and said, "I doubt, Captain, if that arrow was intended for a falconer, so which one of us was it meant for, then?"

A few minutes later, Fenton Layne died at the queen's feet as they tried to lift him onto a litter. Probably with his last remnant of strength, Elizabeth surmised, he'd opened his blue eyes and scanned the sky, either for a sign of the hawks or, God willing, looking up to heaven. His hand went limp in hers; she was surprised to see she'd held it all this time.

"He was ever a good and faithful servant to me," she said in a loud voice. "My lord," she added, turning to Robin, "since it seems it was his last wish, will you be sure someone finds the hawks and gets them safely back to someone who can tend them."

"At once, Your Majesty—*if* you are planning to go in- side now."

She nodded, for she was concerned that Meg had not moved and kept staring at the corpse. Was she seeing this death scene or another with a smaller body, one that Ned had to finally coax from her arms for burial? "Meg," Eliza- beth said, stooping to squeeze her shoulder, "do not blame yourself for this loss—*or for any other.*"

"Aye," Drake put in when the maid didn't move, "the span of our lives is God's will, not ours."

"Captain, I will send for you later, but there is much I must do now," the queen told Drake. "Guards, stay with the body until Sir William tells you where the man might be buried. But first, of necessity, Sir William must summon the sheriff and coroner of the shire. I," she went on, loosing Meg's shoulder and producing a clean white handkerchief from up a blood-speckled sleeve, "shall take the arrow shaft from you, Captain, and the pointed end Meg cut off from you, my lord Leicester."

Both men gave their pieces into her keeping. "Meg, come with me," she added, and started away.

Her guards, who had returned empty-handed from their chase in the direction of the shooter, and her courtiers, who had finally wandered back, all curious, fell in behind her, some asking questions she ignored. Striding quickly, with the rest of her guards surrounding her, all the way across the front lawn of the manor, she forced herself to calm down, to think, not just to react.

Under the stone-arched entry to Loseley House, she turned to face her whispering coterie. "We will hold a service for Fenton Layne later today in the chapel, if Sir William agrees."

Their septuagenarian, silver-haired host emerged from the crowd. "Of course, and we can bury him in the cemetery with the Loseley House servants, if you wish, Your Majesty, though I warrant the local officials will want a look at him first."

Elizabeth nodded in agreement. "And, since our noontide repast has already been laid out for my people under the trees near the meadow," she went on, gesturing behind them, "perhaps that food can be brought inside to the great hall. Until the chapel service, I will be in my rooms."

"Oh, yes, of course, Your Majesty. I'll have the choicest viands sent up to you and your ladies."

"My ladies will partake with the court, so just some things for me and my closest servants."

"Closest *servants?*" a voice behind her repeated, as she turned to go into the house. Norfolk, arms crossed over his chest, leaned against the entryway. "Since you are sovereign, are we not all your servants, Your Grace? I should think a queen would like her closest kin about her at a time like this. After all, I fear that arrow could have been meant for you and someone missed."

She spun back to face him just inside the door. "Someone may have missed, but I'll not miss having closely watched and interrogated every one of those who might be responsible, my lord. Not one!" Though the light was dimmer here than out of doors, and her eyes seemed slow to adjust, she studied Norfolk's face and stance as if he had been hauled before an inquisition.

"Your hose are all grass-stained," she said.

"Leicester told everyone to get down, and of course I always follow the commands of someone new-fledged you've tried to haul up by his bootstraps—or by something."

She almost slapped the man for his continued impudence and vile insinuations. She would have banished him, but she needed to keep an eye on him—a hood on him. Perhaps he was trying to drive her to distraction so she would order him away and he could flee north to his cronies and the Catholic queen.

"See you do not go far—or go *too* far—my lord," she told him. "Should I haul in brigands who had a motive to kill their queen—or harm my new man Drake, either—'s bones, you will be the first in line!"

He bent in a stiff half bow as she spun away and went up the grand staircase. She was halfway up, still holding the bloody arrow, when she recalled that Norfolk had removed his red hat and batted at an insect she didn't see or hear just before someone—perhaps—received that signal to shoot this arrow of death.

Thirsty, Elizabeth drank a goblet of malmsey straight down but ignored the silver platters of food. She gestured to her coterie of trusted servants to sit around the table.

"Jenks, you will ride to the first post on the north road and send the string of messengers on to inform Cecil of what happened. He'll see the import of it. Eat, eat, all of you," she urged, sweeping her hand toward the array of meat,

bread, cheese, fruits, and puddings, "for we are all going to
be busy before nightfall."

"Of a certain, Lord Cecil will want to know if you'll be
heading back to London straightaway or just staying inside
here where it's safe," Jenks said, as he cut off a hunk of
golden cheese.

He should have known by now she'd not be cowering or
fleeing, she thought. Rather, she'd be heading an investigation
with her covert Privy Plot Council. But then the bold, mus-
cular Jenks had a wit for horses, not mental machinations.

Meg's husband, Ned, also ate heartily, trying to coax Meg
at least to try some grapes. She seemed to have retreated into
the dark, secret depths of herself where she'd lived these last
two months.

Carefully, the queen unwrapped the two pieces of arrow
and laid them on her handkerchief on the open end of the
long table. "After we decide who will be delving into what,
I'll send for Francis Drake, and not only to hear of the English exploits in the New World against the Spanish," she
said, leaning stiff-armed on her hands to stare down at the
arrow. "I will need to question him about any murderous enemies he might have, for we know the lengthy list of mine
well enough."

"Should the entertainments be canceled this evening,
Your Grace?" Ned asked.

"Not a comedy, I hope?" she inquired.

"Truth be told," he said with a flourish of his hand toward the open window, "a summer fantasy set in the dark
woods, a ghost story about the evil Sheriff of Nottingham
and the great hero Robin Hood."

Elizabeth sighed. "Though it sounds as if that would not
elicit gaiety and laughter, we'd best delay any entertainments

at least until tomorrow. And for courtesy's sake, please inquire if our host agrees."

"Sir William will no doubt honor your wishes, Your Majesty," Ned said, his mood suddenly somber.

To give the mercurial man his due, since Meg had been despondent, Ned's portrayals of tragic figures had become much more genuine than his saucy dukes or romantic and comic characters. Anyway, there was naught to laugh at now. And speaking of sheriffs, the local one must be arriving soon to view the corpse and interview witnesses, including, perhaps, the queen herself.

"No, Ned and all of you, hear me now. Sir William More may owe me his recent knighthood and the honor of this visit, but he is Catholic to the core and highly sympathetic to the Duke of Norfolk and the northern lords—which is why I charge all of you to keep your ears pricked up for any gossip about our host and Norfolk being closeted together or whispering in corners. Sir William and the duke have a long history, for my lord Norfolk was once, though briefly, the ward of the Mores here at Loseley House, so he knows this entire area quite well."

"In other words, birds of a Catholic feather flock together," Ned said.

"True, and, as put, apropos for this sad day. But to your immediate duties. Jenks, before you ride out, take a look at this arrow. I know you've always been a sword-and-dagger man, but can you tell me anything about this?"

His mouth full of cheese he hastened to gulp down, the tall man came to bend over the weapon—the part of it they could see, until her guards found the bow from which it had been shot. "First thing," he said, "it's not an arrow."

"But—oh, you mean that it's a bolt, from a crossbow? I

briefly learned to shoot a crossbow as a child. I should have thought of that. I remember how hard it was to crank the bowstring taut with either a foot stirrup or hand crank. Yes, I see now this is shorter and thicker than shortbow arrows. A crossbow—so that's why this could fly so far from the forest across the width of the meadow."

"Either that or the bowman had a powerful pull, like the bowmen of old. But those heroic sorts from the great English yew longbow victories—you know, like Ned's Robin Hood—are long dead now. But I think this did fly in an arched path, so that could mean a crossbow, too."

"Did you see the angle as it approached?"

"No, but I was looking straight across the way, and no arrow flew a low path—and then Fenton just went down. Your Grace, crossbow or longbow, we're dealing with a very fine archer."

"And a very clever, long-distance murderer. Since my yeomen guards turned up nothing, I shall send handpicked men to search the area where the shooter hid himself, so return as soon as you can, Jenks. When my lord Cecil arrives, I shall call a formal covert Privy Plot Council meeting— with Francis Drake, perhaps the murderer's target, in attendance, too."

"Or," Meg said, raising her eyes from her clasped hands at last, "it could be someone else."

They all turned to stare at her. The once talkative woman seldom spoke of late, especially when not spoken to. Even Ned looked shocked.

"What do you mean?" the queen asked.

"If the bowman was so good, perhaps he hit who he was aiming at. Most like an assassin would strike at Your Majesty or maybe a sea captain, however obscure Drake is to most—

but what if the person wanted to kill Fenton Layne? I mean, poor Fenton had a life, so he must have had both his lovers and his enemies."

"Meg, what would I—we—do without you?" Elizabeth said, as Ned squeezed his wife's shoulders. "Of course he had a life, and it's the thief of that we must bring to justice, whomever the killer meant to strike down."

As steady and sure as she sounded, the queen began to shake. She could feel a cold spot in the center of her chest and middle of her back—as if someone would shoot her, or as if a spirit had touched her there. Whyever had Ned mentioned that he planned a play about ghosts this evening?

"You are all dismissed," she told them. "Jenks, hie yourself onto the north road and be watchful, even as we all must be."

Chapter the Third

"SHERIFF ADRIAN BARNSTABLE, YOUR MAJESTY," SIR William said, and stepped aside so that the queen might see the man he presented to her. It had taken the sheriff two hours after Fenton's death to arrive. According to Sir William, Barnstable had brought with him the coroner, Richard Gilburne, who was examining the body.

Sheriff Barnstable was built, Elizabeth thought, if not like the barn or stable his name evoked, much like a barrel. His rocking gait and tipsy bow did not inspire confidence, but she knew better than to judge by appearances.

"You may rise," she said. "Have you seen the site of the tragedy?"

"I have, but first, Your Most Gracious and Esteemed Majesty, allow me to beg your pardon for my not greeting you the moment you crossed the boundary to our shire. Of all times for my gout and dropsy to worsen and make me—albeit briefly—bedridden . . ."

"I am sorry for that, but you are here to help now."

The sheriff had jowls like a hunt hound, and folds of flesh hooded his eyes, so she wondered just how well the man could see. He did not look aged, yet acted so, leaning on a stout wooden cane. Why someone so sluggish, ill, and may-hap half-sighted should be a sheriff in the kingdom was beyond her.

"And I shall remain at my task," he informed her, "until I solve this heinous murder of one of your household. I was to lay down the burdens of office after this momentous visit you and the court have blessed us with, Your Most Gracious and Esteemed Majesty, but now I shall stay on. Why, your very being might have been endangered in this murderous attack on one of your own, but I shall lend heart and mind to your well-being during this blessed time you are within our shire."

The man talked in circles; she prayed he didn't work that way. This interview only made her more certain she must take solving this crime into her own hands.

"Then I charge you to find a witness or some clue in the area from which the crossbow arrow must have been launched—and to find the villain himself."

"I believe I heard you have the murderous arrow in your possession, Your Most Gracious and Esteemed—"

"As time is of the essence, you may address me simply as Your Majesty. And, yes, I have the arrow and wish to keep it, but of course you may examine it." She went over to the table where she'd left it wrapped in her handkerchief and brought it to him. As she came closer, the man looked as awestruck as if she were going to knight him with a silver sword to his shoulder.

She handed the wrapped bolt to Jenks instead. "My man Stephen Jenks will go with you. You are dismissed, Sheriff, to go about your important business."

He bowed again, and she could almost hear the poor man's joints creaking. Just outside the doorway, she saw Jenks unwrap the bolt to display it to him. As Elizabeth went back to the work Cecil had sent her by courier yesterday—how she wished he were here already from London—she heard a gasp and a yelp.

"What goes?" she asked Sir William, as he made to follow the other men out into the hall.

Adrian Barnstable came back in, faster than she thought he could move. "The crossbow bolt," he cried. "I recognize the fletching on it from one of our finest shooters in the shire. The man fashions his own shafts and fletches them, too, keeps birds on our tables all the time, even brought them in for your larder here, Your Most—Majesty."

"Who is this man?" she asked, but Barnstable was out the door again. This time, his words alone rolled back in: "I'll have him arrested, interrogated, and charged in a trice, Your Majesty. Fear not!"

She almost sent Sir William after him to demand who it was he suspected, but she trusted Jenks to report back straightaway. If someone local had tried to kill the queen, at least the murderer couldn't be those of national import she most feared might want her dead.

"The battle at San Juan d'Ulua was a disaster from beginning to end, Your Majesty," Francis Drake explained that evening, as they sat over wine and apricots by the open window of her withdrawing chamber. The night was warm, but a western breeze wafted in to shift the velvet draperies. Elizabeth had sent all her women out except for Rosie Radcliffe and kept only one yeoman guard inside the door. When she'd asked Drake if he could have been the target of the fatal attack today, he'd admitted he did have an enemy who might want to harm him—besides the Spanish—but said she'd understand more if he unburdened himself about the battle.

Unburdened, that's what he'd said. "Take your time, Captain, and tell me all that matters," she said.

"All that matters—the bloody defeat and its aftermath, my flight—have haunted me since, but, by my faith, I'll brook no words to tell you how it truly was. As you know," he went on, frowning out the window at the blowing, rustling oak leaves as if he saw the sea again, "my cousin John Hawkins, England's hero for his earlier voyages, was in command of our little band of ships, two of which you had loaned us."

She nodded. "The *Jesus of Lubeck* and the *Minion,* both small and old, but all I could spare. Our royal navy leaves much to be desired, but we shall get to that. Say on, man."

"Preparing to return home from our voyage to the New World last August—'twas almost exactly a year ago—we were hit by a violent storm and had to set in for repairs at San Juan d'Ulua, a small, isolated Spanish outpost on the Gulf of Mexico. We heard from people ashore that a massive Spanish fleet would be arriving soon, so we hastened to be out of their way in time. God's truth, Your Majesty, we had no desire to pick a fight, for we were outnumbered and far from any friendly town to lend us sustenance. They could barely be convinced to sell us water. But too soon we spotted thirteen sails—indeed an unlucky number that day.

"We knew if the Spanish fleet trapped us in their harbor, we were doomed, and all our bounty we had traded for would be forfeit. We trained our cannon on them to keep them at bay until we could slip out. I repeat, we did not want a battle, for more than one reason. We thought they might let us go so their little town would not be caught or harmed in possible crossfire. With our spyglasses, we could see they had cannon on deck and crossbowmen in their rigging, but so did we."

She nodded, picturing the scene, though another dreadful image kept intruding: a crossbowman, perhaps aloft, maybe in a tree, ready to catch her or Drake in crossfire of another sort.

"I warrant you've heard the rest," he said, his voice now harsher, faster. "Deceit, betrayal. The local governor, Enriquez, had signed a pact he would let us leave peaceably. But he began to fire on us from the shore as their fleet closed in for a kill, like—like huge hawks swooping down on pigeons already caught in a trap and disabled," he said with broad gestures. "But, even when they sent fire ships against us—"

"Fire ships? They burned some of their own ships and sent them against ours?"

"Yes. Even then, Your Majesty, our smaller ships maneuvered better, but we were battered. So many were maimed or killed. I commanded the *Judith* and, after six hours in battle, saw the opportunity to escape and did—to save those of my crewmen who were still alive, to hope to fight another day, for I thought all else was lost, that my cousin was lost. I had no idea he'd managed to fight his way free and would be looking for me to back him up—or would have a hellish voyage home. Or that," he said, and heaved a huge sigh that hoisted his shoulders, "he would blame me for deserting him in his direst hour of need."

They sat silent for a moment. Somewhere outside in the darkness an owl called, *who, whooo.*

"I fear my cousin hates me now," Drake admitted, turning to look at her again. "Yet he needs me, for I know those distant waters and how treacherous the Spanish can be. And I hate them as he does—it burns deep in my belly and my soul!"

"In mine as well. Which is why you must, if not put that dreadful past incident aside, learn from it. We must both learn from it. Our smaller, darting ships in the face of their lumbering galleons, the use of fire ships, and the brave tenacity of our men even when treachery strikes are lessons we must hold to. You see, Captain Drake, you and I are much alike."

"Indeed, Your Majesty?" he asked, sitting up straight as a board in his padded chair.

"We both have learned things the hard way, through our losses, and it has made us wiser and stronger," she declared, rhythmically hitting both fists on the arms of her chair. "And we both must deal with cousins who hate us and might wish to make us suffer—or even die."

"Yes," he whispered, "by my faith, that's true. But as that owl out the window is asking again, if someone meant that arrow for one of our hearts today, who? Who?"

William Cecil wished he could look as rested and ready as his favorite messenger, Justin Keenan, who rode abreast of him as they reached the vast grounds of Loseley House near noon. They trailed four guards and four scriveners. Only Keenan seemed to look about with relish, while Cecil felt crazed to get off this horse. He supposed a professional courier who rode so much and so well would have to find the passing scenery of some interest, or he'd go stark mad with all the time he spent in the saddle.

A good courier covered about fourteen miles per hour, and with post horses every ten miles, the man could almost fly. Then, too, if a courier could claim he was on royal business, he could commandeer horses along the way as long as they were later returned by a postboy. Keenan, however, often favored pulling one horse and riding the other to make tracks between Cecil and the queen.

No wonder the man did not seem to have a care in the world. Mere couriers did not have to live day and night with the fear something would happen to England's monarch, nor did the man have to deal with that carping, complaining Spanish ambassador, Guerau de Spes.

"Will you convince Her Majesty to return to the safety of one of her own castles or palaces, then, my lord?" Keenan asked as their horses' hooves spit gravel on the lane to Loseley House.

Usually, the man never spoke unless spoken to, another admirable trait in servants. Keenan was mature, at least thirty, with years of experience in the livery of one earl or another until last year, when he'd come into Cecil's employ. Despite sweat and road dust, he always looked neatly turned out, today even bedecked in new-looking riding gloves and leather doublet. The man's chestnut hair was kept clipped unfashionably short, but his strong, square jaw and broad shoulders made him just the sort the queen wanted in her employ. Like her sire, she favored good-looking servants; Cecil tried to keep Keenan out of her way so she wouldn't pirate the man.

"I fear not even God can convince this queen to do what she will not, man," Cecil muttered, and began to brush dust from his sleeves and breeches. He was certain he'd have little time to rest before he was drawn into the thick of things. It had been three years since the queen had taken it upon herself to solve a murder, but once committed she was always in tooth and nail.

Cecil was only too glad to ride into the huge block of shade the big house threw across the sunny lawn. He had seen Sir William More's county seat but once, years ago, before the queen had suggested More enlarge it to host royal visits—actually, of course, to keep him from spending his fortune supporting Catholic causes. It must have taken thousands of pounds for More to haul in more of the mellow stone from the ruins of Waverley Abbey near Farnham.

Cecil noted well the stone badge of the Mores carved grandly above the central entry: The strutting moor hen and moor cock symbolized the family name—and attitude. The only thing missing, Cecil groused to himself, was the Virgin Mary, or perhaps the unvirginal Mary, Queen of Scots, whom Cecil's spies said Sir William secretly idolized.

Keenan dismounted quickly to hold Cecil's horse for him before his following scriveners or guards could do that service. "Any other task, then?" the man asked.

"After you see to the horses, get a bite to eat, but wait about lest I have need of you."

Cecil gritted his teeth as he took a few steps on solid ground to try to loosen his muscles, for they ached as if he had the ague. House servants spilled through the arched entry to greet his party; one man offered him a quaff of cold wine, which he downed in almost one gulp.

The last wine he'd had was yesterday, with Ambassador de Spes, and, however good it was for a Spanish claret, it had tasted like sand. As ever, de Spes had been sleekly attired with his hair slicked down with some sort of sweet-smelling pomade, the sly fox. Yes, a fox, one that should be sniffed out and hunted down.

"You understand my dilemma, of course, Secretary Cecil," de Spes had said in his heavily accented English. He al-

ways pronounced Cecil's name Ses-*seel.* "On behalf of my
liege lord, King Philip, I must insist that your queen and her
sea captains honor our laws."

"This is old business, Ambassador," Cecil had said, "and
Her Majesty has responded clearly to your claims more than
once."

"But by Spanish law, English ships have no right to ply
the Gulf of Mexico or venture along the Spanish Main off
the coast of the Americas. Spain has strongly stated, 'No
peace beyond the line.'"

"To repeat our stance, Ambassador de Spes, your king
may declare all he wants of 'Spanish law,' but such is not
compulsory for our countrymen, our queen, or our ships,
which have every right to trade in and explore the New
World. As Her Majesty herself has put it, no one country
owns the open ocean. No one can declare some fictitious line
in God's great sea which others may not cross—not but for
the boundaries near one's own homeland."

"But Secretary Cecil, quite simply, we were there first. And
if your countrymen continue to act like brigands and free-
booters, then they shall be challenged and treated as such."

"If your countrymen dare to fire upon sovereign English
ships again, it can only lead to war, de Spes!"

In short, what Cecil had to report to the queen today was
not good news. At least he had every reason to think he
could offer her a motive for someone shooting an arrow at
her—or, for that matter, at the sea captain Drake.

Now that Cecil had joined them, the queen intended to call
a Privy Plot Council meeting later in her chambers. For now,
with Cecil, her court, and the Loseley household, she sat on

the back lawn pretending to enjoy Ned Topside's ghostly fantasy, *Robin Hood Returns.*

The real sheriff, the blustering Adrian Barnstable, was evidently also a blundering one, for he had not yet returned with his quarry as he had promised, though he had sent word back with Jenks that he was personally searching for the man, a hedger and birder named Tom Naseby. If he didn't produce the man by morning—though the queen could not fathom why some rural laborer would want to kill anyone—she was going to send Jenks and her yeoman Clifford after both Barnstable and Naseby.

"Of course, many of fair England's sheriffs are honorable men, but the Sheriff of Nottingham was most disloyal to our good King Richard," Ned, decked out as Robin Hood's spirit come back to life, was declaiming. To glow ghostly in the distant flickering torchlight, the clever actor had smeared some sort of sticky substance on himself, then evidently rolled in crushed flowers—Meg's yarrow, perhaps, which had not managed to save poor Fenton.

The queen's thoughts drifted. Richard Gilburne, the local coroner, had done little more than pronounce Fenton Layne "deceased of blood loss by an arrow to the most vital part of his chest." She was getting nowhere, relying on the local, rustic upholders of her laws. Tomorrow she must take matters more into her own hands, beginning with a thorough search of the area from which the crossbowman must have shot.

From asking other servants who knew Fenton, Ned had learned naught about the falconer's private life that could be a motive for murder. Elizabeth was beginning to hope it *was* just some demented local lad or pure accident, a poacher letting a bolt fly wrong. How much simpler her life would be without some convoluted motive to trace.

She tried to listen to the play, but she could not concentrate. Instead, she kept pondering the Spanish problem, which Cecil had also weighed in on today, and the letter he'd brought from Mary of Scots, carping about "how depressing it is to live in the countryside where chill winds blow, you cannot imagine..." *Chill winds indeed,* the queen fumed—winds of possible civil war.

She worried, too, that Meg had greatly gone back into the shadows of her past. And, as much as the queen intended to trust Francis Drake, she had argued with Cecil over Drake's being a hothead. "Then I'm a hothead against the Spanish, too!" she'd ranted at Cecil, when she'd actually been so glad he had come.

> *"An outlaw bold was Robin Hood,*
> *Clad in Lincoln green,*
> *'Mong Sherwood Forest's leafy boughs,*
> *He could be scarcely seen.*
> *He drew six feet of English bow*
> *To aid plain folk in their despair.*
> *Resistance 'gainst the sheriff*
> *And loyalty to England's throne*
> *Was needed then and there..."*

Ned's fine message drew the queen's thoughts back. She rather liked the words; at least Ned knew how to bolster the monarchy in these tenuous times. Too bad Robin Hood had been dead for nigh on three hundred years, for she could use him now to draw his yew longbow and shoot evil shooters.

It took her a moment to realize that a commotion off to the side, which she'd thought at first was Robin's Merry Men entering the impromptu stage, was obviously some other ado, for Ned, trained as he was to keep in character, finally turned, put his hands on his hips, and frowned. As if part of the fantasy—though it suddenly seemed a farce—Sheriff Barnstable stumbled through the leafy scenery of Sherwood Forest, dragging a man bound hand and foot. Two others, burly lads, entered, too, blinking in surprise to see either such bright lights or the assembled audience.

In the front row, the queen stood as Sheriff Barnstable evidently spotted her.

"Caught and questioned, Your Majesty, one Thomas Naseby, who is in possession of two missiles identical to the fatal one." As if to prove his point, he held a feathered bolt high in the air.

"He's confessed?" she asked, as she walked forward and took it from the sheriff. Yes, in the shifting torchlight, it looked to be the same.

"Not yet, but he will, for he was indeed at the perfect site on yonder hill to launch this weapon of death."

Naseby was disheveled and dirtied by rough treatment, unless a man who followed the trade of repairing hedges always looked like that. She guessed not. He was bleeding from his nose and mouth and looked dazed.

Her first instinct was to instantly question the prisoner herself, but everyone was staring, and she didn't need it noised about that the Queen of England subverted her duly appointed peacekeepers, nor that she personally solved crimes that came close to the crown. Besides, she wasn't sure at this point that Naseby would know his own name.

"I'll keep him close in my cellar 'til morn, Your Majesty," Barnstable announced with a bow, as if he were some sort of *deus ex machina* to end the play. "And then I'll have it all from him!"

Elizabeth indicated that her guards should escort the men and their prisoner off the stage. The unghostly sheriff had made a shambles of Ned's entertainment, but if Barnstable had bumbled into solving Fenton's murder, she would reward him well.

Chapter the Fourth

 THE POUNDING ON SOME DISTANT DOOR DRAGGED Elizabeth from sodden sleep the next morning. She was shocked to see that the sun was well up. Though she had postponed the late-night Privy Plot Council meeting until after the sheriff further questioned his prisoner, she had found no peace in rest. She felt as exhausted now as if she had been up all night.

"Rosie, you let me oversleep," she muttered to her lady-in-waiting, who was already up and dressed. "See who that is making such a racket at the door."

When Rosie went out, the queen arose and pulled on a robe over her night rail. She shoved her wild hair back, then splashed cold water on her face from the basin. She could hear Rosie's high voice in the next room, then a man's deeper tones.

"Well, what is it?" she demanded, as her friend rushed back in. Elizabeth's heart beat hard as she steeled herself to hear that the northern shires had exploded in rebellion or that Queen Mary had been sprung from the custody of Elizabeth's man, Lord Shrewsbury. No, Cecil himself would have come to tell her that.

"He's dead," Rosie blurted. "He hanged himself."

"Who? Not Sir William? You don't mean Drake?"

"I can't recall his name. That hedger who shot the arrow at you. It's Jenks outside in the hall, and—"

The queen swore a string of oaths that would have made her father proud, then threw the basin of water against the wall for good measure.

Barely half an hour later, Elizabeth Tudor presided over the first full assembling of her Privy Plot Council in nearly three years. Cecil sat at her right; Jenks, directly across from her, because she intended to interrogate him. On one side of him sat Lady Rosie, and on his other, Ned, then Meg. Meg looked morose again, but at least she had risen to the occasion when her royal mistress needed her yesterday. Finally, looking curious but uncomfortable, Francis Drake sat on the queen's left, wondering, no doubt, why he was suddenly included in this strange stew of servants and their betters.

"It has been my mistake," the queen began, "to be lulled into inactivity in this matter of murder by the sweet summer setting and by a worthless local sheriff who cannot be relied upon any more than can Robin Hood's ghost."

No one so much as smiled; they all read her temperament well. "I intend to look into this murder myself," she went on, "with the help of all of you—promptly and privily. Is there anyone here who cannot pledge me aid in this?"

No one stirred or even blinked. "I thank you one and all. Jenks, you indicated to me a short while ago that you were surprised that the hedger, Thomas Naseby, took his own life."

"Yes, Your Grace. He seemed steady and sure of himself when the sheriff first spoke to him, afore he was manhandled a bit."

"Quite a bit from the looks of him," Cecil said.

"Aye. He was bloodied and bruised when Barnstable hauled him out of his cottage, so those men of his worked him over inside." The big man hesitated, frowning, his fists clenched before him on the table.

The queen knew Jenks well enough to know he would have liked to interfere. She rued the fact she'd told him to just observe and report to her what happened. "Say on," she urged.

"Nothing made Naseby waver in his story of not shooting the arrow. He insisted some of his bolts had been pilfered—all but for two, to be exact, Your Grace, and he admitted right out that he was in the area. Checking, he said, on a broken part of a hedge where someone of a sudden had built a stile for climbing over it."

"Wait," she said, holding up both hands. "When Thomas Naseby readily admitted he was in the area from which he could have shot that easily identifiable bolt, had Barnstable already cuffed him about?"

"It was those two men with him hurt Naseby, but no. Not yet. Admitted all that freely from the first, like he knew naught about why they'd be asking. Said he'd been out in the fields all day, so I can see why he hadn't heard. That was when I was standing in the doorway of the man's cottage, afore one of Barnstable's louts closed the door on me and latched it inside, too."

Elizabeth groaned but fought the desire to put her head in her hands. "Did this man have a family to—to live for?" she asked.

"Heard his wife's dead but that he had two boys, though they weren't about the cottage then."

The queen saw Meg lift her head and turn toward Jenks; she seemed to come to life at the mention of the children.

"Your Grace," Cecil said, "you are thinking that the sheriff was overzealous to please you, and the hedger may have well been innocent, matching bolt or not?"

"We've come to a pretty pass if you can read all my thoughts, my lord, but yes. Yes, I fear so, and I partly blame myself."

"Your Majesty," Drake put in, "if I may say so, a captain of a massive ship—like you commanding this nation—can't always be at the helm. Your officers, so to speak, are expected to and must be trusted to do their parts."

"Thank you—all of you, for your present and future support. We must move quickly now before we have more dead innocents on our hands, perhaps because they were snared in someone's trap who only wants to harm me—or you, Captain."

Ned put in, "If the man didn't hang himself, that means someone else did, that is, eliminated him so he couldn't continue to claim he was blameless of shooting the arrow. I hardly think Barnstable, bootlicker that he is, is capable of murder. He'd want Naseby to sing like a bird to you so he could get the glory. I'd wager he fully intended to question the man—of course, mayhap under duress—this morning."

"I fear you've all learned your lessons of deduction far too well. Jenks, I am relying on you to go to Naseby's cottage and find his sons. Rosie will give you a pouch of coins for them, and you are both to inquire who might take them in—or are they of an age to fend for themselves?"

"I know not, Your Grace."

"Then assess it when you tell them that their queen grieves the loss of their father, and that we shall try to keep his name from being tainted with accusations of murder or attempted regicide. Ned, you will come with Meg, Rosie, and me to examine the area from which the arrow was supposedly shot. Fetch my guard Clifford to come along, because I need protection and he knows the area from the earlier search."

The queen rose; the others stood, too, as if dismissed, though she kept up her stream of orders.

"My lord Cecil and Captain Drake, I shall leave you here to separately inquire—through casual conversation, of course—what Sir William and the Duke of Norfolk think of all this. They may give naught away, or indirect questioning may implicate them. Besides, I do not want them trailing along nor using this morning for their own covert conferences. Tell my courtiers, if you must, that I simply yearned for a solitary walk. And, when Sheriff Barnstable shows his face here today—with egg on it—hold him until I can fully question him after I examine that gaol of a cellar he mentioned."

"Of course, Your Grace," Cecil said. "But can you not simply send the others to report back to you and not go out yourself this morning? If indeed this hedger was innocent of the attack, someone is still about who can put a bolt in the middle of someone's chest from over a hundred yards away."

"I've made the mistake of letting others look into this, Cecil, and I can hardly wait for nightfall to search for clues."

"I have a partial set of dress armor in my things," Drake said. "It's lighter than some, but it would deflect arrows, unless a shot came from close range. It would be too large for you, but if padded and then covered with a cloak, you could wear the breastplate and backpiece well enough."

Cecil chimed in. "Your enemies are clever, perhaps desperate—and as yet unknown."

"Yes, I warrant that would be wise. Drake, deck me out like a soldier, then, for this is war."

It was such a lovely summer morn that if the queen had not had a murder on her hands—actually, two of them, she wagered—she could have almost enjoyed the walk. But then, too, Drake's armor was a heavy, hard reminder that this was no primrose path stroll.

Yet as her tall yeoman Clifford, who had been in the haphazard search yesterday, led them upland through the screen of trees toward a large hay meadow edged by hedges, they did see yellow primrose and many other flowers, spilling from the base of the head-high hedge. Elizabeth noted cow parsley, hawkweed, and lords-and-ladies, and Meg lagged a bit to bend toward others the queen could not name. Prickly hawthorne, from which the hedge was mostly made by having its limbs cut, bent, and interlaced, was in bloom. Orange-black butterflies and buzzing bees darted along the plump, dense barrier while magpies and finches flitted here and there, and a kestrel sketched circles in the sky.

"I see the stile," Ned said, pointing.

"We saw that on our first pass through this area yesterday," Clifford said. "I just looked over it and saw no one, nor didn't think much of it."

"But now we know," Ned went on, "it's the one poor Naseby claimed someone had cobbled together and hacked partly out of the hedge. Jenks said that meant some sheep got out, so Naseby had to patch it, though he wouldn't otherwise deal with it 'til winter, when it was bare of leaves."

"Be careful, everyone," Meg said, coming to life at last. "I see stinging nettle along here. Devil's Plaything, they call it, and for a good reason. It burns one's skin and makes a dreadful rash. For some folks it's even fatal—see, that's it right there. Steer clear, now."

It heartened Elizabeth to see Meg show some interest as she pointed out the delicate green leaves. "Bad place to build a stile with these nettles nearby," her herbalist muttered.

The stile itself looked makeshift and shoddy, but it did hold Ned's weight, then Clifford's, as they climbed over and came back. "Get down," the queen said. "I'm going up."

She cast off the awkward cloak she wore to hide the armor, hiked her skirts, and climbed partway up. Peering over at the next field, she saw no more three-foot-high blowing hay but sheep and closer cropped grass. The rooftops of the village of Guildford were barely visible far beyond the rolling hills. She turned around and sat on the top step.

"Your Grace," Rosie said, "you were shot at in broad daylight before, and sitting up there like a target . . ."

"And the sun glitters off that chest armor like a shining bull's-eye!" Ned protested.

"I'm coming down. Ah, if I could only forget my troubles and be a country maid, I could reign from this crude wooden throne over this lovely piece of land and not worry for aught."

She sighed and gripped the rickety banister to come back down. But as she gave one last glance at the scene of the great house and gardens below, and the breeze lifted the limbs of the trees, she saw it: She had the perfect view of the very spot where she, Drake, and Fenton were standing when the fatal bolt was shot.

" 'S blood," she cried, "this stile is a shooting platform and this hedge both a hunter's blind and escape route for the murderer!"

Meg was grateful the queen had let her and Ned stay behind to gather some herbs along the hedge. She cut hawkweed, for tinctures for wounds or nosebleeds, and knapweed, which was always good as an astringent. She took some broad-leafed dock, too, useful for rubbing skin stung by the very nettle that grew beside it.

"Nice of the good Lord to give us both the bane and the cure side by side," she told Ned, who was evidently anxious to get back to the house. He was standing on one foot, then the other, but she could tell he was also pleased to see her even momentarily content. Or was he eager not to leave but to say something?

"This lords-and-ladies is poisonous when fresh, you know," she told him, "but if I'd roast the tubers, then pound and dry them, it's good for all sorts of deconcoctions for irritated eyes, even handsome green eyes like yours, Ned Topside."

"Best leave the poison stuff alone," he said gruffly, when she thought he might banter back.

"You aren't fearful I'd use poison on myself?" she asked. "No more chance of that than poor Naseby hanging himself—not a man with boys to tend. Husband, even when things have been the blackest, I wouldn't harm myself."

As if she'd said something seductive, he pulled her to him, and she didn't protest that the herbs were smashed between them.

"Meg, Meg, I've missed you so, being alone with you— the way things used to be."

"I know I've not been a good wife to you lately—since . . . But I couldn't help it. I just can't bear to think of us together like—like we were. Even after we had little Ned, we took our joys so much, and then he died . . ."

"It's all right," he said. "I can wait, but I don't want to. I need you."

"We can't here—in the meadow. Ned, you said we need to get back."

"If we lie down, the meadow grass will hide us. If we can't here, we can't for the entire royal progress. We don't get time alone, we don't live together. My sweetheart, let's just . . ."

She couldn't say she felt what she usually did with Ned, but she was happy to have him hold her. The hay and earth itself smelled fresh and sweet where they crushed it under their bodies. Still, she didn't forget her little lost boy, even when Ned's love embraced and filled her.

When it was over, they heard voices nearby and scrambled to cover themselves. One person howling, one perhaps sobbing or gasping.

"Where's that coming from?" Meg whispered, picking up her knife and gathering her scattered herbs.

"Can't tell. But it's tormented, disembodied voices—"

"Stuff and nonsense. It's hardly your ghostly Robin Hood."

They were barely to their feet when two heads popped over the hedge at the top of the stile—two lads, one a bit bigger than the other, shouting boyish variations of "Ow, it smarts!"

"Oh!" the larger boy said when he saw them. "We got to patch the hole in the hedge. Our father's the hedger, but he been took 'way for now, and we got ourself stung up by some bugs or bees we din't see."

Ned and Meg gawked up at the lads and then glanced at each other. It had to be poor Tom Naseby's sons, and they didn't know their sire was dead.

"You come on down here," Meg said. "I'll just bet you've rubbed against stinging nettle. I've got something that will help with that right here. Come on, then."

They came up, over, and down, burdened with a bundle of limbs and, clanking together, a billhook, a handsaw, and two stonebows, the kind used to kill small birds for pies.

"Now put all that down and let Mistress Meg tend to you," Ned told them. "Then we'll go to meet the queen."

The taller boy looked like he'd argue, but the shorter one seemed in awe of Ned. "You mean the real queen come to visit or the fairy queen, Titania of the forest?" the smaller lad asked. "She flits about with Robin Goodfellow and Will-o'-the Wisp near hedgerows, you know."

The bigger boy frowned and elbowed the smaller to shut his mouth. Meg just shook her head. A dreamer of fancies like Ned, that little one was.

She blinked back tears as she tended to the lads, rubbing fresh dock leaves on the red rashes on their hands and arms. These two had no notion they were orphans now, or that they were about to testify before the Queen of England to help clear their father's name. Her heart went out to them so strong that, for the first time in two months, she forgot for a moment that she'd lost her own little boy.

It was nearly noon when the queen, Jenks, and three guards, over Sir William's protests, rode two miles into Guildford to Sheriff Barnstable's house. The town was charming, she thought, with prettily thatched, half-timbered houses newly whitewashed and a village green bedecked, no doubt, in her honor. Jenks rode the back way to the sheriff's cottage, its lawn abutting a pond with noisy ducks.

The queen dismounted but waited with her guards while Jenks walked around in front, then came out to open the back door with the sheriff himself in tow.

"Your—Your Majesty," Barnstable stuttered. He'd obviously been eating; he had a large, dirty napkin tucked in his collar and grease on his fingers. He went into a bow that bumped him into the door frame. "Such an honor to have you here at my humble—"

"Step aside, man," she said, pushing past him as he stumbled back. "Why did you not come straightaway to tell me of your prisoner's demise?"

"I-I told your man Jenks here, but could hardly presume to come early to you with sad news, Your Majesty, though this does satisfy my suspicions of Naseby."

"But not mine!" she insisted, as she followed Jenks down the hall, with her three big guards trailing.

"Why," Barnstable called after her, "the man was obviously shamed by his guilt and took his life. I didn't move the body but to cut him down, lest you needed to see the proof, and—are you wearing armor, Your Most Esteemed and Gracious Maj—"

"Hold this man here, Clifford," she threw back over her shoulder. She was getting angrier with every step as she gathered her skirts and followed Jenks down creaky wooden stairs into the dank-smelling cellar.

"You'd best fetch a lantern," she told him when she saw that the cellar was lit by a single rush light, which had almost burned down.

"But to leave you with the dead man—" Jenks began to protest, then scurried up the stairs at the look she shot him.

She stood over the poor man, a huddled bulk on the floor, then bent down and touched his shoulder. "Your queen rues your death," she whispered, as if he could hear. "I shall find justice for you—and for my other servant who was caught in a snare perhaps meant for me or my captain. And I'll see your boys are reared by some good citizen here."

The door banged open above; Elizabeth could hear the sheriff's shrill protests before Jenks thudded back down the stairs. The lantern lit the small, square area well enough, once her eyes began to adjust. Yes, she thought, as dark as this got, she must strive to see clearly.

"Ordinarily," she told Jenks, "I would have you examine his head for bumps or bruises to see if he was knocked out before being hanged, but after he was beaten yesterday, I doubt such would be conclusive. That blackguard of a sheriff hasn't even laid him out properly, but left him dumped here like a sack of meal. I'd like to have Barnstable's head as well as his post."

"He keeps saying he's giving his position up after your progress leaves, Your Grace."

"No, he's going to have the post removed from him in disgrace before I leave. Meanwhile, I'll ask you to check on Naseby's person for anything unusual while I look about."

Holding the lantern, she examined the crossbeam from which still dangled the poor man's strap from his quiver tied in a noose. She bent over Jenks to see that the quiver was empty now, either because someone had stolen most of his bolts as he'd claimed or because Barnstable had taken the last two for evidence. It was one of many queries the sheriff must answer.

She noted that the things stored down here were not unusual: a bucket of turnips, a barrel of apples, and a wheel of cheese on a cutting block—with a cleaver stuck in it.

"Are his hands tied?" she asked.

"No, but there are welts on his wrists where they were bound."

"At what point were they unbound, then?" she mused. "I'll warrant he was left tied until he was dead, perhaps with hands behind his back."

She shuddered at that image, of the man struggling as the noose was readied and he was hoisted up to be strangled in it.

"But if his hands *were* tied in front," Jenks whispered, "he could have hanged himself. Why keep carrying around that empty quiver, 'less he planned to hang himself with its strap from the first moment the sheriff accused him?"

"The question is not only about poor Tom Naseby. If Barnstable meant to leave him imprisoned all night in this cellar, why leave that sharp cleaver there so Naseby could cut his bonds or hack through that wooden door to escape? I wager the cleaver didn't matter because Barnstable knew Naseby would meet his fate in a staged suicide quite early in his imprisonment. Ah, look," she cried, and bent into a dusty corner to pick up a gleaming silver shilling with her own likeness stamped on it. "I doubt if this bounced out of a hedger's purse," she said, displaying it to Jenks.

"Or a country sheriff's."

"You've learned a thing or two about devious behavior these years in my service, haven't you, my man? What do you think this means, then?"

"Doubt if a coin worth that much would get lost and not found fast."

"That is, unless the person who lost it was in a rush or so well-off it didn't really matter. Or unless it was part of a large bribe and so, amidst other coins, wasn't even missed.

Worse, Jenks, this coin looks new minted, and that means it must have come from London recently."

His eyes widened under his thatch of hair as she handed the lantern back to him, keeping the shilling tight in her sweating palm.

"I'm going to have Clifford search the rooms upstairs," she said in a rush. "I ask you to stay here with the body until I send a party from Loseley House to see to his burial today. And we'll not worry that the sheriff protests an accused murderer's being buried in hallowed ground, for he will be too busy answering Francis Drake's questions in this very cellar of a makeshift gaol."

Chapter the Fifth

WHEN DIVESTED OF DRAKE'S DRESS ARMOR, THE queen breathed easier, yet she still felt a tightness in her chest. From her privy withdrawing room window overlooking the back gardens of Loseley House, she watched Cecil walking under the grape arbor in deep conversation with the Duke of Norfolk. She had no idea where Drake and Sir William were, but at least he and Norfolk weren't together. She could only hope that both of her allies were worming information out of those who secretly opposed her will.

She heard someone at her door and turned to see Meg, looking as if she'd been rolling about in a haystack. Crushed bits of herbs or leaves clung to her tousled hair, and she looked most distressed.

"Your Grace, Ned and I are feeding the two Naseby lads in the kitchens, for they came to fix the hedge," she blurted, wringing her hands. "Gracious, we didn't have the heart to tell them their father is dead, but he really is, isn't he?"

"He is, to my great regret, because I vow he was innocent. Meg," she said, gesturing for her to come closer as she glanced out the window again, "I've sent for Captain Drake, but the moment he is gone, bring the lads up here to see me."

"By the back stairs? They're a bit afraid."

"Aren't we all?" she whispered as if to herself. "Yes, by the back stairs, though I'm sure everyone I'd like to keep their presence from will soon know they're here."

Someone knocked on the door, and it opened again. "Captain Drake, Your Majesty," her guard stepped in to announce, even as Meg darted out.

Drake crossed the chamber and bowed adroitly.

"I like how you can lose your sea legs when you are on land," she told him as he straightened. "In short, a man I can trust who can adapt in dire circumstances is exactly what I need at this moment. I would like you to take two of my yeomen guards with you and ride into Guildford to stringently question the former town sheriff, who has just been removed from his duties."

"Stringently, Your Majesty?"

"I believe he either hanged the hedger, Thomas Naseby, in the makeshift gaol of his cellar or let someone in to do the deed, and mayhap took money for it, too. I warrant the poor man was hoisted to his death by strangulation in a noose made from his own leather quiver strap. But I'd bet my kingdom that Barnstable's too rocky on his feet to accomplish that alone, even with Naseby's hands bound.

"And," she went on, displaying the shiny coin in the sun pouring in the window, "since I found on the cellar floor this new-minted shilling, which I did not mention to Barnstable, you have much to work with. Did Barnstable pay someone to help him? Or, more likely, did someone recently in London—of some means—pay Barnstable?"

"I see," he said, looking shaken and yet still solid, a man of passions but power, too, she thought with approval.

"My guard Clifford is there now," she added, "searching

the former sheriff's house. He will let you know if he finds aught else that would be fodder for your interrogation. Yet I regret to involve you so, and if you would prefer to remain aloof from this, I will certainly understand."

"My own safety aside, I understand that my sovereign could be in danger, and I shall do all I am able. But best I have your man Clifford stay close, for if I get out of the Barnstable wretch that he knows aught of that crossbow or bolt that could have been meant for either of us . . ."

He said no more but smacked both palms to his thighs.

Not a hothead as Cecil claimed, Elizabeth thought, but one who knew his own limits and could control himself, and a man able to inspire others. Though loath to change the topic, she said, "You have been with Sir William, have you not? Have you any suspicions he would be so daring and devious as to parade us out to the little hillock for hawking, having hired someone local to shoot in our direction— perhaps even as a warning that went awry?"

"Forgive me for speaking frankly of one of your nobles, Your Majesty, but I believe Sir William More is not clever enough to hoodwink me—or us—in that way. Except for his servants and his family, whom he orders about at will, I would wager he is a man better at taking orders than giving them."

"Yes, I agree. But taking orders from his queen or some other?" she mused, gripping the shilling and tapping her fist on her chin.

"I dare say, Your Majesty, as for your cousin the Duke of Norfolk or my cousin John Hawkins," Drake said with a shake of his head, "best we both reserve judgment."

———

The two Naseby lads looked not so much afraid of as awed by the queen, Meg thought, as she and Ned escorted them into Her Majesty's presence. At least that might keep them from elbowing each other as they'd done on the bench at the table in the servants' quarters downstairs. Now, in the queen's suite, from which she'd sent everyone else out, they sat stiff-backed, side by side in a broad-seated, low lady's chair, made for wide skirts and embroidery over one's lap. Each took but two sweet comfits from the plate the queen herself offered as she leaned across to them from her matching chair.

"So, your father sent you to patch a piece of hedge under that new-built stile," Her Majesty said with an encouraging nod and smile. Elizabeth Tudor would have been a good mother, Meg thought, that is, if she could curb her temper when things went to pieces.

"Not 'xactly, Majesty," the larger boy, Simon, called Sim, said. She and Ned had coached the lads to address the queen as *Your* Majesty, but, surprisingly, Sim was not as bright as the younger Piers. Yet the smaller lad wasn't a bit practical and seemed not to separate the fanciful from the actual.

"You see, our sire got hisself took by the sheriff," Sim went on. "But the sheep squeezed through by the new stile. So I tell Piers here we better fix it for him. We're 'prenticed, 'specially me, 'cause I'm older."

"Could the shepherd or the owner of those hay fields have hastily put up the stile?" the queen asked.

Sim shook his head. "Heard not."

"That was very good of you to try to help your father."

"Neighbor said he shot an arrow that hit someone, but he wouldn't—but at birds," Sim explained, his high boy's voice almost shrill now. "He'd never miss. We're stonebow boys, help his birding, too—not poaching, though!"

"I'm sure you don't."

Meg yearned to stroke the stubborn cowlick that poked up from Piers's head. What industrious lads they were, learning hedging and shooting at low-flying game for partridge or pigeon pies.

"I've seen stonebows with their double strings and pebbles for shot," the queen said. "And I hear your father was a fine crossbowman."

"Still is," Sim said. "But someone stole his bolts, all but two he was making, he said."

Meg blinked back tears. These lads had said their mother, Polly, died two years ago when the dreaded sweat swept through this area. She'd been buried in a common grave behind the church rather than in the graveyard. That's where Meg was going to suggest the queen allow their sire to be buried, too. Wasn't the queen going to tell them their father was gone?

"When was this—that his bolts were taken?" the queen asked.

"Four, five nights 'go. Out o' his quiver when he was checking hedges. 'Course, he said the best bolts was 'talian or Spanish, but cost too much, and never had none o' those."

At the word "Spanish," Meg saw the queen startle, then quickly recover. *From the mouths of babes,* Meg thought, for more than anything, Elizabeth Tudor feared that her own English folk who were Papist would side with the Spaniards to throw her off her throne.

"Do you have any idea who built that stile over the hedge?"

The lads conferred, whispering. "Don't tell that!" Sim hissed at Piers.

"You may tell me, Piers," the queen corrected the older boy.

Piers, who reminded Meg so of Ned for some strange reason, spoke at last. "Someone did it o'ernight. He's strong for sure and mayhap invis'ble, too. Don't know, but could of been that naughty fairy Will-o'-the-Wisp, what skips over hedgerows and disappears and befools anyone watching."

Meg saw the queen bite back a laugh. "But if it wasn't a fairy, who else could it have been?"

"Someone," Sim said with a shake of his head at his younger brother, "who knows that hedges make the birds fly up and not skim the fields. That way they can be shot, that's what I think. See, he wanted a quick way to get to birds he shot—maybe poached. So he used the stile for a place to steady his crossbow, too."

"I believe that could be it indeed," the queen said. "I thank you for your help and warrant you will make a fine hedger and birder yourself someday, Sim Naseby."

"But I really want to see the world, Your Majesty!" the boy blurted. "At least far as the sea!"

Meg saw the queen press her lips together hard and nod before she said, "I understand your longing for the sea. But now I want you lads to know you will be well cared for, though I have some sad news. Your father, who I believe was a good man and was wrongly accused by the sheriff, has died. I am going to punish the sheriff and have you stay here with my friends, at least until we can bury your sire and find a place for you here in town. Do you understand what I just said?"

Sim squared his shoulders and nodded, but little Piers sucked in a sob. Before Meg knew she would move, she knelt behind their chair and put her arms around the little boy from behind. His body was trembling. He suddenly dug at the nettle rash on his arm, though she'd bathed and tended it. Meg leaned her cheek against his tousled head, and he quit scratching. The queen leaned forward to put her hand on each of the boys' knees, but Meg just held on tight, so tight.

A thought hit her hard, and she had to say it right then: "Your Majesty, whoever hacked that hedge or built that stile or shot that bolt might have a real bad rash of stinging nettle."

"With all that's happened, you surely won't keep to your announced schedule to proceed with this progress into Hampshire," Cecil said to the queen that evening. Courtiers buzzed outside the door of her privy chamber like bees, waiting for her to appear. Ned's interrupted entertainment from last evening was to be held for safety's sake in the great hall, though Elizabeth had put out word the new setting was merely to avoid the chance of rain.

As if the walls had ears, though she had sent her ladies out ahead of her, the two of them spoke quietly and quickly as they often did in snatched bits of conversation when others crowded close.

"I believe we've beat this subject to death, my lord—at St. James's last, I recall," she said, and fanned herself in the overly warm chamber. "I am not canceling my journey into Hampshire."

"But the dangers to your person are greatly increased over what I counseled before, Your Grace," he countered, gripping the high-backed chair he stood behind. "Hence, I know you will look at this with a more wary eye. Our next stay is with someone we can trust, but after that we're into the frying pan again with a Catholic and Queen Mary sympathizer, and all the time you're dragging Norfolk along, and God knows who else who wishes you harm."

"Cecil, I repeat, the bolt might not have been intended for me. And if it was, I will not be affrighted in my own kingdom by someone who wishes me to cower in terror." She flipped her fan closed and pointed it at him like a tutor's finger. "I will not become a prisoner and build walls between myself and my people. I want and will have again the freedom to wade into a football game, for instance, or stop on the road to speak with a rustic laborer who brings his children to meet their queen!"

"That reminds me, Your Grace, you are quite certain you want to take the Naseby lads along when we depart on the morrow?"

"I won't leave them here where that pompous maggotpie Barnstable and those louts of his might harm them. Jenks will serve as temporary guardian of the older boy, Sim, and Ned will keep an eye on the younger one, Piers. Besides, I'm not certain I can pry Meg Milligrew away from the younger, who is grieving sorely over both his parents' deaths."

"A transfer of affections for her?"

"One I heartily approve of if it helps the bleakness of her soul. However, the transfer of affections which both Sir William and my cousin Norfolk have undergone to turn their loyalties from their rightful queen to Mary of Scots is something else."

"Yes, Norfolk's wily at hiding his true feelings—or thinks he is. I just wish there were some way to get more answers about these two murders before we move on. But," he added, holding up both hands as if to ward her off her next sally, "I don't mean that we should change our schedule to stay to find out."

"I'm not turning tail to run back to Windsor or London, so there you are. As for staying here, it would gain us nothing. Barnstable's henchmen, who must be questioned, seem to have fled the area. Drake says Barnstable won't admit that someone bribed him or helped him to get rid of Naseby, and Clifford found no sack of money hidden in his house, though he could have buried it."

She sighed and began fanning her flushed face again. "Barnstable claimed if a new-minted coin was found in his cellar, he has no notion who dropped it there—and, since he has no wife to question . . ."

"Who would marry the wretch?"

"He is wretched—like that vicious stinging nettle, clinging and prickly that leaves a dreadful rash," she said with a shudder. "I hate to leave him simply deposed from his little sheriff's kingdom, but I can't imprison him on the evidence we have."

"I've a suggestion, then. My best courier, Keenan—"

"Oh, yes, I know the man. Rugged and handsome, sits a horse as if he were born to it."

"Ah, yes, that Keenan. At any rate, he rides back and forth, hither and yon to London and beyond for me on a frequent basis, so, as we move on farther south, I could have him stop in Guildford en route to inquire whether Barnstable seems to come into sudden money. Or if those henchmen return, he could question them. But I'm not sure whom to trust to be Keenan's informant when he comes through, because I could not spare him, nor do I want the important papers he brings me delayed."

"What about that thatcher who was bold enough—and loyal enough—to approach me on the road with his two little girls?"

"Ah, the ones I hear you gave the gloves to?"

"For which I was sternly lectured by Norfolk. Can you have someone locate that man and have him be the one to keep an eye on Barnstable and his louts?"

"I'll see to it. Keenan's been sent to London, but he'll be back soon, so I'll have one of my other men set everything up with that thatcher, once we track down where he lives."

The queen nodded and fanned herself furiously. "Someone is sure to slip up and give us the clue we need to track Fenton's—and perhaps Tom Naseby's—murderer. We simply must be patient and keep an eye out for the little things as well as the big."

"As for small details—you said in the Privy Plot Council meeting you'd like to check everyone for that rash. But that would mean rolling up the sleeves of hundreds of people— those with us—or even more if it's someone local. Besides, the man who erected that makeshift stile or shot the bolt—"

"Could be miles away by now or could have worn gloves and wouldn't show the nettle rash, or—'S bones, I had thought about letting Meg offer treatment to anyone who was suffering from such, but that would be—too obvious—laughable."

As if to punctuate her words, laughter boomed outside her door, led, obviously, by her dear Robin's deep voice.

"I'm glad someone's having a fine time on this progress," she groused, smacking her folded fan on the back of the other chair.

"One more thing, Your Grace, if you promise not to hit

me with that fan," Cecil said, his voice coaxing rather than
contrary now.

"Say on, and then we'd best go out and put on a happy,
brave face."

"Drake didn't break Barnstable as I had thought he
would."

"Which argues against your argument, my lord, that he is
a hothead," she cut him off before he could say more. "He
didn't lose his temper, didn't beat him to a pulp, though he
admitted he would have liked to."

"Just a word to the wise, and that is you, Your Majesty.
After all, Francis Drake arrived here with dress armor as if he
planned some parade for himself, some grand show, when he
had been summoned to simply explain about that disastrous
battle. Now if running off in the heat of battle isn't a hot—"

"You'll not call him that again! He ran to fight another
day and has learned his lesson well. I believe he will not
desert me, my lord! Besides," she said, lowering her voice,
"we're all hotheads with this sticky, warm weather tonight."
She made for the door so fast he had to hustle to keep up
with her and open it. "Besides, dear Cecil, perhaps it will be
cooler tomorrow, for we will soon be staying in a solid castle
with a host I can trust."

"But deeper into Hampshire, a wilder land," he said, as he
opened the door nearly in Robin's face.

He must have been going to knock, she thought. Or was
he trying to make her jealous by all this laughter without her?
Was he endeavoring to punish her again—to make her fearful and to admit she needed his protection? After all, when
that bolt hit Fenton, it was Robin who was there to take over,
to protect her and give orders to the courtiers just the way

she'd always feared he would if she should wed him. She desperately wanted to trust Robin of all people, but she had seen too often and too well that even those dearest and closest could be corrupted by the passion for power. No, surely her Robin hadn't known beforehand of that bolt so that he could rescue and comfort her.

The queen flipped her fan open and waved it in his face with a little laugh as if she had not one care in all of England or the vast, wide world.

Chapter the Sixth

AFTER THE SABBATH CHURCH SERVICE AND A MID-
morn meal at Loseley House, the queen and her
entourage processed farther southwest toward
Farnham. She was much relieved to put Sir William More
behind her, though her burden for the deaths of two stalwart
men seemed to ride apace with her coach. Each time she
glimpsed the Naseby boys during the day, guilt shook her as
hard as the rutted road, for she had failed to solve what must
surely have been their father's murder. She wondered if that
killer—or the one who had well paid such a demon—was
along on this journey, too.

Even the sporadic cheers of her subjects did not lift her
heart today. Yet Elizabeth of England smiled and waved gaily
at the drovers of wagons loaded with wheat as they pulled
off to the sides of the roads to permit her entourage to pass.

"Wheat from Hampshire for flour and bread in London,"
Robin leaned down from his horse to tell her. Not only did
she have him and Norfolk riding abreast of her coach for
protection, but she had again donned Drake's armor under
her cloak. Cecil had wanted her to close her leather curtains,

too, but she must show them all she feared naught—though she feared greatly.

"I can recognize wheat, my lord. Shall I give you a lesson on the geography of my realm, then? Farnham is the crossroads of this area, and," she added, turning to him and lowering her voice so that Norfolk would not mark her next words in the din of the cheers, "I know well enough that Farnham Castle was the place my sister Mary stayed en route to wed King Philip of Spain at Winchester, so never mind a lesson on that. At least this district is now firmly in my loyal Protestant bishop's hands. I dare say, it will be refreshing to have a host who does not have his love and loyalty fixed elsewhere."

"Your sister should never have wed a foreigner or a king, my love," he whispered back, leaning so low he could have toppled off his horse into her coach. His eyes lit and a saucy smile crimped his lips. "How I wish my glorious and beautiful queen would wed a true Englishman, one whose passionate love and fervent loyalty is ever hers and will be my entire . . ."

His low words were drowned by rapid hoofbeats that stopped a short way behind them. As they were once again passing open meadow with no people lining the road, Elizabeth turned and craned her neck to look back, despite how the armored breastplate made her feel like a turtle in a tight shell.

It was the courier Keenan pulling an extra horse and coming from somewhere to hand Cecil, who rode just a ways back, a packet of letters. They spoke in hurried bursts, both frowning.

"Robin, tell Cecil and his man to attend me now. And, my lord Norfolk," she said, turning to him and raising her voice, "I shall have you ride ahead to gauge our distance yet to Farnham."

"And to get me out of earshot," she heard him mutter as he put his spurs to his horse's flanks, while Robin rode away in the other direction. As her guards closed ranks close to the coach again, the queen noted well that, unlike many in this warm weather, Norfolk wore fine leather gloves. She had been offering her gloved hand to her courtiers overmuch to-day, then scanning their wrist and finger skin for a nettle rash like those the Naseby boys still sported and scratched at, de-spite Meg's skin-soothing concoctions.

She turned to face Cecil as he rode up on her left with Keenan on his outer flank. Robin returned and kept his horse on the other side of her coach where Norfolk had been.

"What news, my lord?" she asked Cecil. "Not just more tedious correspondence from London, I warrant."

"Sometimes I am certain you have eyes in the back of your head, Your Grace. Yes, Keenan has brought news from one of my sources in London, who, in answer to my query, informs me that the new Spanish ambassador, de Spes, has a man in his employ who is a fine archer and crossbowman."

"Ah. And can said archer and crossbowman be located in my capital at this time, or could he have strayed to the coun-tryside for a summer respite?"

"We are working on that, Your Grace. Thus far, we can-not locate him."

"Keenan, what do you know of Spanish shooters?" she asked. "You are back and forth to London and about the countryside a great deal. Have you heard aught of how such a one might compare with my best English-born bowmen in skill and distance?"

"I know little of that, but I must admit, Your Gracious

Majesty, I have heard Spanish crossbow bolts and arrows are the best."

"Yes, I have heard that, too," she said, thinking of what young Sim Naseby had blurted out yesterday. "So, would such bolts or arrows be simple to purchase here in England, or are they far too dear in price?"

"Available but dear, I would wager," Keenan said, as Cecil nodded.

"Only affordable by someone with means, someone with coins?" she mused aloud. "So, though poor dead Thomas Naseby made fine bolts, the best and truest—as you say, Keenan—could be Spanish made."

"But the same with leather goods of all sorts, Your Majesty," he added. "Most Spanish imports are fine quality."

"Robin," she said, turning his way, "do you, for example, own Spanish arrows or bolts?"

"I, Your Grace? I would wager most of your nobles do. As Cecil's man says, it's just like owning Spanish leather gloves or a fine Cordoba leather jerkin."

"My lord, gloves and jerkins are not shot from bows to maim or kill people! And you have prettily danced around the question."

"But the bolt which killed your falconer was made by that dead thatcher," Robin protested.

"And if that man were innocent and had his bolts stolen as he and his sons say, someone was clever enough not to use his own bolts but try to blame someone else—someone local. Can you not answer a direct question?"

"Yes, I suppose I, like most others of some means, have Spanish-made bolts or arrows," Robin admitted, looking most annoyed.

"Your Grace," Cecil cut in, "granted the Spanish are a danger, but we have no evidence to tie them to—"

"Just find where that imported Spanish bowman is and see that he is somehow detained, with or without de Spes's knowledge, Cecil."

"Yes, Your Grace. It is being seen to."

"I'd say," Robin cut in, his voice almost petulant, "you'd best look to someone closer, one not usually part of your entourage. Your fine Captain Drake didn't come alone to attend Your Majesty, you know. He brought two ship's crewmen with him, one, I hear, a fine marksman with the bow, good at hanging about in swaying rigging and yet striking true."

Trying to cover her surprise, Elizabeth swung around to gape up at him. She almost accused Robin of jealousy. More than once she had suspected that he might stoop to something low to get her trust and affection, so how dare he implicate Francis Drake! Still, she did not know Drake that well, and here she'd included him in her Privy Plot Council—she'd let him interrogate Sheriff Barnstable, for all the good that had done. And, though she'd instinctively trusted Drake from the first, Cecil evidently thought he was a climber and rather rash.

No, 's blood, she told herself, she *was* a good judge of character. Even if Drake had let down his cousin and master, John Hawkins, even if he needed her goodwill to build his influence with her, she trusted Drake, at least as much as she did Robin.

But then, hell's gates, hadn't her father long ago taught her to trust no man?

Despite her worries, the queen's bright and boisterous welcome to the market town of Farnham raised her spirits. Robert Horne, the Protestant bishop of Winchester, tall, solemn, and thin as a rail, met her at the town boundary and made a lovely speech of welcome before they all set out again. Yet Drake's armor, chafing and heating her, was a constant reminder of what had happened and possible future danger.

The castle where they would stay two nights had been built in 1138 by the grandson of William the Conqueror, and she felt today like one indeed. Despite the unsettling events of late, the Queen of England smiled and waved and nodded at her subjects. All along the way, carpets and tablecloths hung from windows; flowers pelted into her path from upper stories of tall buildings that shaded the streets. Cheers and huzzahs oft roared as loud as the sea.

The twisting River Wey glinted in the sun as the royal progress turned from East Street onto Castle Street. From here they could see the gray-stone castle and its ramparts on the northwest hill overlooking the black-and-white-timbered and thatch-roofed town. Emerging from the tight streets, they were thrust into sunlight again and then into the massive shadow of the walls and castle towering over all.

The horses strained as they pulled the coach and wagons up toward the massive gatehouse set in thick, stalwart stone walls. Within the main building and its towers lay a grassy inner bailey. It would do well, Elizabeth thought, to tether tents there for the fringe folk and to be a place of refreshment and sporting—including an archery match she meant to stage.

As the entourage halted and the queen was assisted down from her coach, servants immediately proffered cool goblets of wine to her and her main party. Elizabeth couldn't wait to get out of her armor and dusty garb; she had a good notion to dump the cool liquid between her breasts, but she sipped it as she scanned the lofty castle battlements. She breathed a sigh of relief. No one could hide behind trees or build a stile on hedges here to shoot a bolt or arrow. Nor would danger lurk in the upper parapets or crenellations where bowmen once stood, for she would order those well guarded and explain to her host why.

Waiting at the inner bailey door of the castle was Horne's family, his wife, Joan, and three daughters. As each of the little girls curtsied and then rose, Elizabeth touched their heads as if in blessing, just as she had the thatcher's girls on the road last week. She turned to the bishop's smiling wife again, a pretty but plump woman, plainly yet richly garbed.

"Is it difficult to go back and forth like a shuttlecock between your home at Winchester and this castle, Mistress Joan?" the queen inquired.

"We do well enough, Your Majesty, when my dear husband's enemies let us dwell in peace," Joan replied, as they walked into the castle. Elizabeth noted how the bishop frowned and shook his head at the woman's quick comment.

"Forgive my wife, Your Majesty, for I asked her to mention none of our problems to you, not on this holiday where all is bright and gay."

"I appreciate a woman with a strong backbone, Robert." She nodded to Joan and walked farther inside with him. Bishop Robert Horne was a handsome man, if a bit austere even for a dedicated scholar. "Tell me plain," the queen said, "what problem pains you sore enough that your Joan would mention it at once? Has there been some sort of danger or threat here?"

"She refers to an ongoing dispute with an influential family, the Paulets, from the next shire of Hampshire, Your Grace, Catholics, who cannot abide the changing times and are hostile to a Protestant bishop—and are fast friends with your next host, the Earl of Southampton at Titchfield."

"Ah. Then the Paulets and Southampton are hostile to my bishop's queen, too—as I full well know. Say on."

"The Paulets and Southampton yet resent that upon your accession you immediately removed your sister's Catholic Bishop John White and his Catholic justices and put in your own Protestant men." Once mentioned, his woes spilled from his lips. "I have followed your suit in promoting and advancing local men of the new faith, you see, not popish leaders in this region."

"I do see," she said, as Robert, with his wife now close again, escorted her to the bottom of the large, curved stone staircase. "It is much the same in some other places," she added, more to herself than to her hosts, "so why not in Hampshire, eh?"

"Forgive me, Your Grace," Robert said, speaking quicker and quieter as others of her entourage came near, "but Hampshire is—well, is different, and I believe you have not been there before."

"That is true, but I have heard it is beautiful."

"Yes, in its wild and primitive way. The forests are deeper, the people more isolated and, therefore, more independent and wayward. I swear, some of them are so peculiar and backward—so otherworldly—that you would think we had a struggle on our hands between the ghosts of the old Saxons and the pagan Roman conquerors, not the current Catholics and Protestants."

Strangely, what came to her mind was Ned Topside's little

fantasy with its dark depths of Sherwood Forest full of both the evil and the good. She shook her head to banish the thought.

"Then, too," he went on, "Fareham's being a seaport with exports and imports means that foreign thoughts and foreign people influence the area quite as much as London does."

She drained the rest of her wine and put the goblet on a servant's tray. "I will hear more of this later, Robert, in private, but for now, this cool, old castle feels good on this warm day. I pray it will serve as a most welcome haven from all that lies outside these walls—including that strange, heathen shire of Hampshire I am determined to see for myself."

The next day the queen requested a tournament of sporting events. It pleased her people well to have diversion from their travels. Elizabeth herself had shot the first arrow of the match but now watched from the upper parapet walkway that encircled the castle. Besides the breezes being cool up here, her view of the events was good—and, unless some villain flew overhead like Icarus with waxen wings and with a bow like Cupid, she felt safe.

She had been using both Jenks and Cecil's man Keenan to summon certain ones to her for conversation, which was actually interrogation. Drake stood by her side now with his bowling ball in his hands, for those not shooting at the butts were bowling on makeshift grass alleys servants had hastily laid out.

"I was not aware you had brought two men with you," she told Drake after some small talk. "When I heard, I sent word they were to participate today in the shooting match with the others and not hang about in the shadows."

"I believe I did not mention their presence, Your Grace, but I did not want to be alone on the roads. I wasn't certain of the situation with ruffians or outlaws. Besides, since my summons to attend you on your annual progress was common knowledge among my shipmen, I thought word might get back to my cousin, and that would make him even more—ah, embittered toward me. In short I, like you, thought I could profit from some protection."

"Of course. A good idea. Are your companions strictly sailors, then?"

"Sailors and soldiers."

"Skilled in what sort of warfare on your ship? Must each soldier at sea be adept in both firearms and archery, or do they focus on one task?"

"Hugh there at the butts, for instance," he told her, pointing at the man she had already identified and had been watching closely below, "is a fine bowman, even swinging from the rigging, though I did not realize you would include my men in the shooting match today."

"He has been included at my special request. Is he more adept at longbow or crossbow?"

"Both, but—" He dropped his arm and turned to look her full in the face. "Your Grace, you aren't thinking that . . ." He cleared his throat. "Both of those men are fully loyal to me—and you. That is why I brought them."

"But can you vouch for their whereabouts when you and I were shot at?"

"I—no. They told me later they were in the servants' tent catching a few winks until they heard the hubbub. But I know my men, Your Grace."

His brown eyes were so steady as he faced her, his expression slightly alarmed yet steadfast. She believed him, didn't she?

"You see, they were both with me that disastrous day at San Juan d'Ulua, Your Majesty," he went on, his voice calm and deliberate. "They covered my back and may have saved my life."

"And could not have been corrupted since by an offer of coins from—say, your cousin?"

His gaze wavered for a moment, and she sensed that his inward fears pressed hard on his heart. She understood that fully.

"If a captain can't trust his men, Your Grace, the battle might not be worth the fight, and it would certainly be impossible to win. A captain can't go it alone."

Elizabeth nodded and looked away from him at last, down at her people playing their games—councilors and courtiers with servants looking on. "You are right, of course, Captain Drake, and there are some of my folk I can vouch for, too. After that, it becomes most difficult. Come with me, won't you, while I see how things are going down there at closer range? A captain cannot always hang about the cabin or even in the crow's nest but must mingle with the crew."

The queen noted that even Bishop Horne was on the hastily laid out bowling alleys. Accompanied by Francis Drake, she watched her courtiers cast their six-inch balls from knee height toward two cones. The winner was the one who laid his bowl nearest the cones, called marks. Most courtiers traveled with their set of balls, termed jacks or bowls, often in a tooled Spanish leather case. Much money, time, and curses were spent on playing bowls in her kingdom. Men wrangled over a hair's breadth to declare a win.

"What the deuce! A pox on it! You've cut me off!" Robin yelled at Lord Suffolk as she and Drake approached and stood a ways back to watch.

Chuckling, Suffolk cast his second ball, then jumped and danced about, shouting, "Rub! Rub! Rub!" as it rolled toward the mark.

"Ha!" Robin retorted. "Now there's the rub—you've lost, my lord!"

The queen was surprised to see that Cecil had left his papers to take on Norfolk on another alley, but maybe he, too, saw this opportunity to observe those who might be guilty of evil intentions. Still trailing her sea captain, Elizabeth strolled over.

Cecil and Norfolk were bowling on the bias, a game that was much more of a challenge than regular bowls because it used jacks that were not quite round, so they rolled obliquely. It was Cecil's turn, and Norfolk waited impatiently—and kept unwittingly scratching his left wrist, now not covered with his Spanish leather riding gloves.

She sidled up to him, though when he noted how others turned his way, he swung around to face her. He bowed to her but ignored Drake.

"Your Grace," Norfolk said, "will you take a turn, then? One never knows which way the ball will go. Much like dice which are not loaded or a deck of unmarked cards, it is all so much more interesting."

"I warrant you like things veering off the way they should not rightfully go."

"At times, I do indeed."

"But I already play some such game with you, Norfolk. Best remember I make the rules in this land, and you will go by them or forfeit much. Are you all right? You have been digging at that wrist, scratching like a dog."

His eyes narrowed; he jerked his hand away from the other. "I swear, the beds at Will More's place were full of fleas," he muttered.

She glanced down at the wrist at his side. He had shoved his cuff up during play but now yanked it down again. It was, of course, impossible that Norfolk himself had shot at her and Drake, for he had been standing not far from them with a gauntlet and hawk on his wrist. But Norfolk had many followers, perhaps allies of Queen Mary, Catholics and their ilk, even the Spanish—or simply others who liked his wealth, his coins he could leave scattered about and not miss one lost.

Yes, she recalled how readily he let poor Fenton place the gauntlet on his hand, perhaps to hide his wrist. Had he mayhap been up near the stinging nettle hedges, not to build the stile but to ascertain its position? Though she had insulted him by giving him a falcon far under his rank, he could have been grateful to have his wrist covered. And then, perhaps he'd given that signal where he appeared to swat a fly away . . .

"Let me see that wrist," she said, and he, perhaps realizing too much protest gave away guilty motives, lifted his cuff and held it out for her.

"I don't see bites, but rather a red rash you've made much worse."

"It's nothing," he insisted, avoiding her eyes.

She fought to keep calm when she would like to cuff him at the least or to toss him in this castle's old dungeon at best.

"I only ask because some on this journey have contacted stinging nettle, and that leaves a bad rash," she said, hoping her nonchalant tone carried true. "See my herbal mistress for a cure, lest that could be your problem."

"I could not have something like that."

"I believe," she said, aware that Drake and Cecil hung on their every word, "nettle seems pretty to look at but carries its poisonous ways within. Captain Drake, shall we take a turn bowling with jacks which do not slant astray, then?"

She put her hand on his arm and turned away. Again she felt that strange circle of chill in the center of her back and between her breasts, but she could hardly wear Drake's armor among her closest kin and courtiers. She shuddered and tried to shake a strange sense of foreboding as she strode swiftly on.

Chapter the Seventh

 THEIR FIRST NIGHT ON THE ROAD, WITH JUST OVER half of the distance covered to their next stop, they stayed at the tiny town of High Cross. The queen and her closest courtiers were ecstatically welcomed into an ancient inn, though one newly whitewashed and scrubbed for her visit. The rest of the entourage had to make do in rented chambers or their own tents.

The next morning, after smiling and nodding through a concert of off-key madrigals and numerous fare-thee-well speeches, queen and court were offered a huge breakfast by local farmers who spread their plain but plenteous fare on plank tables on the village green, from which the sheep had been lately shooed away. Then it was off toward Southampton's grand home at Titchfield near Fareham, where everyone looked forward to a more hospitable haven—but for the fact, Elizabeth brooded, that she could not trust her future host worth a fig.

Her bishop's warning about Hampshire haunted Elizabeth as her entourage plunged into another deep forest of that shire. Wolves and wild boars still inhabited these woods. More than once horses pricked up their ears, and her people's chatter stilled at the sound of a howl or as a snorting, big-tusked boar charged across the road.

"Rather like a black cat, eh?" Robin joked before she frowned him to silence.

Once in a while, the royal entourage emerged to clearings and hamlets where people stared and even cheered her on. The day was sunny, but that made the forest roads they plunged through much like tunnels by comparison. Giant oaks loomed overhead, which Drake told her were just the sort used to build ships. They passed through deep banks of spiny, yellow-flowered furze where the faint smell of wood smoke from remote, invisible chimneys or campfires wafted on the air. Erratic dirt tracks led from the main road into mazes of thickets. Whether such paths were beaten bare by beasts of the animal or human kind she was not sure.

Norfolk rode with her a while, but she found his presence more oppressive than the scenery, so she sent him back into the procession and made do with Robin and Drake, however much Robin seemed to dislike him. It pleased her to think he might actually be jealous of the man.

In truth, she needed some diversion, for the fortified Place House mansion at Titchfield where they would stay was yet several hours away. The nearest town was Fareham, which some of her courtiers had been confusing with Farnham, the place they had left behind this morning. Robin tried to make light of the similar names with poems and puns but soon fell silent again.

"You've seen our destination, Captain," she called to Drake. "Describe it for me, then."

"I was surprised to see that Fareham, where I left my ship and the rest of my men on the River Meon, is such a flour-ishing seaport, Your Grace. The quays are bustling with exports of timber, bricks, and wheat and imports of wine, coal, and salt. Shipbuilding abounds there, too. I hope you will deign to visit my men and my ship."

"I will indeed. Is the Meon of Fareham like that pretty little River Wey we saw at Farnham?"

"The Meon has much more—well, character, Your Grace. It's a chalk river, flowing from the downs and the marshes, and its size and strength vary with the weather, as if it had moods of its own. With the shipbuilding there, it reminds me of the River Medway, where I grew up after my family left Dartmoor."

She saw Robin roll his eyes and dramatically pretend to stifle a yawn. She would have liked to slap him as Drake went on. "That was where, under your father's reign, ships of the new royal navy laid up for repairs. I was fascinated by sailors and their stories. And it was an area ever fully loyal to the Tudors, unlike—well, I fear unlike the area around Fareham."

He may have realized he wasn't helping her low spirits, for he seemed to sink into silence after that burst of information. She sent Robin away and ordered one of her guards to fetch Meg Milligrew from the vast parade of people. Would they never get to Fareham? she fumed. If they could but escape all these huge trees and deep woodland, she could breathe the free air of the sea.

Worse, Cecil had begun her day by daring to argue again that she should have canceled at least this part of the journey, for, he said, backing up Bishop Horne's warning, their next host, the second Earl of Southampton, was a dyed-in-the-wool Catholic and ally of Norfolk. Their stop with her bishop had been a short respite, but between Sir William More at Loseley House and Lord Southampton at Place

House in Fareham, it was out of the frying pan and into the fire, he'd lectured her.

"I know that, and I have said I know that!" she'd exploded at Cecil. "This is one way to keep an eye on them and use up their funds, which could go for more dangerous purposes than entertaining their true queen and her court! Best to beard them in their dens, so no more, Cecil, even from you!"

Now, though, in the dark heart of endless forests full of feral dens, she wasn't so sure she was right. Yet certainly there was safety in numbers, and she had that. Her guards rode before and behind the coach and at each of its wheels, so they did not block her view of the scenery or people she summoned to her.

She turned to question Drake about how many men guarded his ship in Fareham. But his head bobbed in exhaustion, and he now rode just slightly back so his horse's head was all she could see without twisting her neck. 'S blood, this was a long, boring ride today, and, after she spoke with Meg, she would nap, too.

"You sent for me, Your Grace." Meg's voice interrupted her thoughts. Her herb woman had made her way through the guards and appeared on the other side of the coach from where Drake rode. Elizabeth thought Meg rode a horse well—a good-looking palfrey, too—as she jogged abreast the coach.

Elizabeth scooted toward the edge of her seat so she wouldn't have to speak too loudly. She held the leather curtain farther back with her hand and leaned her cheek against its heavy folds. "Meg, has Lord Norfolk been to you for a cure for a rash or flea bites?"

"Asking for the broad-leafed dock tincture, you mean?"

"Whatever it is. Has he asked you for aught?"

Elizabeth knew she was growing short-tempered even with those she favored and trusted, but she could not help it. And this progress was to have been not only for politics but for pleasure!

"No, Your Grace, he hasn't asked me for a thing. Piers's and Sim's rashes are finally better, though."

"I am glad to hear that. How does the little one? Still crying?"

"Some. I dare say, Your Grace, I am a comfort to him. I—I understand his grief."

"And I pray he, in turn, will be good comfort for you, my Meg."

"Nothing will ever replace our little Ned, but—" She sniffed hard. Their eyes met. Elizabeth wondered if her own griefs ever showed so on her face. For one moment, watching Meg was like looking in a dark glass, not at her own stoic countenance but as she would appear if she ever dared show fear or grief in public. Meg's face was so like her own, her form so similar. She even wore a velvet cap, one of the queen's castaways, perched on her red hair. Elizabeth was glad to see it, for the woman hadn't given a fig what she looked like for weeks after her babe died.

"But what, Meg?" she prompted.

"The lad reminds me so of Ned, it's uncanny, Your Grace. Oh, I mean not so much in looks but in his flights of fancy and his way with words, once he gets going about fairies and ghosts and such. Ned's taken to him, too, encourages him, says he'd make a fine boy to play the children or ladies' parts—so maybe we can just keep him, Your Grace."

"We shall think about that, if Piers is willing, but I'm not certain the two lads should be separated. Jenks and his wife say Sim is just the opposite, you know, all solid fact, dedicated to taking over for his father back home, yet he loves the unknown and is thrilled to be on a journey."

"Jenks also says Sim keeps saying he can't wait to see the sea. I thought maybe Captain Drake would want a cabin boy or such."

Elizabeth's hand was getting tired of holding the stiff curtain back; it kept rubbing against her cheek and temple as the coach bounced along. Besides, it was time to send Meg back to her place in the entourage so Norfolk or others would not wonder what was afoot that the queen spoke over-long to her herbalist.

"A cabin boy? A fine idea—I repeat, *if* we agree the two lads should be separated. I know how sore it pained me to be continually separated from my brother years ago—and, yes, sometimes from my sister, too, though she ever detested me." She heaved a sigh. "We shall worry about the Naseby lads later, for there are other things to fret for now and—"

Meg screamed. Her tidy cap and coif seemed to rip free of her head as she fell forward on her horse's neck. In that brief second, Elizabeth screamed, too, as something sliced through the leather curtain she held against her head.

Drake was half dozing in the saddle on the rear starboard side of the royal coach when a woman's scream and then another cut the air.

He looked ahead, right, then left. Had the queen screamed? No, more likely her herb girl, Meg Milligrew. It must be she who screamed twice.

In an instant, he spurred his horse, but the queen's guards engulfed the coach, shutting him out. Again he tried to ride forward but the Earl of Leicester, the Duke of Norfolk, and others edged him away.

"What's amiss?" he shouted, as a yeoman guard turned away from the coach and rode past him.

"Got to fetch the physician."

"What befell, man?"

"Arrow shot . . ." he called over his shoulder before the rest of his words were drowned by the buzz of voices.

Drake's first impulse was to ride into the forest in the direction from which the attack had come, but several yeomen guards were already doing that. He glanced behind him for his men. Neither was where he had been and should be.

Once he heard the queen's commanding voice up ahead and was certain she was safe, he swung his mount back along the now halting flanks of the entourage. People looked frenzied, but no one knew a thing, and he did not want to create panic by telling what he knew—which wasn't much, wasn't enough.

His stomach twisted. Without Elizabeth, England—and his wild, passionate ambitions—would be not only becalmed but sunk. And to think he'd been insulted that she had asked him about the loyalty of his men yesterday. Where in creation were they?

Her Grace had even ferreted out earlier that his man Hugh was a fine shot—and that sailor suddenly seemed to have extra coins for gambling. His other man, Giles, did, too, for that matter, though not shiny, new-minted ones.

By God's faith, where were they now when he hadn't given them leave to depart their posts? He'd question them stringently, as the queen had commanded him to interrogate that blackguard Barnstable. After all, both men had been on his cousin's ship before he'd transferred to the *Judith* just before the battle at San Juan d'Ulua. Then, too, their covering his back as he'd boasted to the queen was *before* he'd let his cousin down by inadvertently leaving him behind.

He passed the royal physician, riding with the yeoman guard in the opposite direction, as he broke from the rear of the royal entourage and thundered down the road the riders and wagons had left even more rutted than they'd found it. If his actions looked suspicious, as if he were fleeing, he'd simply stand his ground and explain to Her Grace. And he'd flog those two if they had just dropped behind—or, God forbid, gone into this deep forest for their own devices, especially since the arrow obviously came from there.

Around the next turn in the road, he saw the two of them emerging from the fringe of forest. Their horses were tied to a tree trunk. How long could they have been gone? Had they stopped this far back, and he'd been dozing and not noticed?

"Where in heaven's name have you two been?" he roared, as he reined in between them and their mounts.

Slack-jawed, they gaped up at him as if he were a ghost. They had nothing in their hands, at least, so he hadn't caught them with bows or a quiver full of bolts or arrows.

"Just had to relieve ourselves, Cap'n," Hugh said, shrugging. "Too much rich food and ale, e'en for the likes of us last night, you know, more'n a quick stop would do for. And can't hardly plop one's bum over the side rail and just fire away off a horse like at sea, eh?"

The man's rational explanation and jovial mood calmed Drake somewhat. But Giles didn't look a bit innocent. No, he looked pained, green at the gills over something.

"And you, man?" Drake said, putting one arm across his saddle and leaning down toward him.

"Ne'er was seasick a day, Cap'n, but got the runs bad today."

Drake decided not to grill them now but to watch them better, much as he'd seen Her Majesty deal with those she did not trust.

Then it hit him, and chills shot up his back: Today, as at Loseley House, just like the queen, *he*, too, was in the vicinity of the arrow's path. Granted, he rode a bit back and on the other side of the coach, but thank God he had been ready to nod off, so perhaps his head had dropped then, or the coach had bounced just a whit to make the arrow intended for him miss its mark. No. No, it must have been meant for the queen, and she or her herb girl had been slightly wounded. He prayed that was all. He must ride back to be sure.

Worse, he was suddenly affrighted that the queen might think he'd turned tail and fled just now—and believe him a coward or traitor, as his cousin no doubt still did.

He turned his horse to ride toward the upheaval around the queen. He muttered a string of sailor's oaths he never used, no, not even when he'd fled the massacre at San Juan d'Ulua, not so much, as he always claimed, to fight another day but because he was terrified he'd lose his first ship and never be trusted to command one again. His only opportunity for a future now was to convince the queen that she could trust him and that he'd never flee again.

After Dr. Huicke had come in haste and examined Meg, who was not even bleeding, Elizabeth had sent him away. Then fear and fury flooded in, and she came back to herself again.

Though she'd screamed in shock, since she'd been certain Meg was not hurt, the queen had stared silently at the arrow that had stuck in the gilded wood of the coach beyond and barely above her head. She glanced at the terror-struck Meg, still ahorse, with her hair wild, then to the arrow again. Other than that, Elizabeth could not move, could not think. Her guards had reacted, though: Some had gone into the forest.

Slowly her thoughts settled. Someone had shot through the trees expertly, exactly through Meg's hair and the curtain beside the queen's head and into the coach. Or else the shot had gone awry and missed what it was meant to hit—either Meg or her, but either way, the shooter could have meant to hit the queen.

Her mounted guards and closest courtiers had made a solid wall of protection around her, but they were now crowding Meg away from the coach.

"Get in here, Meg!" She found her voice at last. "Get in here!" The woman half fell, half dove into the coach. The queen slapped the pierced curtains shut on the side from which the missile had come.

Outside her coach, chaos continued. She watched out the other side as more yeomen guards peered in. Robin, Norfolk, and Cecil appeared at the side she had open.

"Shall I lead the search, including for the arrow?" Robin cried, leaning down to look in.

"It's stuck in here."

"I'll stay close. Guards!" he shouted, and began to give orders. "However deep the thickets and foliage, more of you, go! On foot if you must! Boonen," he cried to her driver, "we can't coast along here like sitting ducks. Onward! We are far closer to safety at Titchfield than in turning back. On, man, and at the fastest clip you can safely manage!"

Elizabeth was both moved and annoyed by his taking over. "And Robin!" she cried, as her brain began to really work again, suspicions and all.

"Yes, Your Grace?"

"Send someone back through the entourage to tell the others I am well but to beware. They should strive to keep up even if we leave the baggage carts behind. And someone fetch Ned Topside here to his wife!"

"But he mustn't leave little Piers unattended!" Meg cried, and that made the queen realize she, too, had recovered her wits.

"At least the bolt only grazed your skull," Elizabeth said.

"My cap flew off, though—it was close."

"Very close," the queen said, and scrutinized the offending bolt stuck in the painted and gilded wood. Her own head might have been there had she been sitting straight up in the center as she usually did, or perhaps if the curtain had not slowed or deflected the shaft. Then, too, Drake had been nearby again when it hit, but where was he now?

She kept her hand firm on her friend's shoulder, hoping to comfort her. But indeed, Meg could have been mistaken for herself on that horse, and she began to shake harder than her herbalist or the bouncing coach.

Though it was no doubt but a few moments, it seemed to Meg an eternity until Ned rode up to the coach. She cried when she saw him and knelt to reach up to take his hand through the crack between the pierced curtains. He rode quickly and jerkily along beside them, since the queen's driver was going at a good pace.

"Slow down, Boonen!" the queen shouted, and yanked the curtains open wider on Ned's side. "Boonen, we are away from the attack, man, and my bones and teeth can't take the jolting!"

"Better you keep the curtains closed, Your Grace," Ned piped up, "than face another bolt from the blue."

"From the greenwood, you mean. And no jesting! I can't abide this dark, damned forest. Take Meg back with you and sit her down in a wagon, not up on the seat. It is possible that the shooter believed she was me, although the fact the bolt plunged into my coach may make that a pointless point."

Meg saw Her Grace shake her head at her own inadvertent punning. Meg held hard to Ned, but, in the stronger light now, she studied the bolt the queen had mentioned, stuck deep in the wood. The vehicle slowed as Francis Drake rode up hastily on Ned's other side.

Meg frowned up at the bolt. She'd seen the first one at close range, and this one looked pretty different to her. "Your Grace," she said, her voice trembling, "this one looks like an arrow, not a bolt, doesn't it? Maybe it wasn't even shot by the same man—or shot by someone who is skilled with any sort of bow."

As Ned rode away with Meg sitting before him on his horse, the queen clenched her hands so hard that her fingernails bit into her palms. She was furious with herself for letting panic command her actions and cloud her brain. While she cowered, her herb woman, no less, who had been as endangered and shaken by the deadly missile as she had been, had the presence of mind to see that the bolt was not a bolt at all but an arrow!

Two attempts on her life—if they were that. By more than one person, as Meg had suggested? She had a bolt and an arrow for evidence, yet perhaps was no closer to knowing who was the expert marksman or men, who had, thank the good Lord, evidently missed everyone this time.

Then, too, Drake had been nearby, on his horse, his head probably even visible to the shooter above the height of Meg's head and the top of the coach. It was feasible that the marksman had mean to hit Drake, she reasoned as, on her knees to give herself some height and leverage, she tried to dislodge the arrow. She amazed herself by not being able to budge it from the wood, at least not without perhaps snapping it off. Yes, indeed, this was not a bolt but an arrow, a fully fletched one with a shaft longer than a bolt.

"Drake," she cried, "climb in here and pull or pry this arrow from where it stuck."

He tied his horse's reins to something outside and slid in from the saddle as if he were walking the yardarm of a tossing ship. He adeptly avoided her wide skirts and looked where she pointed. She opened the curtains of the side it had shot through to give him more light, for two guards blocked her view of the forest now.

"Ah," he said, "driven deep, as if the shooter were close, when he obviously was not or someone would have spotted him. And to place it so, through all those thick trees and hanging foliage . . ."

"You sound as if you admire his skill."

"I'm afraid I do, though I am thankful he was just a whit off—unless, of course, he was right on target."

"Who was his target, do you think? It was not my falconer, Fenton, who stood between you and me this time but my herb woman. Had you thought that you might be the target as well as I again?"

"Yes—yes, of course."

"Then what do you mean that the shooter might have been right on target?"

"That he might have only wished to affright you— again—or to warn you this second time. Or me."

"Exactly, Captain. Both of us—either of us—could have been the bull's-eye again, to be warned or killed. But warned to do what—to flee from whence we came? To simply fear whoever hates us? For it seems the marksman is lurking in each place we stop or pass, and that, of course, means it could be someone either stalking our progress or *in* our progress."

"Yes, I agree," he said, frowning. His usually commanding voice sounded shaky now, but perhaps that was from the jolting of the coach.

"I can hardly turn everyone in this large retinue into spies watching each other for who disappears into the forest from time to time," she muttered.

Hastily, as if to change the subject, he said, "I shall pull the arrow out and try not to snap it off." He started to say something else, then tugged and wrenched the arrow out. "At least four inches into that hard oak," he reported. "To come the distance it did—but longbowmen are few and far between in this modern age," he added, as if to himself.

"Longbowmen? You think that arrow was shot from a longbow? Those went out with my father's reign."

"I say that because this arrow," he said, glaring at it in his big hands, "must have come a long ways, and an arrow cannot be shot by a crossbow, which also would have the distance. A shortbow would have been useless from a ways within the forest fringe."

"Yes, surely someone would not have shot from the first line of trees, or he could have been seen. And if he were farther back, the thick foliage should have gotten in his way, especially with a shortbow. So I—or we—may have now been shot at by a crossbowman and mayhap a longbowman who should be nearly extinct but for decrepit, old men . . ."

"Well, it cannot be a marksman back from the dead or some sort of forest phantom. Your Majesty, I must tell you that I noted both my men were missing when this arrow was shot," Drake blurted. "I searched for them and found them emerging from the forest far behind the end of the procession. They both had loose innards today, they say, and were seeing to nature's urgent call. They had no weapons of any sort on their persons and, I believe, could not so swiftly have covered the distance in the forest from the place from which this came to where they emerged, nor, I can assure you, do they have crossbows or longbows in their saddle packs."

"I see," she said, taking the arrow from him. "That was quite a lengthy recital—confessional, perhaps. It is good you acted quickly and told me quickly. I charge you to keep an eye on them both."

"I shall. I told you also lest someone who does not appreciate my attending you on this progress should report to you that I fled like one guilty."

"Another thing we share then, Captain," she said, carefully placing the arrow on the opposite leather seat, "is necessary devious thinking for our own personal protection and advancement."

Their eyes met and held.

"Yes," he admitted, then added, "and one more thing I must confess."

She frowned. "Which is?"

"I have—Your Majesty, I have seen arrows like this, not

with the same fletching, but the shafts are much the same. Look," he said, gesturing toward it, "a pyramid point that tapers to a square base, cleverly carved."

"But what's this wrapped around it?"

"That's quite characteristic and also gives it away," he whispered, then cleared his throat. "It's wrapped tightly with a strip of soft leather so it rotates in flight and digs deep into its target—much more deadly. These were the very sort some of the Spanish bowmen shot at us at San Juan d'Ulua."

She sucked in a quick breath. "Spanish! I knew it. I feared it. Then—your men, like you, perhaps, could have collected such arrows for keepsakes of your deliverance."

His fine features seemed to clench around his narrowed eyes. "True," he said. "I have a few yet in my captain's cabin. *Quadrellos,* the Spanish call these arrows, Your Grace. They bored so deep into the bodies and bones of my men, we call them homicidal arrows."

Chapter the Eighth

AS THE AFTERNOON WORE ON, THE ROYAL EN-
tourage, tired and distressed, pushed on through
fields, villages, and a final forest. Never more
than on this day had Elizabeth regretted England's law that
each local parish must maintain its own roads by spending
but four days a year repairing them. That included cutting
back brush and filling holes larger than pots with stones, neither of which had been done here. And if an obstacle was in
the way, such as an ancient tree trunk or thicket, the road
might take a sharp jog around it, so the queen's progress
must, too.

Yet Elizabeth was certain she could smell the sea, and that
kept her spirits up a bit. She thought the horses pricked up
their ears and pulled harder at the scent, too. As they burst
from the shaded tunnel of the last deep woods, the sun-
struck scene awaiting them before the town of Fareham startled them all.

It looked as if the entire population of the village, perhaps of the whole area, had turned out for a grand and glorious welcome. Cheering, waving people, six or seven deep,
packed the rutted dirt road into the town. Banners, many

improvised from tablecloths or petticoats, smacked smartly in the breeze as people waved them or held them aloft on poles. Some sort of low wooden scaffolding had been erected and was strewn with leafy boughs, evidently as a stage for a pageant. In the midst of it all, Henry Wriothesley, the Earl of Southampton, and his wife, Lady Mary, rode to greet them on flower-bedecked matching horses.

Elizabeth called to Cecil and Robin from the depths of her coach, "I was expecting hard looks and meager cheers. Perhaps I was in error to judge, though I know well enough the tricks of pretense and artifice."

"But you had ordered," Cecil said, bending down a bit to look in at her, "that we would ride straight for the shelter of Place House. Your Grace, after that possible attempt on your life today . . ."

"My people, Cecil, are awaiting, and in an area I had been fretting was not strong for a Protestant queen. I will not cower from terror, even in this open area with many about we do not know. Especially, their queen shall not sit, as if some guilty prisoner, in her coach to watch these festivities. But," she went on to stay the further protest coming from him, "I am not disillusioned that those white-teethed smiles coming this way may not be the bared fangs of wolves. Boonen, halt here!" she shouted. Then she added quietly to Cecil alone, "Deploy my guards carefully, my lord, and do put on a pleasant face."

The twenty-four-year-old Earl of Southampton, Henry Wriothesley, whose last name was pronounced Rise-lee, was a young whelp Elizabeth still had hopes she could tame. These last few years, he was much more at court in London and was becoming a vocal member of her nobles, though she was afraid he listened far too much to Norfolk. What galled her most about Southampton as a covert supporter of her rival, Mary, Queen of Scots, was that his father had been one of her father's staunchest supporters when the old religion was being supplanted by the new.

The first Earl of Southampton, Thomas, had worked for King Henry VIII and his chief advisor, Cromwell. Twenty-seven former monastic manors, including Titchfield Abbey but a half mile from here, had been awarded to this earl's father for "his good and true and faithful service" to the Tudor king. Young Henry had inherited the earldom at the tender age of five but had somehow turned back to the Catholic faith while yet wallowing in the wealth that had flowed from the Tudors.

Perhaps, Elizabeth thought, as the young couple dismounted and approached her coach still all smiles, Henry Wriothesley was somehow trying to atone for his father's headlong ruination of the Catholic faith in England. 'S blood, she'd smarted silently for the brutal way it had been accomplished by her father, but she'd never say so. After all, Great Henry had done it to wed her mother as surely as he'd meant to get his hands on the wealth of the corrupt old church—and for his conscience's sake, of course.

"Your Gracious Majesty, it is our honor and delight to welcome you to Fareham," the earl declared as he, then his wife, Mary, dismounted and bent to kiss the beringed hand the queen offered them.

"I am pleased at the fine greeting, my lord, and look forward to our time with you."

"If you would deign to delay your further progress for but a few moments," he went on, "we—my family and the town folk—have prepared a short fantasy in your honor. If you would but mount the rural throne we have built under the leafy bower on the dais, we can commence and then, afterward, head onward to our domicile, which we have readied for you and the court."

"I would be pleased to see the play," she said, nodding and smiling as a footman put down the wooden steps for her to dismount. Behind the Wriothesleys, she could see Cecil frowning and shifting from one foot to the other. "*If*," she added, "you, my lord and lady, will both stand close beside me during it all."

"A great honor," the pretty, green-eyed Mary declared with another quick curtsy. "I have been looking forward to this moment ever since we heard you would bestow a visit on us, here in the deep south country."

It was a good thing, Elizabeth thought as she climbed down, that noble marriages were arranged early, or this skinny, sallow-faced boy, however fine his attire and smooth his manners, would never catch a beauty like this one.

Elizabeth made certain she walked close between the two of them, keeping a light touch on their arms as if to escort them to the leafy bower they had built, which arched over the silk-draped wooden throne. "Sit," she said, "each of you on one of the arms of my chair, yes, like that."

The poor girl blushed a bit to be pulled so close, perhaps to have her satin skirts overspill the queen's own costume. Elizabeth knew she would have taken to the earl if Cecil's spies and the young man's intercepted notes to that traitor Norfolk hadn't revealed his true colors. Now he fidgeted, too, and spent a long moment getting his clanking sword and scabbard out of the way as he perched on the outer edge of the other arm of her chair.

Among the crowd turned expectantly her way, the queen

noted well that Cecil had deftly deployed her red-liveried yeomen guards. Most were facing out toward the crowd, keeping a good eye on them, though a few closer watched her courtiers and scrutinized the approaching players. In this imagined forest setting, she wondered if her guards who had plunged into the real forest several hours ago would find the shooter or any sign of him.

Well, Elizabeth thought, as she settled back to watch the little fantasy, just let someone dare to shoot at her right now.

A handsome lad began the entertainment by reading from a scroll in a loud voice, proclaiming that "the great deer hunt park of the Earl of Southampton at Titchfield near the town of Fareham in Hampshire welcomes the queen of the realm, Elizabeth of England, the great virgin goddess of the hunt, as was the Roman virgin goddess Diana!"

Everyone nodded and whispered at that. The queen did love to ride and hunt, but she had no desire to do so in the near future, not since she was evidently the hunted lately.

Glancing off to the side, she saw Ned Topside studying each gesture on the stage, no doubt wishing he were the principal player this time. He had on his shoulders the younger Naseby boy, Piers, all eager eyes at the stage before him.

She saw that handsome courier of Cecil's, too, Justin Keenan, perhaps just arrived. Off to the side, he still held his lathered horse with his wheezing second horse behind, so he must have ridden them hard. Cecil had sent him, not to London this time, but only back to Guildford to learn if Sheriff Barnstable's men had come back into town so they could be questioned.

"And so, we begin," the prologue went on. "As our queen has emerged from the forest, so once did the virgin goddess Diana return from the hunt!" The man rolled the scroll closed, bowed to her, and exited.

Traipsing in from the side of the makeshift stage depicting a forest, to stand before the queen's seat on the dais, came a beautiful, red-haired, slender girl in green satin with a fine leather quiver over her shoulders and a bow in her hand against which rested a ready arrow.

Elizabeth realized she was leaning forward and sat back in her seat. No, the arrow bore no resemblance to the *quadrello* that had been shot at her earlier.

What else caught her eye was that the woman was played by a female and not a young boy whose voice had not deepened. Behind the goddess trailed a bevy of beautiful nymphs—actually girls, too—ones to rival the queen's own ladies in fair countenance if not in poise, for they were, no doubt, women selected from the town. Two of them squirmed in their tight-laced bodices, and one scratched an itch under her arm. Their stilted dialogue told of the fine aim and skill of the goddess Diana, who was tired and wanted to bathe and rest after the long hunt on this day.

Her nymphs divested Diana of her weapons and cloak, then stood around her as if to block the view while she supposedly bent to bathe in a forest pool, made from a circle of shimmering blue silk laid on the rough floor of the stage.

"Now comes Actaeon on the scene, Your Grace," Mary Wriothesley blurted in a whisper, as if, like a child, she could not help but tell what was coming next.

Elizabeth knew the mythological tale of Diana and Actaeon well, as did most of her court, no doubt. She watched as Prince Actaeon, the comely son of King Camus, entered with four hunt hounds at his heels. He spoke of his own hunting expedition on this day. Now he was, he said, "led thither to my destiny."

The prince accidentally came upon Diana bathing. He gasped as he peeked past her nymphs to gaze upon her nakedness. Beside the queen, Lady Mary sighed so hard she inadvertently elbowed Elizabeth's shoulder.

The nymphs screamed and tried to protect the goddess from the eyes of a strange man and mere mortal. Diana stretched her arm for her bow and arrow, but they were out of reach; instead, she splashed water, cut pieces of silk, in Actaeon's eyes.

Then, cleverly for a rustic player, the queen thought, as Diana's curses met the man's ears, for his punishment, he began to turn into a stag. From under her garment, one nymph slipped a deer hide on the actor, and another passed him stag's horns he cunningly strapped on his head.

Staggering about the stage, horrified at feeling himself turning into the animal he had oft hunted, the doomed man gasped as his hounds bayed at his heels. Surreptitiously dropping pieces of meat to them, crying out in horror, he rushed headlong away through the counterfeit trees before the pack supposedly attacked and devoured him in the unseen forest depths.

When his cries halted and the audience heard only the howling of the dogs, everyone grew quiet for a moment before exploding into cheers and applause. They hushed again when Diana held up her hands for silence, then turned sideways between audience and queen and spoke.

"Just as," the red-haired maiden declared in a clear, high voice, much like her own, Elizabeth realized, "when the ancient Romans lived in this area and replaced the old Anglo-

Saxon deities like Woden, later Catholicism came to conquer all pagan gods, so I, the virgin goddess Diana, a mere figment of foolish minds, was displaced by the true faith."

The queen wondered if she would mention that Catholicism, too, had been replaced by the truer faith of Protestantism, but then this area was yet a stronghold for the old religion.

"And so, in honor of that," the young woman went on, "I, the virgin queen of the hunt, must give way to the Virgin Mary, the rightful queen of heaven."

Elizabeth stiffened as another fair young woman, draped in a blue robe, even over her head, came out and took the place of the banished goddess Diana, who fled offstage with her nymphs. This woman's hands were clasped as if in prayer, and she gazed up toward heaven while the awed crowd finally began to cheer again.

The queen's wide stare snagged Cecil's. He had suddenly appeared in her line of sight, just over the shoulders of Robin, who looked most annoyed, and Norfolk, who seemed to be stifling a grin.

Elizabeth's eyes narrowed as her brain took in the clever words: *the virgin queen . . . must give way to Mary . . . the rightful queen . . .* Surely they did not dare to insult her with clever treason favoring Mary, Queen of Scots! Still, it was not blatant, and she would appear a fearful, weak woman if she acted like one.

"An interesting turn of words at the end," she said, rising so quickly she almost toppled her hosts off their tenuous perches. "'Tis much more pleasant, I warrant, to be queen of heaven than queen of this earthly realm, for everyone in heaven is good and true."

Ignoring the wary expressions on their faces, she turned to wave at the crowd as their cheers swelled and broke over her.

At least, despite Southampton's—or maybe Norfolk's—duplicity, the common folk, who probably didn't discern the deeper meanings of this play, were simply glad to see their queen.

Elizabeth marched straight back to her coach and told Boonen to head for Place House, following their hosts on their fine horses.

"I'm not running away with the dogs at my heels," she muttered to herself as the coach jerked into motion. "I intend to stay and fight."

"I was not deceived for long, I'll tell you that!" Elizabeth ranted to her Privy Plot counselors—without Drake this time—as they met in her chamber in her suite of rooms at Place House that evening after dark. Fortunately, a thunderstorm was raging outside, for she was finding it difficult to keep her voice in check. The more she realized how slyly her hosts had pulled her into the snare of their pageant, the more she wanted to shake down the rafters of this place.

"I was dead set against it from the first," Cecil put in, his voice eternally calm, as he tapped a stack of documents together. "But, as you realized from the first, Your Grace, that little farce hardly affected the local people's goodwill."

"But to be forced to ignore the badwill of my hosts, after all my family has done for theirs! I could barely choke down those fine dishes at the feast this evening, especially the venison! However much I love to hunt, I'll not go prancing through their damned deer park, mayhap to be attacked from the forest again as was poor, hapless Actaeon!"

"I was thinking, Your Grace," Ned put in, "that you were meant to be the goddess Diana instead of Actaeon."

"Do you think I am some claybrained ninnyhammer?" she demanded. "You missed my point. I know that!"

"Then, too," he went on, evidently as used to her tantrums as Cecil, "since the main role of the virgin goddess Diana was played by a female instead of a boy, I had another thought. Could that have been a snide reference to the fact that as a woman you should not rule, but it should have been a boy—a male—in that part? I mean, after all, your brother became king at an early age, and Southampton was but a boy when he took the earldom, so perhaps the message is that you should wed and bear a son who could rule."

"Too far-fetched," she muttered, lowering her voice at last. "That is, unless it's a half-cocked reference to the fact that Mary of Scots has produced a son and heir who has more right to rule than I do, too. But he is only three years old now. Besides, the pro-Papist forces in this country and abroad adored having my sister Mary on the throne and would hazard all to have my cousin Mary in my stead."

"We could keep for evidence," Cecil said, still shuffling papers, "the next correspondence that passes between Norfolk and Southampton about support for your cousin, then arrest them on suspicion of treason."

"Oh, indeed I would like to toss them in the Tower and the key in the Thames. But I want to give them more rope to hang themselves first, my lord—hang themselves by the neck and not just by their thumbs, which is all we'll be able to do if we can't completely establish the fact they've been financially supporting the northern Catholic lords. If a rebellion explodes there, I'd actually like all the traitors in on it tooth and nail, so we can catch them in the same trap and be done with them."

She jolted as someone knocked on the door. "Jenks, see to

that and step outside to speak to whoever it is without letting them look in," she ordered. As he hastened to obey, she
told the others almost in a whisper, "I do intend to have
Southampton give me a thorough tour of this place and
these grounds, rain or shine, on the morrow, for I am looking
for evidence he's been training troops here. If he can stage
that play, perhaps he can stage help for a northern uprising."

"He's had weeks to hide any such troops or evidence, Your
Grace," Cecil said.

"That is why I—we—shall also search the outer grounds
and surrounding area if we must. I refuse to just—Jenks,
what?" she asked, as he stepped back inside, holding a small
hempen sack out stiff-armed, as if it would bite him.

"The guards who searched the woods after the arrow was
shot are here," he said, bolting the door behind him and returning to the table. "The yeoman guard outside handed
this in."

"Well, what news? What is in the sack?"

"They found sure evidence of where the man shot from,
about twenty feet off the road, but not the man himself," he
told her, extending the sack.

"Twenty feet—a longbow, indeed, then," she said, as she
took the sack. It was light, as if empty. She opened it to peer
inside while everyone leaned her way. "It can't be more than
the string of a bow," she said, tipping it toward the lantern
in the center of the table, not wanting to just plunge her
hand in.

It was empty! No, something here—fletching feathers
from an arrow?

Instead, she pulled out a calfskin tab that protected the
skin of two fingers, the thumb, and the bend of the hand
when the shooter drew back the bowstring. Some shooters,

especially ladies, used gloves instead. This leather tab trailed strings by which it could be tied over the wrist, but one of the strings had broken.

"A shooting tab to avoid calluses," Ned said.

"Stained with dirt and sweat. Well used," Meg put in, squinting at it.

Cecil stood and leaned closer. "Someone with quite large fingers, unless it is simply, as Mistress Meg implied, well worn and has stretched a bit."

"At any rate," Elizabeth said, as she sank into her chair, staring at the very tab that had surely belonged to the shooter, "I'll wager this, too, is Spanish leather."

Elizabeth's body was exhausted that night, but her brain was wide-awake. She plunged in and out of disjointed sleep. Again, again, she saw in her mind, like scenes in a play, that first arrow racing in her direction. Again, Fenton fell to the ground with his life's blood pouring from him. Again, she saw the poor, hanged Thomas Naseby.

Her mind skipped to her brief interview with Cecil's courier, Keenan, this evening after the banquet. He'd reported that the former sheriff Barnstable, like the two louts who had been his henchmen, had disappeared from Guildford; he'd not even taken clothes or coins from his house, his manservant had said. Keenan had added, extending a newly minted silver shilling to her, "I made the man give me one of the coins, and I warrant they are all like these."

It was identical to the one she'd found on the floor of Barnstable's cellar, the room where Tom Naseby had been hanged.

Clever, Keenan was, as well as handsome and strong, she

thought as she teetered on the edge of sleep. Cecil's best courier, no doubt, a man she'd like to have working more directly for her. But what Keenan did was important, bringing intelligence back and forth from London and parts north for Cecil. She should have a messenger who could report directly to the Privy Plot Council . . .

Drifting away again, once more she saw the arrow that had barely missed her and Meg. It hissed at her as it sliced through the leather curtain of her coach and thudded deep into the gilded wood just over her head.

Elizabeth turned over and tried to find a more comfortable position. She'd churned her sheets to waves, waves like those that buffeted Drake's ship, just as homicidal arrows had hit its decks. He and his surviving men had kept them as bizarre tokens of the enemy . . . she could see the death arrows when she visited his ship . . . arrows, bolts, finger tabs, quivers, she was quivering in fear when she must show none . . .

She sat bolt upright in bed, her heart pounding. What had wakened her? She heard naught but Rosie's heavy, steady breathing from her trundle as if she slept the sleep of the dead.

Finally, Elizabeth got out of the big bed and in her night rail padded barefoot to the window overlooking the central courtyard. The storm had ended, but clots of clouds still scudded across the sky, sometimes obscuring the pale three-quarter moon. Drake was riding at dawn tomorrow to prepare for her visit aboard the *Judith* the day after that; she looked forward to seeing his ship and the River Meon. But nothing else, except seeing the sea beyond the river lifted her spirits. She felt weighed down by burdens and frightened when she could not afford to be.

She went into the deserted privy chamber and lit a fat beeswax candle from the low-burning lantern and sat at the table to read her Bible. She knew just where she would find the passage she wanted. Let her enemies present their plays of pagan virgin goddesses supplanted by the great symbol of Catholic queens, the Virgin Mary. Elizabeth of England would somehow prevail; she would see this through.

She moved her lips as she read the words in Psalm 64 she needed so desperately for comfort: *Hear my voice, O God, in my prayer: preserve my life from fear of the enemy. Hide me from the secret counsel of the wicked; from the insurrection of the workers of iniquity; who whet their tongue like a sword and bend their bows to shoot their arrows, even bitter words: that they may shoot in secret at the perfect: suddenly do they shoot at him, and fear him not. They encourage themselves in an evil matter: they commune of laying snares privily . . . but God shall shoot at them with an arrow . . .*

"Yes," she mouthed in the flickering light. "And I shall find a way to shoot back at them, too."

Chapter the Ninth

MEG STIFLED A SCREAM AS A MAN BLOCKED HER WAY. She was cutting through the wilderness gardens behind Place House. This area was left to run riot in its natural state. With all the tall, leafy bushes and bowers, it was much like walking through a maze. Worse, dawn hardly reached here, and people, but for the kitchen servants, were not yet astir.

She gasped and jumped back. It was the Duke of Norfolk himself and evidently alone. Crushing a sweetbag of rose petals and lavender to her breasts, she managed a tipsy curtsy on the deep grass.

"I thought that was you, herb mistress," Norfolk clipped out. "I've a rash that plagues me like the very devil. The queen says you have something for it."

He pulled up his sleeve to display a bumpy, livid red rash that showed its fierce color even in the pearly light. It covered his right hand and crept up from his wrist toward his elbow. She squinted at it and had a good notion to ask if Elizabeth Tudor on the throne didn't plague him like the very devil, too.

She knew her place, though, at least with this man. Just

wait 'til she told the queen, for Her Majesty had suspected such. Now Meg could testify that the highest lord in the land had stinging nettle just like the lowborn Naseby lads, stinging nettle he might have touched at the site from which that fatal bolt was sent—or he could have caught it from scores of other places, she supposed.

Surely the queen's own cousin, however haughty and condescending, wouldn't stoop to hiring someone to shoot deadly darts at the queen. Still, Her Majesty suspected he was secretly planning to offer himself to Mary, Queen of Scots, in wedlock. That alone could get him tossed in the Tower, but an assassination attempt would get him tried and beheaded. Either way, a mere herb girl had to tread carefully here.

"I've the very remedy for it, my lord, if it's stinging nettle," she told him, wondering if he'd seen and followed her into the gardens or was here for some other purpose. Most unusual for a man of his stature to be out without hangers-on.

"Yes, I warrant that's it. Hie yourself for the cure, then, mistress, and don't stand there gawking. I'll wait here."

Again, she had to bite her tongue. She'd like to say she suspected that he'd gone five to six days with it itching already, so why the rush now? "Do you have a notion where you came by it, my lord?"

"What in all creation does that matter?"

"If I knew how long you had suffered from it, I could better judge the amount and strength of the cure," she lied. Oh, if only the queen's Privy Plot Council would meet soon again, she'd act out each word they exchanged, with Ned's playing the duke's part.

"Just give me the strongest cure and dosage you have and be quick about it. It's getting worse daily."

She curtsied again but could not resist one more rejoinder. This man was a plague on her beloved queen and, right now, there was no cure for that.

"Such minor earthly maladies when we've done naught to deserve them," Meg said, "make one think how dreadful the fires of hell will be for those who truly transgress the laws of the land and of heaven, too." She rushed to get away from him before he could cuff or curse her.

She kept up at a good clip back toward the royal servants' rooms to fetch the broad-leafed dock tincture. No good to have Norfolk's nose so out of joint that he complained to the queen she'd been sassy or tart with him.

She lifted her skirts to sprint but soon came to a halt. At first she thought she'd come upon one of Norfolk's men lurking nearby to guard him, but no. A well-dressed man all in black bent over something, holding himself still for a moment before he moved. Was he going to be sick on the ground?

Then she noted the young man was bent over some sort of iron stick he was holding to hit at a small, round ball. It was the Earl of Southampton himself.

A little, flat piece of metal was stuck on the end of the iron stick with which he tapped the ball away from him, again, again, until it rolled across the grass—the only sod cut quite close she'd seen in these gardens—and dropped into a hole in the ground she could not see from here. He walked over to the hole and bent to retrieve the little ball before throwing it down farther away and then standing over it to tap-tap it into the hole yet again.

Some sort of new game. She'd never seen the like.

Meg glanced up to the windows of the mansion to see if

anyone was watching, but no windows, let alone faces, were visible from here among the tall bowers and bushes. She backed away so he wouldn't see her but tripped and toppled over something on the ground.

"Umph!" she grunted as she hit. Her petticoats flew up, but she quickly righted herself to a sitting position as other little balls came rolling around her.

Southampton turned, frowning, holding the skinny stick like a club. "Who goes?"

"Pardon, my lord," she said, scrambling up. "Meg Milligrew, Her Majesty's herbal mistress, just cutting through the gardens, but the Duke of Norfolk sent me on an errand, and I didn't see the log. Oh, not a log," she said, as she shook her skirts out. Why, she'd stumbled over a three-foot-long leather bag full of other iron sticks. Fine-looking leather, too, it was, all tooled, matched, and stitched to make pretty patterns.

"On your way, girl, and don't be so clumsy."

Meg curtsied and started away. Curse that man, too, but she hadn't been clumsy since the queen took her in and ordered Ned to tutor her in carriage and speech, so that she could stand in for Her Majesty at a distance if need be. Clumsy just because she fell over his bag of iron sticks and little bleached-white leather balls? And why didn't he have a servant along to carry that thing for him? It must have been weighty. Did he not want anyone to know he was out at dawn hitting at little balls with a stick?

She wondered if the Duke of Norfolk had been heading through the gardens to meet the Earl of Southampton. Otherwise, why should two such powerful, important men be alone at such an early hour in a thick-grown place? If that was true, she doubted if the young earl intended to teach the older duke a new game, unless it included their old one of plotting against the queen.

With obvious pride, Henry Wriothesley, Earl of Southampton, escorted his queen about his large, fortified mansion and its vast grounds. Many courtiers trailed behind but at a distance, for she had requested a private tour without everyone talking at once. Besides, as well as looking for signs of troops that had trained here, Elizabeth intended both to question the young lord and to try to make one last attempt to sway him to her side. All the while, she made certain he did not take her outside the shelter of the walls, for she wanted no more arrows flying at her from the forest—or even a well-tended deer park.

"Our gatehouse sits in the middle of the old church," he told her, gesturing at the massive, three-story redbrick entry through which the queen's progress had entered yesterday. "The great hall of Place House was once the monastic refectory, and the old cloisters beyond became the central courtyard, where we are planning the afternoon's pastimes. The rest of the church was converted into domestic apartments—the two wings there," he added, pointing at each in turn.

The mansion was so large that, for once, it housed not only the visiting court but servants, too. No one had to scramble for local shelter nor live in tents. Seldom did the queen visit houses on a summer progress that could offer her a presence chamber, privy chamber, withdrawing chamber, and bedchamber in her suite. Place House also had a room large enough for a council meeting, should she need one. She'd given it over to Cecil for his secretaries and his couriers, through which they kept in close contact with London and other parts of the realm. How she wished for a letter telling them that the newly imported Spanish crossbowman, working for the Spanish ambassador de Spes, had been captured or at least located.

"I believe, my lord Southampton," she said, gazing at the ruins of the old abbey, "your sire gave no thought to living where the monks once worked and worshipped, but how is your conscience on that?"

He looked taken aback and cleared his throat. "I did naught to feel guilty for, Your Grace."

"Yet I sense you do feel guilty about something. Do you fear the sins of the father shall be visited upon the next generation, so to speak? I admire a man of loyalty to his conscience and also to his rightful monarch. In my kingdom, I believe that is obvious, for I have kept about me such as the Earl of Leicester and the Earl of Norfolk—both of whose families have gravely failed the monarchy in the past. You see, I can forgive, and I judge each man on his own merits, as, my lord, I shall accordingly judge you," she added, leaning closer to him and forcing him to look full into her face.

"Yes, Your Majesty. I would expect nothing less," he said, but his tremulous voice did not match his bold words or stoic expression.

She said no more for now and let herself enjoy the beauties of both the formal gardens and the wilderness area. Especially intriguing was a long mound, a barrow, where, he explained, the ancient Anglo-Saxon pagans used to bury their dead. Some thirty feet in length and at least ten feet high, it lay just inside the wall encircling the wilderness gardens.

They strolled along the turfy mound. "There was once an old pagan church there," he went on, warming to this topic as he had to his description of his home built on the ruined church. "It was dedicated to Woden, local legend says, their god of the dead."

She noted the broken stone foundations of a small building next to the mound. Moss and lichens etched themselves into the old stones as if they held cryptic runes that would not divulge their secrets. How she wished she could read this man's face and voice—and heart.

"Woden," she echoed. "Yes, he was mentioned in the closing by the goddess Diana in your pageant yesterday. I know little of what the Anglo-Saxons believed before they were converted to Christianity. Can you tell me more?"

"If you vow you will not laugh at me for repeating local superstitions."

"Say on."

"The area folk, especially those in the smaller forest towns, believed Woden was always attended by a pair of ravens—some say hawks—and a pair of wolves. Ravens have been spotted in great numbers this year, and wolves still inhabit the depths of these southern forests, you see. He wore a black cloak, too, said to make him invisible in the forest depths."

"I believe I have heard some howling as we passed through, but hawks and ravens are omnipresent in the kingdom. So this dead god of the dead supposedly used to haunt these forests?"

"Ah, yes. He rode through the tall trees, sending arrows right and left at those whose souls he coveted, some of whom he warned before he killed them."

A chill shot up her spine, and she shuddered. The spots

between her shoulder blades and her breasts grew cold, then hot. "And untutored folk still hold that Woden haunts these woods?" she demanded, her voice rising in pitch.

"The thing is," he said, frowning, "they claim he's been reborn and lives again—that some have seen him of late, I know not who."

Her insides cartwheeled, but she protested, "Stuff and nonsense. Shame on Christians, Papist or Protestant, believing such pagan drivel."

"Agreed, but if you ask folks hereabouts, especially old men like Hern the Hunter, they claim his spirit has been reborn not as Woden but as someone called the Hooded Hawk. At first I thought they'd stolen the notion of a sort of Robin Hood figure, but they say this spirit is vengeful and dangerous like Woden."

She tried not to show her annoyance or her alarm. No, she lectured herself, these were not the days of yore with pagan superstitions, however much the surroundings here promoted such. This man was subtly trying to prey on her fears again for his own purposes, as he had during the pageant yesterday, or perhaps even dissuade her from venturing outside these walls into town.

"So," she said, keeping her temper carefully leashed, "this Hooded Hawk is said to haunt especially these nearby woods?"

"All deep forests of Hampshire, it's said. Of course, he's just in people's heads. If anything happens amiss, the superstitious need something or someone to blame."

"Who is this Hern the Hunter you mentioned?"

"No one of consequence. An old, blind man, a recluse. I've been too busy to look him up for years, and he may be as dead as the Anglo-Saxons, for all I know."

He forced a smile as if he'd made a joke, but she saw nothing humorous, especially since she'd gotten him alone to unnerve him, and all his foolish chatter had managed to further rattle *her.*

With Giles and Hugh riding behind him, Francis Drake kept his face turned away so they wouldn't see his eyes fill with tears as he sighted his ship. The *Judith* awaited him, still safely moored along the most seaward quay on the River Meon in Fareham. *Foolish man,* he scolded himself, but he hadn't missed his new wife as much as he had missed the ship, and if his bride of but six weeks knew, she'd be jealous indeed. He saw few of the crew about, but he'd told his first mate that one-third of them could go ashore each day as long as she was kept tidy and safe. Yes, she looked good— graceful, with her sails tied fast to the yards as if she'd pulled her petticoats up for him.

As he rode up to her side, he recalled again how strong she'd been in battle, his first ship, even with her powder-blackened guns glowing hot and her sails and tidy trim riddled by shot and bolts. He'd saved her from more than one fire ship that day, and just in time to avoid flaming arrows, too—those damned Spanish flaming arrows. They'd pay, the bastard Spanish. If he had to spend a hundred other ships, spend all the years of his life—if it cost him his life—the Spanish would pay.

Could they know of his wish for vengeance, and so were still shooting at him, and before the queen's very face to shame him or make her think he was dangerous or cursed?

"Keep an eye on the horses, Giles," he said, and gestured to Hugh to board with him. Of the two, it was Hugh he mistrusted more, so he'd take a page from the queen's book and keep him under close watch.

He didn't see the man who sang out from the shrouds above, but he heard him: "Cap'n 'board! Cap'n 'board!" It thrilled his soul.

Jeremy Haverhill, his first mate, stocky and sturdy, appeared from the captain's cabin, and Drake wondered if he'd made himself at home there in his absence.

"Cap'n Drake!" he clipped out with a stiff half bow. "I'll call up the crew."

"It's you I needed to see, man. I want this entire vessel made shipshape—immaculate for an inspection on the morrow, and by midmorn. Decks sanded, scrubbed to the scuppers—and a fine meal with fine wine laid out in my cabin, too."

"Yes, Cap'n. And, pardon my askin', but you seen the queen herself?"

"It's the queen herself who is coming, Mr. Haverhill, with how many I'm not sure. I'll give you coin from the lockbox to lay in victuals—the finest this little town of Fareham has to offer."

"Don't know a fig 'bout what's good wine, Cap'n Drake."

"Nor do I, but buy what's expensive. Besides, Her Majesty seems taken by—enamored of the sea. She may want grog or beer for all I know, but lay in the wine. Get going now. With Her Majesty, it is best to be prepared for all possibilities. I'm relying on you, for I can only stay a little while and must head back."

"Oh, Cap'n, near forgot. A letter come from your cousin Cap'n Hawkins 'bout two days ago. It's in your cabin, and I can fetch it."

"I'll see to it now. And Mr. Haverhill, do not tell the men who's coming. I don't want—well, I don't want a crowd gawking at her."

Or the possibility, he almost added, that someone would take a shot at her, however joyously the crowds had welcomed her upon their arrival. He climbed the stairs to the halfdeck but hesitated before going into his cabin. Scanning the shore, he was relieved to see that there were no deep forests near this quay but rather fields and marshes. Still, he planned to send men up into the crow's nest and along the yardarms tomorrow, partly for the impact of the scene with their skyblue shirts, but also to keep his queen as safe as he had vowed to keep the *Judith*.

He went inside with Haverhill and doled out thirty shillings to him, a fortune equal to nearly a gold sovereign, a month's wages for a good craftsman. As the man put them in his purse, Drake noted they were new-minted, very much like the coins Her Majesty had found in Barnstable's cellar—no doubt, like the one she'd said Secretary Cecil's courier had retrieved later from the former sheriff's house.

Suddenly sapped of strength, he leaned back against the dark wood wall. His cousin never sent payment for the *Judith*'s crew in such new coins; Drake had known the money was coming but had left before it arrived this time. The queen had said such coins must have come from London, and he'd thought Hawkins was in the west country. Was this all sheer coincidence, or should he show this to Her Majesty? If he fingered Hawkins and his cousin turned out to be guiltless, he'd harm a man England admired and needed— and he might need, too.

He dismissed Haverhill and grabbed the letter that lay on

his small table. Yes, sealed with wax impressed with his cousin's signet ring of a merchantman under full sail with a hawk swooping in the sky overhead.

> *Drake—*
> *I command you back to port in Plymouth. Stop playing courtier immed.—If the queen wishes a report, I, sr. cap'n of the fateful battle, shall give it to her. Take care of your new wife and let me take care of the queen—or I will take care of you—*
> *Yrs., J. Hawkins, London*

John Hawkins was in London? That aside, the last cryptic line of this order sounded like a threat, a double-headed threat against not only him but the queen, and that could be treasonous to boot.

Chapter the Tenth

AGAIN, THE SEEMINGLY SOLICITOUS YOUNG EARL OF Southampton was the queen's host as he escorted her out to observe and partake in the sporting events of the afternoon, held at the edge of the formal gardens nearest the house. Some of her ladies trailed after them; other courtiers were already outside at play. A fountain splashed merrily, and she recalled the amusement she'd had at Whitehall Palace spraying Robin years ago when they were both younger—when she still foolishly believed she might marry him.

"Watch your step here, Your Grace," Southampton said.

"I always do so, my lord, for I am ever vigilant and canny, to use a Scots word. Remember that well, even as we oversee the sporting. Which reminds me, my herb mistress mentioned you were playing a game she did not recognize in the gardens this morning." She smiled sweetly at him, for she felt herself well armed with that bit of knowledge.

He looked like a schoolboy caught with his hand in the Yuletide comfit box. "Ah, yes, Your Grace."

"What was that particular game you played?"

"A game from the north, I take it. I know not much of it."

"You are in communication with someone in the north? How far north?"

"I'm not sure—how far north, I mean."

"I repeat in different words, lest you did not grasp my first question, my lord. What is this northern sport called?"

"I believe it is named golf, Your Grace."

"Named so by whom?"

He still did not look her in the eye. He had much to learn, she thought, from his wily guest Norfolk. Meg supposed, and no doubt rightly so, that the two men had met privily in the wilderness area of his extensive gardens this morning. The queen rued the fact Meg had not hung about to eavesdrop on the two of them, but if Meg had not returned to salve Norfolk's nettle rash, then hied herself away, he would have been more nettled yet.

She smiled again, not at her own private pun but at how very discomfited Southampton obviously was. She was almost enjoying herself. He kept looking away, as if gazing deep into the splash of the silver fountain.

"Called golf by whom, Your Majesty?" he echoed her question. "I—I wouldn't know who named it. The word means naught to me."

"You see, my lord," she said, tapping his arm with her folded fan until he was forced to face her, "I have had a letter from my Scottish cousin, Mary Stuart, now my guest *in the north* of England. She asks that she might be permitted to play a Scottish game called golf. She's always writing to beg some favor or other. Anyway, no one truly English seemed to know one whit about golf, so how interesting that you want to learn. Perhaps when you have mastered it, you could give the Duke of Norfolk lessons."

The poor man's eyes darted wildly toward the courtiers playing various games beyond the fountain.

"But," she plunged on, "I asked Cecil's messenger, Keenan, who brought the letter I just mentioned, if he had heard aught of this foreign game of golf when he was in the north. He knew little but that it takes much practice. I am certain you will soon be very adept at it, playing in private first thing in the morning, as if the sport were a jealous mistress you must please."

She could tell he was uncertain if she goaded him or not. How different he was from clever Norfolk, who usually behaved as if the best defense was to be offensive. All this answered her question about who had planned the pageant yesterday, for this young whelp and his pretty little wife could not have concocted it. Rather, Norfolk's double-dealing hand was in it somewhere, just as it was in planning the unrest to the north, which could explode to full-blown treason.

She was tempted also to demand why and from whence Southampton had such a finely tooled leather bag for his golf equipment, but she kept that to herself for now.

"Shall I have you teach the Scottish rules of golf to my courtiers today, my lord? No, perhaps not," she mused aloud, now tapping the fan against her chin. "I much prefer for them to concentrate on good English games with English rules—but for Norfolk, of course, who dangerously does as he wishes."

Though the breeze was delightful, Southampton looked as if he needed air, and his sallow skin hue had gone grayish; she feared he might pass out. She hoped his tat-taling of all this to Norfolk, who had taken to glancing at her and the young earl from across the crowd of courtiers, might settle them both down.

"I—of course—I favor good English games, too, Your Majesty," Southampton stammered. "I am praying you will d-deign to observe matches of fives today, for I have not yet built a court for tens, nor purchased the racquets or a long net."

At least she could give him credit for attempting a sudden change of topic, she thought. "I believe you mean ten-*nis,* my lord. That's the way we always say it in London, but perhaps tens is the northern—or Scots—way to say it."

She smacked his arm with her fan and left him as she joined the others.

"Would it please Your Majesty to go hunting with us on the morrow?" Elizabeth's hostess, Lady Mary, asked, as the two women walked down the great staircase to join more sporting and gaming in the courtyard after a noontide respite. Evidently, Southampton himself had not wanted to face her again so soon.

Elizabeth had been waiting for an invitation to the hunt, especially since the fine local deer park had been touted in the pageant. No chance she was hazarding a trip into a forest hunting, however much she excelled at the sport, but she had been surprised Southampton had not invited her this morning. Did he think that letting the invitation come from his lovely wife would make his queen more likely to accept?

"I'm still too tired from my journey for a great deal of fast riding," Elizabeth told Lady Mary. "Best I just send my courtiers. They will be avid to take advantage of your park and its game. And on the morrow, I'm going the short distance to the River Meon to see Captain Drake's ship."

"Oh, how exciting. But—Your Grace," she said, pausing at the bottom of the stairs, "I pray it is not because bows and arrows would be involved in the hunting."

At the banquet last night, the queen had explained to her hosts her misfortune to be near two bolts from the blue, as Ned Topside termed them. As she had recounted those events to them, she had watched their faces for signs of guilt or unease, neither of which they'd displayed. Though when Cecil had mentioned that a far worse fate awaited whoever was responsible than that which had befallen poor Actaeon, the hunter in their pageant, Elizabeth was certain she had read sudden alarm on Lady Southampton's pretty face.

"But who," the queen asked, "is the man called Hern the Hunter whom your husband mentioned? Is he the former master of your lord's hounds or deer keeper?"

"Old Hern?" she said, with a shake of her head. "Oh, no one that is worthy of your concern. Just a recluse in the forest to the east, a demented old man, I hear."

The queen noted well that both her hosts had seemed eager to dismiss the man's importance. Then, too, Southampton had looked angry with himself when he'd let Hern's name slip. Perhaps the "demented" old soul was worth a visit.

Much as during their stay at Farnham Castle, the courtyard that afternoon echoed continually with the queen's courtiers playing and wagering at their games. Two exquisite, inlaid shovelboard tables had been brought outside from their usual place in the great hall. Standing on sturdy legs, the boards were some thirty feet long and three feet wide. With little shovels, players pushed round, weighted pieces toward lines that were worth points. Women were as skilled as the men at this game, for oft the men shoved too hard and their pieces flew off the end of the board.

On green baize tables, others cast dice in a popular court game called hazard. The rest, including Norfolk, Leicester, and Southampton, bent over a card game called primero; Elizabeth had turned down the offer to join them. By peering over shoulders, she noted that the queen cards were emblazoned with her own face, a very young, pretty face, too.

She felt smug about that until she noted that the king card was not her father or brother or any Tudor ruler. It was her sworn enemy, the Spanish King Philip. She would have ripped that card from Norfolk's hand and stamped on it, but she did not want to show her Tudor temper, which she knew they all joked about. Besides, when Philip of Spain had been wed to her sister, he had indeed been King of England as well as Spain. Worse, after her sister's death, he had dared to propose marriage to Elizabeth, so dead set was he to control England again. Even worse than that, she fumed, that deck of cards must be at least ten years old, and that was perhaps why she had been rendered so young and fair. Suddenly she liked this pretty and young Lady Mary who squired her about less than ever.

"Oh, let's see how the men playing at fives are doing, Your Majesty," Mary said for at least the fourth time, and Elizabeth let herself be led back into the courtyard.

As the earl had mentioned earlier, the game of fives was played by both courtiers and local men. It took five men at once, flinging a ball against a courtyard wall divided by chalk markings into four areas. In this sport the French called palm play, each man wore a white glove on his right hand with white cords bound around that hand to make the ball fly faster when it was bounced back against the wall. She supposed those cords had inspired the racquets used in the more refined version of the sport.

The brick court on which the players stood, like the areas on the wall, was square with four marked sections, each assigned to a particular man, with one floating player. Yes, it must indeed be the rustic game that had become tennis, played on an open, double-sized court with a net between two teams of five men each. As women never played, it hardly interested the queen. She always liked to be at the center of the action, not merely observing it.

Amazingly, Lady Mary, looked entranced by the heated game. The players sweated through their white, half-laced shirts as they lunged and flung the ball, their powerful thighs straining against their breeks and hose. At the break, Lady Mary and several other ladies applauded; Mary even bent to retrieve a ball and press it into the hand of one of the players.

Elizabeth recognized the man: the handsome youth who had played the part of Actaeon in the pageant yesterday. She was going to jest that she was glad to see he had managed to escape the hounds at his heels, when she realized the obvious. So obvious she'd almost missed it, and no one else seemed the slightest bit aware.

Mary Wriothesley, Lady Southampton, had not only returned the ball to the man but slipped him a note she'd hastily wrapped around it, one he now stuffed quickly up his sleeve.

Elizabeth remembered that Mary had called her attention to his entrance in the play yesterday, not to mention that she'd nearly fainted. And, when Cecil last night had remarked that anyone who tried to harm the queen would meet a fate worse than Actaeon's, Mary had actually looked alarmed. The queen could only hope that the message was a *billet doux* and not some treasonous correspondence. Still, it did give her a good bargaining card if she interrogated the woman later.

"If we don't hurry, we're going to miss evening meal, and I don't want little Piers going hungry to bed tonight," Meg groused, as she and Ned, with the boy between them holding their hands, headed into Fareham in the late afternoon. "And all to find out where some old man named Hern the Hunter lives in the forest, when Her Grace said she wasn't going into any forest again, except in her closed and guarded coach."

"Not the first time she's changed her mind, my sweet," Ned said. "Besides, Piers is glad for the adventure, yes, my boy?"

"Yes, Ned. We can practice our lines on the way."

"What lines?" Meg asked. "Something to present to the queen?"

"Perhaps," Ned said, and winked at the boy.

"Real lines from a play about Robin Hood," Piers blurted, giving a little skip between them. "From *Robin Hood Returns*." He began in a singsong voice. "A ghostly fantasy by Ned Topside. *An outlaw bold was Robin Hood,/ Clad in Lincoln green,/ 'Mong Sherwood Forest's leafy boughs,/ He scarcely could be seen.* That's all I know real good so far."

"I know *well*," Ned corrected.

"Sure you know it better than me," the boy insisted.

Meg laughed.

"It's good to hear you laugh again," Ned told her. "Especially when it just hit me that Robin's *scarcely could be seen* does make him sound a bit like that Hooded Hawk the queen described."

"And Woden," she said, "is supposedly invisible in the forest, too, in his black cloak."

"It's all fairies and phantoms in the forest what does the mischief," Piers piped up. "With cobwebs for reins, they could ride the backs of hawks, I know they could."

Over the top of the boy's head, Ned rolled his eyes, but tears stung Meg's. Would their own lad have been so taken by flights of fancy and clever with words, so eager to please Ned by learning lines? For one moment, she almost burst into tears, but she kept taking one step and then another. For Ned, for this boy—for her dear queen—she could now go on.

Elizabeth had invited Francis Drake to that night's Privy Plot Council meeting, for, after the most recent attack, his fate seemed mingled with hers again. She felt a bond with him and admitted she needed all the help she could find to ferret out her—perhaps their—enemy. Both of them had hostile, powerful male cousins they wanted to rely on but could not, cousins who held grudges and might be dangerous, each in his own way.

As they sat around the table, it was deathly silent in her presence chamber, which had finally emptied of courtiers after a late supper and dancing in the great hall. Even Cecil didn't shuffle papers but gripped his hands before him on the table. She had excused Meg Milligrew, for the boy Piers had a sour stomach, evidently from eating too many of the sweets they'd bought him in Fareham. She'd sent Meg and Ned there to discover all they could about Hern the Hunter and the Hooded Hawk and to ask if there had been men passing through town to the mansion who were not local inhabitants.

Both Jenks and her yeoman Clifford looked jumpy, but then she knew that, like Cecil, her longtime loyal guards wanted her to abandon this summer's progress and return forthwith to Whitehall Palace in London. Lady Rosie was the only other woman in the room, and she had been driving the queen to distraction lately, sticking to her like a burr in-doors as if she could protect her from flying missiles from each corner or turn of the hall.

"Tomorrow morning I am going to visit Captain Drake's ship," Elizabeth announced. "It is but a mile away, and I shall take a full escort of guards and several of my closest courtiers."

"Wearing Drake's armor under your cloak," Cecil put in.

"Yes, which I shall remove once on board. The captain as-sures me," she went on, with a glance at Drake, "that there are no sites for a bowman to hide within shooting range of the ship, and he will have men aloft in the shrouds."

"In the shrouds," Ned echoed. "Strange name for some-thing people are usually buried in."

"If you cannot speak more to the point or simply stick to your report without dark and pointless puns," Elizabeth told him, "I shall ask you, as difficult as it is, to keep quiet, Mas-ter Topside. We are all on edge here."

"Yes, Your Grace," he said, shifting in his chair as if prop-erly chastised. "Shall I recount what I learned in Fareham about Hern the Hunter and the Hooded Hawk legend that may be connected to the shootings?"

"Do so. Meg has already told me you learned of no strange men coming to the manor, though I don't know whom to trust anyway. It seems the people hereabouts are more concerned with figments of their imaginations than with reality. Say on, but—Yes, Captain?" she said, as Drake gasped, then lifted an index finger to speak.

"This Hooded Hawk—it's a nickname for a myth of sorts, is that right? But—connected with the shootings at you, possibly at us? I only ask because of this—and this."

To Elizabeth's surprise, he placed a shiny gold sovereign on the table, then withdrew a letter from his doublet. He opened the parchment with shaking hands and laid it before her on the table next to the coin.

"The coin—with others—arrived in my absence as pay for the crew."

"From your cousin Hawkins?" she asked, picking it up.

"Yes, Your Grace. This brief epistle was waiting for me in my captain's cabin today, from the same."

"A bold seaman," Cecil put in, "so I hope to heaven he's not behind these attacks—though, forgive me, Drake, I'd rather have you be the target than the queen."

"I understand, my lord," Drake said. "By my faith, I, too."

"Sometimes," Cecil went on, as Elizabeth bent over the epistle, "I think Hawkins's many merchant ships are the closest thing we have to an adjunct navy, and that includes your ship, too, Drake. That's why I think it's important that, despite certain risks of late, Her Majesty make a great show of visiting your vessel on the morrow. And that note, Your Grace?" he said, and left the question dangling as Elizabeth read the epistle—twice.

"It is carefully worded and can be read either way," she said, and handed it to Cecil. " 'Take care of' could mean for good or ill, though it is clear here Hawkins wants for himself whatever glory he thinks you are basking in, Captain.

After all, he is the senior man, as he notes here, and you are yet employed by him. How interesting that he must have been in London for some reason," she added, and spun the sovereign on its edge. "Or else someone in London sent him such coins."

"But his insignia in the wax by his signature . . ." Drake said.

"What?" she cried. With Cecil, she bent over it as Drake moved the lantern at the end of the table closer to them. Yes, she hadn't seen that at first, as she hadn't clearly seen too much of late. No wonder Drake had suddenly looked so shaken.

"I understand what you were thinking and fearing when we mentioned the Hooded Hawk," she said. "It is hard to make out the lines clearly in the wax imprint of his signet ring, but I do see." As she looked up, her wide gaze met first Cecil's, then Drake's.

"Yes," Cecil observed, "this hawk could be a pun on Hawkins's name, and so harmless enough, even as the note could be read in a guiltless way. And the hawk is in no way hooded."

"I rather thought," she said, as Cecil passed the note to Lady Rosie, "that the hawk's head is nearly shrouded by the sails of the ship and so could be considered hooded in that regard."

"Yes, a bit far-fetched, but I guess that could be," Drake said. Both Cecil and Rosie nodded.

"At any rate," Elizabeth plunged on, "it would align with the theory that your cousin Hawkins—through a hireling— could be behind these attacks, which then would be focused on you. But since the bolt and the arrow missed you, does that mean Hawkins thinks I would send you away because you are some sort of target? More like he should worry I would find out and have him hanged for endangering my life—and he needs my goodwill!"

"Perhaps, Your Grace," Drake said, "he means in a way to reenact the battle of San Juan d'Ulua. He taunts or dares me to flee as I—I did during that battle."

"Too devious for a blunt, straightforward man like Hawkins," she insisted. "It's a trait of you west country sea-farers, I warrant. Though that wax seal could represent a hooded hawk."

"But he's oft at sea," Drake insisted, "so how could he know to take advantage of a myth local to this spot? I doubt if he'd hear of it either in London, where the note came from, nor when he was in our home port of Plymouth to the west, where he's ordered me to go."

"Ned," she said, "tell everyone what you reported to me about Hern the Hunter and this Hooded Hawk legend, and without another clever wordplay on shrouds or hoods, either."

"Yes, Your Grace. Meg and I learned Hern's a real man," he began, "maybe almost in his ninth decade of life now, and lives in the forest east of town."

"Which could be the forest we came through," Jenks said, "the one where we found the finger tab after the arrow was shot. But a man of nearly ninety years could hardly shoot so well anymore."

"Yes, I warrant it's the same forest," Ned went on, "but closer to Fareham than in the heart of the forest from whence that last attack came. Anyway, Hern used to be an excellent bowman, a longbowman even, but in the last forty years or so, before he got too weak or his eyes went bad, a shopkeeper told me, he was a bowyer and a fine one."

Clifford, who seldom spoke at these meetings, put in, "Not many make quality bows and arrows anymore, not for battle e'en if for hunting. That's why poor Tom Naseby's death back in Guildford dealt a double blow."

"So this Hern has bad eyes," Cecil said. "Then it's hardly been Hern placing that bolt and that arrow so precisely—if it was precisely, and he didn't actually miss his target."

"I also learned" Ned said, "that longbowmen have powerful shoulder muscles, and I warrant that old man hardly does."

"So," the queen said, "can we link this Hern in any way to the legend of the Hooded Hawk?"

"A legend he may be," Ned said, "but many folk hereabouts seem to believe he either was or is real—reborn or some such nonsense. A fine marksman, they say, both with the crossbow and longbow, but he seems to have a mean, destructive streak of late."

"How late?" Cecil asked. "Someone's seen him recently?"

"Seen his cruel handiwork, at least, off and on this summer. He's rumored to be the one who shot and killed a few sheep for fun, poached deer from Southampton's forest, and put flaming arrows into a thatched roof or two."

The queen's gaze snagged Drake's again. "Like fire arrows," she said, "shot at a ship in battle, a Spanish trick. So," she added, turning to Ned again, "the reasons we should find this Hern are to see if he could name someone who might still shoot a longbow in these parts and to inquire what he knows about the so-called rebirth of the Hooded Hawk."

"My thoughts, too, Your Grace," Ned said with a little bow as if his part were finished and he awaited his usual accolades.

"I'm desperate enough to want to visit him myself," she vowed, "for all else seems to lead to dead ends, and that is not a pun."

She jumped as someone rapped on the door to the room.

"Why," she said, lowering her voice, "each time we sit down for a privy meeting, must we be interrupted? And who, this late, would know?"

"A message could have come from London," Cecil said. "I've kept Justin Keenan here for now and put him in charge of the couriers. I told him if something key came up—namely anything from my man who is watching the Spanish ambassador de Spes—to fetch me. I'll see to it," he added, and started to get up.

"Let Rosie go," Elizabeth ordered. "If it isn't Keenan, I don't need someone else knowing that anyone but her is with me at this late hour."

As Rosie went to the door, the queen said to Cecil in nearly a whisper, "I think we could use Keenan on this covert council. He's back and forth, here and there. I know you repeat things to us from your intelligence, but he's observant and, I wager, closemouthed, which is exactly what we need."

"Your Grace, I really can't spare him, if you mean to have him work directly for you, but . . ."

He let his voice trail off as Rosie opened the door and stepped out into the hall, then came back in. She closed the door behind her, walked a few steps in and said, "Master Secretary Cecil's right, Your Grace. It's his man Keenan with a letter in his hand for the master secretary only about—about what you said, my lord."

"Cecil," Elizabeth said, "I will not gainsay your wishes on this to allow him entrance, if you don't trust the man, but you have shown that you do, and therefore I do, too."

"Very well," he said. "I will need to retain him in my employ, but I believe he should be able to report directly to this group, if there is some need."

Rosie nodded and went back to the door to escort him in. Elizabeth could tell that Keenan, however stiff-faced Cecil's aides had learned to be, was surprised to see the mix of servants and their betters sitting with the queen. For one moment, he nearly lost his poise and gripped the letter he held in his hand so hard that he bent it. He started to bow to Cecil, then realized he must bow first to the queen, which he managed a bit jerkily.

"My correspondence from London and other parts of the realm is always sealed," Cecil said, "but I know full well the men I pay to pass it on to me through relays sometimes pass on what they know man to man. Right, Keenan?"

"Yes, my lord," he said as he hastily advanced and laid the letter before his master. "I am to speak straight and fully here?"

"You'd best or your queen will have your head, man. Say on."

Keenan cleared his throat and backed a few steps away from the table again, facing Cecil and the queen before he spoke. "The man you have in London, my lord, that is, the one who watches the new Spanish ambassador, de Spes, has discovered—in a way—the whereabouts of the crossbowman recently arrived from Madrid."

"In a way?" Elizabeth repeated. "Explain."

"That letter may have more complete details, Your Majesty," Keenan said, as Cecil broke its seal, "but I hear that the bowman was sent out of London almost as soon as he arrived, with an escort who can speak good king's—ah, queen's English."

"Sent where?" Cecil demanded, as he unfolded the letter.

"Sent south, that's all your man could learn. South, not

only with his weapon but with an ornate leather quiver full of Spanish-made missiles called something like *quadros.*"

"*Quadrellos,*" Drake spoke up, "not shot from a crossbow but from a longbow, if you want sticking power and good distance a shortbow cannot give."

"A longbow?" Keenan said. "So he could be skilled at both crossbow and longbow? But no one shoots the latter anymore, Captain Drake, though I saw it demonstrated once when I was young."

"You've done well, Keenan," Cecil said, "but you may keep childhood memories to yourself, as well as all you have said, seen, and heard here. Is that understood?"

"Perfectly," he said with a smooth bow that showed he had fully recovered his composure. "Secrecy and quickness are, after all, my lord, thanks to you, my stock-in-trade."

Chapter the Eleventh

 SHE NEEDED THIS GLORIOUS DAY, THE QUEEN thought, as her entourage's horses clattered through Fareham and headed toward its harbor. The sky was blue; the salt-scented air was crystalline. The sun was warm but gentle. And again, her people cheered.

This was not a planned parade, but those working or walking along her route bestowed upon their monarch their spontaneous fervor, which made it all the better. Surrounding her and Drake rode seven guards, including Jenks and Clifford. So as not to overtax Drake's hospitality, she had brought only two of her ladies-in-waiting and Robin. Let Norfolk and Southampton fume and do their worst, for she'd left them behind—being covertly watched by Meg, Ned, and Keenan.

Elizabeth ignored how Drake's armor bounced against her hipbones when she rode, for it made her feel secure, even as his own protective arms would. She blushed at that wayward thought and shook her head. He was a man newly wed and her captain, who served her purposes nationally, not personally—and yet, though no one would ever know, he did move her that way. Maybe Robin had been right to instinctively dislike the man. Perhaps he had sensed that to which she had paid no heed at first—that Captain Francis Drake, in many ways, social class aside, was a man after her own heart.

"There she is, Your Majesty," Drake said, and pointed into the distance. He grinned and added more quietly, "The other 'she' in my life beside my wife and my sovereign."

She laughed with him but felt her face grow warm, and not from the midmorn sun. It was almost as if he had read her mind.

"Why are ships always referred to in the female gender?" she asked, keeping her voice light.

"Forgive me, Your Grace, but ships, like females, may be beautiful, yet they can be difficult to control."

Robin laughed too loudly at that, but it reminded her that he was here, watchful as ever. She lifted herself slightly in the saddle to see the place on the wharf Drake had pointed. Evidently thinking she was responding to their cheers, the crowd of sailors, vendors, and workers bellowed louder.

She knew then that she'd like to come again, without all the din and danger. If only she could be a woman friend of Drake's just dropping by the *Judith* without this entourage in tow . . .

"She's much more of a sight at sea, Your Grace," Drake was saying. "When she's bare sticks and rigging like this without her sails full of wind, without breasting the waves, she's hardly what she's meant to be."

He wasn't looking at his queen now but at the ship as they reined in where it was tethered to huge mooring posts. Yes, Elizabeth thought as both Robin and Drake helped her dismount, she'd like not only to come again but to see this ship in all her glory out at sea.

The crew, wearing sky blue shirts and caps, lined the deck railings and clung to the highest riggings. When their queen smiled up at them, they waved their caps and huzzahed with three crisp cheers: "The queen! The queen! The queen!"

It was a thrill for her to walk the gangway to board the ship. Why must a ruler be land-bound? Her father had sailed more than once to France. Was not the water lying beyond this pretty river and the broad bay called the English Channel, so was not she queen there, too?

Drake introduced her to his beaming first mate, Haverhill, then took her on a tour of the ship, pointing out places where his men had fallen in the battle with the Spanish, showing her numerous patches in the sails and the plugged holes where *quadrellos* had pierced a mast or the deck.

"Driven deep, just like the one in my coach," she observed.

"Driven deep if they weren't first stopped by flesh and bone." He frowned, evidently recalling the horror of the battle—and yet, she thought, it had made him dedicate himself to fighting the Spanish, and she needed him for that. Didn't his cousin Hawkins, who seemed so jealous of and angry with this steadfast, younger man, realize they both needed men like Drake?

The only part of her visit she did not like was eating in the small, crowded captain's cabin, though the food was adequate and the wine surprisingly good. She felt closed in, however safe. She wanted to walk the deck again, to crank the windlass he had showed her that hoisted the anchor, to push the capstan herself to raise the topmasts and cargo, and to take the helm in her own hands to steer this ship.

As she prepared to leave the table, Drake slipped her something wrapped in a linen napkin. At first, she wondered if it could be some sort of private gift, but he whispered,

"One of the *quadrellos* the blasted Spanish left aboard as a token of their deceit and destruction. You can compare it with the other one."

She nodded her thanks. Though she was eager to look at it, she put it up her sleeve and carried it out that way.

At the bottom of the gangplank when she was ready to depart and the others couldn't hear, she asked Drake, "Is there any reason—excuse—for you to put briefly out to sea in the next few days?"

"You mean, Your Grace, besides obeying my cousin, who does not realize he cannot command me to leave you when you sent for me?"

Cannot command me to leave you when you sent for me echoed in her head, as if they were hurried words between two lovers.

"Just for a short while, I mean," she said, feeling her face heat up again. "To show me how it is at sea. Perhaps to check the sails or some such."

"Of course, if that is your desire. How many should I plan to take out, then?"

"In these times, I would not come as the queen," she told him, speaking even more quickly since she saw Robin coming their way. "I would be in plain garb with but one woman and four guards."

His eyes widened; his lips parted.

"There have been times of need," she rushed on, "when I have briefly traded places with my herb woman, Meg. She stays in my rooms, then, of course . . ."

"What's this about a course?" Robin asked, wedging his shoulder between the two of them.

"We were discussing," Drake put in before she could answer, "the course the ship must take when I sail her out of the river and into the waves of the deep."

"Soon, I hope," Robin said, as he offered the queen his arm and she took it. "For a sea captain should be guarding our shores against those Spanish dogs, eh, not riding ahorse through forests and towns. The sea must remain your realm, Drake, not the queen's *terra firma*."

All the while he spoke, Robin slapped his leather riding gloves, held in one hand, against his thigh. He'd drunk a great deal of Drake's fine wine, so she hoped there would not be some sort of scene. Drake stood as if made of stone with one hand on his sword hilt and his other in a fist at his side.

"The queen's *terra firma*," she said to break the palpable tension, "will too soon hurt her feet in these new boots, and I am ready to ride back. Are you coming, then, my lord Leicester? I believe Captain Drake has work to make his ship seaworthy again, but years ago I put you, man, in charge of my horses."

She pulled her arm from Robin's and walked away, but he quickly caught up with her and, before Jenks could, linked his hands to give her a boost up into her sidesaddle. When Jenks left to get his own horse, Robin said up at her, "You hang on his every word, that is all, my queen."

"I would hang on yours, too, if you would stop talking of such petty concerns as—"

"Petty?"

"Do not interrupt me," she whispered down at him. "And let go of my foot!"

"If it indeed hurts, I could tend to it, rub it until it feels much better."

"Stop!" she hissed. "Both the queen and her captain need your help and support in these tense times."

"The queen and *her* captain?" he muttered, as if he hadn't

heard her order to desist. "It sounds like a romantic drama, perhaps one your master of revels, Ned Topside, could write and stage."

She yanked her foot from him. "Keep away from me unless you amend your topic and your tone, my lord. I need support and protection from those who would harm me with arrows, so if you are not *for* me, I will assume you are against me. And the others are starting to stare!"

"My queen, the only darts I would ever shoot at you are Cupid's arrows, and you deflect those—perhaps to others. You don't think that I had aught to do with the attacks on you—or on *your* Captain Drake?"

"Why would I think that? Because you are madly jealous and can neither control your temper nor take orders from your queen? Because you'd like to scare Drake back to sea or worse—or frighten me back into your arms?"

She moved her horse away, and Robin scrambled to mount and keep up with her. He was sullen and sulky all the way back, but she couldn't have heard him over the cheers and sporadic shouts of "God save our queen!" anyway.

Yes, she thought, *please, Lord God, save the queen. Save her from the dire possibility that someone she cares for, someone she trusts, someone she is even kin to could want to take her throne and her life.*

Late that afternoon, the vast halls and many chambers of Place House echoed only with the footsteps of servants, for, at the queen's insistence, her hosts and her courtiers had gone hunting. Keeping Lady Rosie with her, Elizabeth was supposedly lying down to rest. The truth was, she, disguised as Meg Milligrew, was going hunting, too—hunting for Hern the longbow maker. Meg stayed behind with Rosie in the royal suite, guarded, as it were, by Cecil, who was working on business in her outer presence chamber.

With Her Majesty rode Ned, her guards Jenks and Clifford, and Justin Keenan. At the last minute, over Cecil's protests, she'd brought him along. No one else, not even Robin or Jenks, sat a horse as well as Keenan.

"I pray," Elizabeth said to Ned, as they rode into the woods east of the mansion, "that your directions from that shopkeeper are good enough to get us there and back directly and quickly. If any of the servants ask Meg later why this party rode into the forest, she is to say she went to bring back curing herbs, and I insisted she take guards."

Even though she had donned Meg's clothes, she wore Drake's armor again under her cloak. She was getting used to it, and it made her feel not only safer but more alert. Then, too, it reminded her she was looking forward to her second visit to his ship on the morrow.

"Hern's hut is supposed to be a few furlongs in, east and then to the north of this path," Ned told her, as he rode just slightly behind her horse. "A boy from town sometimes takes him bread and cheese. I couldn't find the lad to lead us in, but I can go ahead of Jenks now if you'd like."

"No, let him lead. Ned, Meg is much better—in spirit and temperament—isn't she? I would not have left her in my stead if she were not."

"She has moments when she stares off into emptiness, but fewer of those. I'd like to claim credit for that, but it's the boy Piers who's changed her—that, and your bolstering her through it all."

"Perhaps," Keenan spoke up from behind, "we'd best stop talking. If the old man is blind, as I have heard, his hearing might be quite acute. We could startle him or even make him hide before you can question him, Your Grace."

"Point well taken," she said, as they turned in single file onto a narrower path through the thickening stands of trees, taller ones here, stretching for their share of the sun.

Yes, Elizabeth thought, she had been wise to demand that Cecil share Keenan with her. The man was useful for more than just carrying messages hither and yon; he spoke not often but always circumspectly. He'd even managed to pick up the fact that this old man was blind.

Still, Keenan had reported earlier that he hadn't seen Norfolk and Southampton together while she'd been at Drake's ship, whereas Meg and Ned had reported the opposite. It turned out that the duke and the earl had been huddled over a card game in the center of the sunny courtyard for hours, where they could be seen but not overheard. Yes, Cecil kept his chief courier closeted with him too much these days, or he would have informed her of that, too.

On this narrower path, branches and bushes seemed to reach in, grabbing at them. They even snagged her narrow skirts and smacked against her new riding boots.

In a whisper, Jenks asked, "Can this be the way? It doesn't look like many come through here."

"He's a recluse," Ned hissed, "and the only one allowed to live this close to Lord Southampton's deer park. They know, however skilled an archer the old man once was, he'll not be poaching game."

Even here, outside the boundaries of the earl's hunt park, they saw and startled several deer, which bounded away to be swallowed by the depths of deep foliage. A snorting boar charged across their path to drown the rat-a-tat of a lone woodpecker, as if someone were knocking on a door. Chattering squirrels and twittering birds suddenly went silent, though Elizabeth noted well, through the screen of leaves above, a hawk soaring aloft in an updraft as if spying on them.

Again she recalled her poor falconer, Fenton, who might have died in her place—or in Drake's. But for the occasional creak of a saddle and the sighing of a breeze through the trees, their horses' hooves became the only sound.

"There!" Jenks whispered, pointing ahead of them. "A clearing."

At first the sight of the rough stone cottage with its ragged shake roof reminded Elizabeth of another place deep in a forest she had once come upon during an investigation of a murder, the very autumn she became queen, eleven years ago. An enemy, the first one she and her Privy Plot Council had delved into and discovered, was a poisoner, and they'd found her hut and a garden of poison herbs deep in a forest. Unlike then, no deadly plants grew here to guard the premises, only a strange-looking wooden hedge. No, she saw it was a row of barrels and piles of wood stacked high.

They dismounted and walked their horses closer. In a single shaft of sun, which had somehow found its way through the thick canopy of oaks and horse chestnuts, a hump-backed, white-haired man with gnarled hands sat, holding a great, stringless bow.

"Heard you coming," he called to them, looking up with vacant pale blue eyes as he rose slowly to his feet. His eyebrows looked like snow-covered thatch, and his pale beard was scraggly. The gaunt but wide-shouldered old man seemed as ancient as the trees. He held on to the longbow as if it were a staff to support and steady him.

"Greetings to you, Hern the Hunter," the queen called out.

" 'Tis five or six of you, I'd say," he went on, "all ahorse, and hardly the earl or his lady with a retinue. To what, then, do I owe this honor?" His voice sounded muffled, as if he spoke from within one of his barrels.

"Your fine reputation as a bowyer is well known in these parts," Elizabeth went on. "No, we are not the earl and his lady, but how did you know that?"

"They ne'er visit, but would know the way and ride quicker." He inclined his head in her direction and seemed to study her as if his blind eyes could take her in. "You one o' her women, then, or someone come in wi' the queen's party wants a bow for her lord, milady? If so, it's for display or sport these days, not to defend the realm no more."

So he could tell by her voice that she was at least a lady, she marveled, and, even in the forest, word had spread of the royal visit.

"Yes, I would like to buy a longbow," she said.

"Making 'em keeps me young, you see," he added, and his shoulders shook with silent, wheezing laughter. "There's some ready enough out back, in their last stage of seasoning after being soaked and bent in here." He gestured broadly at the barrels, where she could see raw-cut bows soaking.

"Can't take yew wood inside the cot, you know," he went on. "Yew brought into the home can lead to a death in the family. E'en damaging the tree is bad luck, 'less it's treated with all due honor and worked with outside. But it's that strange quality 'bout yew wood makes it so good for an instrument of sudden death."

The queen shuddered. That same haunting feeling returned with sudden impact: Her breastbone and the spot between her shoulder blades seemed to grow fiery hot, then instantly icy.

"But you'll not shoot it yourself," he went on. "Takes a

man's pull, and one wi' broad shoulders at that. Stooped as I
am, I used to be the best."

"Don't you want to sell one, man?" Ned put in, evidently
impatient.

Elizabeth gestured him to silence. At least Clifford and
Keenan knew to let her do the talking. Without being asked,
Keenan stood far back, holding the horses, though they obvi-
ously weren't going to wander off in this thick forest.

"I want one for old time's sake," she told the hoary-
headed man. "You are Hern, then, called Hern the Hunter?"

"At your service, milady. You come from London wi' the
queen, then?"

"Yes, from London."

•"This queen's sire was a fine bowman in his youth. I went
to France in his army once nigh on a quarter century ago,
saw him close up, too, heard him address his troops. There
used to be a song," he said, then chanted in a scratchy voice,
*"Great Harry could outshoot all archers and e'en hit a ring/ No man
drew the longbow with more strength than the king/ Nor could shoot further and with truer aim at anything."* Suddenly shy, he bowed his
head and shuffled his feet.

She blinked back tears. Her father had been dead for
twenty-two years, and of all the myriad songs she knew, she'd
never come across that one. It was like finding a bright coin
on a dark floor—yes, she was obsessed with shiny coins
right now. The one Drake had showed her had perfectly
matched the one found on the cellar floor where Tom
Naseby had been hanged. Treachery and perhaps treason
were afoot, and she must stick to the task at hand and not let
emotions rule her.

"I have heard King Henry tried hard to maintain the use

of the longbow, but it has certainly been replaced by cross-bows and shortbows," she said. "I warrant that the advent of powder and shot as well as better armor will make those obsolete, too, but does anyone you know still shoot a longbow?"

He gave a little snort. "Nary a one, not enough to speak of. It takes big shoulders, lots of pull. Just for show now, sad to say."

"None of these are to be given for gifts?"

"Forgive me, milady, but no one's worthy of that no more—not that I know."

"So no one else has come to buy a longbow from you of late, even if it is just for show?"

"Not sold 'em for years, though some blackguard stole two o' them in the dark 'bout a fortnight ago. I called out, 'Who's there,' but only heard him walking 'way, quick strides, with the bows snapping the bushes back. The thief coulda had a lantern and I wouldn'ta knowed it. Otherwise he could see in the dark—like a ghost or phantom."

Ned and Jenks exchanged quick glances. Elizabeth felt the too familiar chill race down her spine. "Surely you don't believe in such, Master Hern."

"Lived too long not to, milady. The folk here 'bouts tell you the Hooded Hawk is back?"

"I've heard it mentioned. What do you know of him?"

"Used to use blackthorn arrows, he did. Could shoot with any sort of bow, shortbow, longbow, even crossbow best of anyone ever."

"He sounds like a fantasy indeed. But have you ever heard of arrows wrapped with leather?"

"Not in this land, nor from the Frenchies. The Hooded Hawk wore a hood, they say, to cover his grotesque face been gored by a stag. Him and his hounds ride the forest at night—it's not just the wind in the trees. Sometimes it's real still when he passes."

"You've heard him in this forest or ones nearby?"

"All forests in Hampshire, they say. Aye, I've heard him, and the trees whisper, 'Here, here, here,' though some say 'tis really 'Hawk, hawk, hawk,' real breathy like a strange sigh."

"Then maybe he's the one stole your bows," Ned said, but the old man only shook his head. His blind stare, which had been turned her way, now darted past her toward the depths of the dark woods, as if he heard the Hooded Hawk even now. She shuddered, then silently scolded herself for falling into this old man's morbid mood. Yet, despite his talk of ghostly events, his brain seemed sharp and his senses even sharper.

"So you truly believe in the Hooded Hawk?" she asked, gripping her hands so tightly together her fingers went numb.

"Someone's out to make the whole shire believe in him. Speak of the old times, used to be he was an avenger for good, could shoot a yew bow full three hundred fifty yards, while the best I ever did was three hundred. Now he's turned to harm and hurt, what they call Woden's way 'round these parts, maiming and killing animals, setting hayricks and thatched roofs afire. Just pray he don't come here, 'cause my shake roof goes tinder dry."

Elizabeth noted Hern's nostrils flare as he spoke. From fear, or was he trying to scent her perfume? However keen his sense of hearing and smell, he had a heightened sense of the dramatic. Ned hung on his every word, and Clifford and Jenks, big and brawny as they were, reminded her of little, lost boys. Only Keenan, at a distance, stood calmly watchful.

As if she'd requested it, the old man shuffled around his

small yard to explain the process of hewing the slightly **S**-shaped bows from sapwood next to the heartwood in the yew. "Cut the sapwood, then it's three months in clear, running water in a brook, then to a damp place for o'er a year, then bit by bit to drier surroundings. Their last year's in open air and wind—from my line o' those seasoning in back, the two bows were stolen," he said, and repeated that story almost word for word again.

He took her around to the back of his cottage, where nearly twenty beautifully crafted longbows, which would never be wanted or used again, she thought sadly, weighed down wooden poles. To pay him well for the bow she would take, she dug in the purse she'd brought. He obviously heard the clink of the coins.

"No recompense," he said, raising both knotted hands. "Don't want money laying 'bout someone might come for. Your visit, your wanting a bow's worth a fortune to me, milady. But," he said, whispering now, his blank stare boring into her face as if he saw her, "compensate me this way. You are more than a lady, eh?"

"Why do you say so?" she whispered back.

"Your voice, your sweet scent, the squeak of new boots. Your lesson to me of England's war weapons, and from a woman. The way your man quieted when you musta but frowned or looked at him. But mostly, your coming a purpose here to have a fine longbow 'cause your royal sire loved and honored them."

Tears blurred her view of the old man, and she bit her lower lip. He had miscalculated the reason she had come, but, however blind and old, he had the wits to know who she was. Yet she herself, young and healthy, could not be certain who her enemy was, even perhaps someone close by daily.

"Yes, Hern the Hunter," she told him, "I am the daughter and heir of the one who could outshoot all archers and even hit a ring. No, don't kneel," she said, and caught at his hands as he started to go down. "I'm in plain garb with plain purpose, and glad I have come to see a great bowyer and one who fought well and proudly for our England."

Tears puddled in his eyes and tracked down his pale, wizened cheeks. She let him cling to her hand before he leaned back on his longbow again. He turned away to choose by touch a finely grained and elegantly carved, huge bow for her from off the line of them on the drying pole.

She hefted it and noted how long it was—three-fourths of her height, and so heavy that it pulled at her shoulder muscles simply to lift it as she handed it to Jenks to carry.

Of all she had learned on this visit today, what sobered her the most was that whoever had shot a longbow at her or Drake from the forest was not only wily but more skilled and strong than she had imagined. But surely, whoever had dropped a finger tab and shot a very real Spanish arrow could not be the phantom of the forests.

Chapter the Twelfth

"FEAR FOR NOTHING, FOR I WILL BE BACK JUST AFTER sunset," Elizabeth told Meg, as the sun rose over the treetops of the distant hunt park to light the queen's bedchamber. "Cecil has put out word that I will see only Lady Rosie and himself today. Things worked out well when you were queen for a few hours yesterday, and I know you can do this."

"Queen for a day but queen away from everyone—that's me," Meg said with a pert nod. "Today's the longest I've ever ruled, but I'm still in exile. Just hope someone doesn't wing another arrow my way."

"You are to keep clear not only from people but from these windows," Elizabeth ordered, though she was relieved that Meg sounded so lighthearted today. "And no waving down to those strolling in the gardens, for the queen is supposed to be resting. Can you do this, my Meg?"

"Of course, though I'll miss Piers something awful, especially since you're taking Ned and Jenks. He feels comfortable with them."

"But he'll be with his brother and under the care of Jenks's wife and quite well."

Elizabeth endeavored to sound calm, but she was as excited as a young girl. She had changed her mind and garbed herself as a man in Ned's clothing instead of riding out disguised as an herb woman to visit Drake's ship, though that meant not wearing the armor today. She'd decided to leave Rosie here and take only three guards. She was planning to sneak out the servants' entrance, for the entire Southampton household was here today, and someone might recognize that she was not the herb mistress, even if she were dressed as Meg. The way crowds had cheered for her in the streets, if she wore any sort of women's garb or took as pretty a lady as Rosie with her, folk might notice and create a fuss again.

She shoved wayward tendrils of hair up under her cap, where she had the bulk of it pinned close to her head. Her heart thudded as she went down the narrow back staircase to meet Ned, Clifford, and Jenks, who had the horses waiting below. She held her breath when she heard footsteps coming up the stairs toward her, but the young woman who passed by—either a Southampton servant or one from her own courtiers' households—had her arms full of ale jugs and gave her neither word nor glance. That alone was a heady experience. She felt drunk with the idea that anonymity and freedom were hers.

She was relieved Jenks had changed her sidesaddle for a man's and brought her a more common-looking horse; he gave her a quick boost up. How strange but good it felt to ride astride, as if one were really part of the horse and not just sitting on it. *So many adventures on this day,* she thought, as her pulse pounded harder.

Then, as the sun crested the treetops, she saw in the distance a flash of shimmering light—surely not a forest phantasm. All this talk of the Hooded Hawk was starting to affect her. No, it was a woman in pale silk or satin running beyond the edge of the gardens, evidently heading for the Anglo-Saxon burial mound.

Elizabeth squinted in the pearly morning light: A second figure, a dark-cloaked man, met the woman, and arm in arm they darted into the depths of the wilderness garden. Not the Duke of Norfolk and the Earl of Southampton skulking off today, she thought, for even from so far away she recognized the graceful woman and could guess at the man.

"Ned," she said, "I've changed my mind about your going with me."

"But I—"

"Listen for once. Southampton's wife, Lady Mary, just met a man I'd wager is the one who played Actaeon when we arrived, and they've darted off into the wilderness gardens. I already have some things I can use to question her about her husband's doings, but if you could be certain she is meeting another man, it could be invaluable. Try to follow them and do not be seen."

"As invisible as Woden or the Hooded Hawk?"

"No jests. And walk your horse and go in on foot."

"Yes, Your Grace," he said, dismounting.

She could tell he was disappointed not to be heading out to sea with her, so she said, "It will buck up both Piers and Meg to have you here today. Go now," she urged, and turned her horse away.

Drake had hardly dared to believe she would come. And dressed as a lad! The boldness and bravado of Elizabeth Tudor never ceased to amaze him. He strode down the gangway to welcome her.

"I do have a gown in my saddle packs," she greeted him, as he helped her to dismount on the wharf, "but I believe this garb might be better with the wind strong today on deck. The wind will be up beyond the coastline, will it not, and the ship will go fast?"

She seemed as excited as a child as he greeted her and assured her they would unfurl every sail. A woman after his own heart, indeed. He gave her three horses over into the care of his man Giles again, for he'd taken to keeping Giles and Hugh not only watched but separated after they'd gone into the forest without his permission.

Both men were silently fuming over that and because he'd relegated them to subordinate positions, for he'd ordered Hugh to be put on scullery duty to keep him belowdecks today. Drake could not fathom that they had actually shot at him or the queen—not with a longbow, anyway—but they could well be spies for John Hawkins, whom he was coming to trust less and less. Besides, Hawkins probably now considered Drake himself insubordinate for not racing this ship back to Plymouth as he'd been ordered.

Drake gave the queen's tall guards, Jenks and Clifford, over to his first mate for a ship's tour and made a joke about showing them the ropes at sea. He began to give his own orders while the queen stood at his elbow on the halfdeck.

"Square course mains'l only! Short sail, others fast to the yards 'til we're out of the river!" he shouted, as men scurried along ratlines above their heads.

The anchor cable creaked up; the ropes tethering the ship to the wharf were loosed and drawn aboard. The mainsail canvas flapped like cannon shots as it caught the wind and bellied out. Mostly for show, since they didn't need the foremast or mizzen sails yet, sailors hung from the yards and the

masts. Drake saw the queen clasp her hands together, looking up, then out as the *Judith* began to move.

"It will be slow and steady at first," he told her, as they
looked over the starboard rail to watch the ship clear the
wharf. "Not a lot of rain lately means the river's not as deep
as when we came in. The Meon's not much of a tidal river, but
she's always fast-moving. Her depth and flow depend on all
these marshes that drain into her, so she has her own moods."

"I remember you said that before." She smiled at him before squinting up at the sails and waving to the sailors again.
He and Haverhill had passed the word that they had a very
special guest who was here *incognito*. They were not to speak
of it off the ship, but, however much bad luck it supposedly
was to have a woman at sea, the men were excited to have her
aboard.

It touched him that she recalled what he had said before,
and when she turned and smiled at him, he knew exactly why
Elizabeth Tudor was not only queen but a great queen, his
queen. Wily and wary, but willing to throw caution to the
winds when she must. Her surface moods might vary like
this river—high or low, calm or tempestuous. Yet she was
deep like the sea and always, ultimately, in control, the leader
of men he longed to be. And the impact of her personality
and power, however slender she was with her thin but sturdy
legs encased in man's breeks and hose today, even with that
feminine, almost flirty demeanor . . .

"It's nice not to see a forest for a while," she was saying. "I
must tell you later what Hern the Hunter told me yesterday,
but right now, I just want to feel safe at sea."

"Safe at sea. But there's always an element of danger at
sea, Your Grace, from storms or hostile ships—or the unknown. As for forests here, there are hardly any trees along

the Meon's banks except right before the coastline at Hill Head where the river broadens to the Solent and the Channel. Then the *Judith* will roll a bit, and if there's wind enough here to fill these sails, in open sea you'll really feel her."

"How wonderful," she said, grasping the newly sanded railing again and leaning, stiff-armed, back away from it. "It's one thing to be rowed in the royal barge up and down the length of the Thames, but I want to feel I've really been to sea. You must love it passionately."

"I do," he said, facing her again as they left Fareham behind, and their gazes met and held. "It is unlike anything else and to be treasured and remembered always."

Soon, but not soon enough, Elizabeth thought, the river flowed into the Solent, the body of water between the mainland and the Isle of Wight, and they set sail eastward through a narrow strait called Spithead toward the broad English Channel. "That's Portsmouth off the port side," Drake said, pointing.

"That makes sense to me," she said, and they both laughed. She'd been drinking his good wine again, though she noted well he stuck to plain ale while he captained his ship. "But where did you leave your wife? Surely you miss your new wife, if not the jealous and commanding Captain Hawkins."

"Mary Drake, *née* Newman, is in Plymouth," he said, squinting up at the trim of the sails again. "We wed earlier this summer, but she's a good sailor's wife and knows her duty when duty calls her husband."

"I regret that my summons to join my summer progress took you away from her."

"Your Majesty," he said, his face and voice solemn now as he looked into her eyes, "whether you regret it or not, you will always take England's men away from their wives, and rightly so. An island nation needs defending from such as the Spanish devils, but she also needs explorers and traders going out to bring the knowledge and riches of the world back to her shores—and to her queen."

"It's a good thing you are not of a political bent, other than for building the navy and your own career, Drake, or such speeches would outdo those of my parliamentarians who make endless and ofttimes pointless speeches. But the other thing is, if married sailors are at sea, does that mean their children are fewer? You do hope for children?"

"Truly, one of the reasons I wed," he admitted. "I'd like above all a son." He looked taken aback that he'd blurted that out.

"Always," she said, putting her hand on his wrist where he gripped the rail, "when I ask a question, tell me the truth straight out like that, even if you think it will hurt me. I have asked the same of Cecil, for I need men like that. God knows, I'm surrounded with the other kind too much."

"It seems to me Norfolk always speaks his mind, Your Grace, and he's not to be trusted any more than a leaky ship."

"Norfolk speaks his mind only on the surface, but he hides things. Southampton, too, although he doesn't have Norfolk's backbone or wit. You may have wondered why my Privy Plot Council includes several of my servants. It has taken them years, but they know to tell me the truth at any cost now. I need people I can trust, Drake!"

"Then I shall be so when I am near. And if I am at sea for queen and country, I shall be true to you yet."

As the ship rocked, she almost toppled into him. She

wanted to, and to tell him how much his friendship and this day meant to her, but that was both delicious and dangerous.

She took her hand back from his wrist. "Yes," she said, looking away, "I'd elect you to Parliament. But in all seriousness, I rue the fact that perhaps I have endangered you by summoning you to me and keeping you close for a while."

"Because you have given my cousin a second reason to hate me besides that I let him down at San Juan d'Ulua?"

"That, too, but what if that Spanish longbowman who headed south with a translator is loose in these parts? And he's seen I value your presence and counsel and has decided to take shots at you as well as at me? Oh, Drake, I don't know. Privy Plot Council meetings or not, I keep trying to—to sail along, but I think I'm getting nowhere in solving these attacks and murders."

They were silent a moment, staring out over the gray-green waves. She could tell he wanted to say something. He cleared his throat. "Your Grace, may I ask one question about your privy council of servants and courtiers, then?"

"Of course."

"I assume you have never used the Earl of Leicester on it, and yet you seem to be close to each other."

"Close enough to argue too often. You don't in any way suspect him, do you?"

"Not really. We all have our boiling points, but he seems to continually seethe—at me, at you. But forgive me for suggesting that—"

"No, it's a good question, for he has been—and is yet—dear to me, but he's mercurial, and our tempers too often tangle. Besides, he is hardly shuffled off to the side. Since my ascension, when I named him master of the queen's horse, he has sat on my public council of advisors. The thing is,

Drake, I care deeply for him, but I cannot trust him fully—as I am coming to trust you."

He nodded and bit his lip. Was he so moved he could not speak after all those fine, heartfelt words earlier? She saw him blink back tears and look out toward the horizon, where sky met only sea.

"Well," she said, turning away and starting down off the halfdeck to the main deck, "enough philosophizing, I warrant. I want to stand on the very beakhead of the prow and see how this realm looks from far away instead of plop in the middle of it wherever I travel. Lovely to be in a place where arrows can't come flying past one's head."

That long morning, Meg took a nap and stuffed sweetbags with lavender and rose petals while Lady Rosie Radcliffe embroidered on a huge frame nearby. Lady Rosie seemed fine, but Meg felt as if she were in prison. Her Majesty went riding out and even sailing while she was stuck in here, and on a lovely late-summer's day. Secretary Cecil had popped his head in once to tell her that, at the last minute, Ned had not gone with the queen, so at least he was around to take care of Piers, but that made the walls close in even more.

"Warm day in here, isn't it, Meg?" Lady Rosie asked, and stayed the steady thrust and pull of her needle.

"I just wish I could sneak Ned and Piers in here for a visit, that's all." Meg walked behind the embroidery frame to see what Lady Rosie was working on. It was a lovely needlepoint garden with white wild roses climbing a wall. "I'd like to escape to that pretty scene, my lady. Being queen is not all it's cracked up to be," she added, beginning to pace the length of the room as the queen often did.

Lady Rosie laughed. "I can tell you, from being close to Her Majesty, even as you, Meg, that is truer than true. On one hand, you can have everything, and on the other hand, sometimes nothing that you want. You are blessed to have Ned."

"And now Piers," Meg put in, as she watched Rosie knot her thread and reach for another in her sewing basket.

"But the boy's not really yours. I mean, I thought there was some discussion that, when their home was safe again, the Naseby lads would return there and be apprenticed or some such—"

"No! No, I believe Her Grace has other plans for them, and if Piers is apprenticed it should be to Ned to become part of the court players."

Rosie arched one graceful eyebrow. "I see."

"I mean not to speak for Her Grace—even when I *am* Her Grace," Meg amended, hoping she hadn't sounded too forward. Lady Rosie was one of the women closest to the queen. After a disastrous romance with a man who had turned out to be a villain, Rosie had declared that she'd never wed and that she trusted men even less than the queen did. More than once, Meg had heard them laughing over that, however bitter their tone seemed.

"What's that?" Rosie said, turning to peer out the window behind her.

"What's what?"

"That 'cuckoo' sound. I haven't heard a cuckoo anywhere hereabouts in these thick forests, and—Oh, it's your Ned, master of revels, reveling in this day, I take it—and the boy Piers under this very window."

"Are they all right? Her Majesty said I should not look out. I'll just take a quick peek."

Meg rushed over and peered out past the drapery, much

as the queen had peered past the coach's curtain when they'd been shot at. Ned and Piers both wore green capes and feathered hats, costumes Meg recognized from the Robin Hood drama Ned had done back in Farnham, and Piers carried a painted bow Ned had used in the play. She saw no one else. Since she was dressed like the queen, looked like the queen, surely she could show herself at the window briefly.

She thrust one arm out to wave, then stepped out and bent down a bit before popping back behind the drape. Then she heard what Lady Rosie had mentioned, the clearest, sweetest song of the cuckoo. Why, she realized, peeking out again, it was coming from Piers.

"And now, Your Gracious Majesty," Ned declared in his deep voice, "a song to lighten your day and enlighten your heart from the Topside and Naseby Company of Players."

Meg had to laugh. She showed herself again and mimed applauding as the two dearest males in her life began to sing.

Soft spring did a creep right in,
Loud sing cuckoo.
Sweet summer laughed and had its fling,
Loud sing cuckoo.
Windy autumn coming soon,
Where is cuckoo?
Wild winter then blows in next,
Cuckoo quiet in his nest.

Meg's eyes filled with tears. Not only did Piers's clear voice ring out, but he knew all the words and did the most charming gestures and motions with the song, not to mention mimicking the cuckoo call after each line.

Meg leaned out and blew them both kisses.

Then, to her abject horror, she saw that both the Earl of Southampton and the Duke of Norfolk were standing together and watching from behind the fountain.

Her first impulse was to shriek and dive behind the drape, but she boldly, grandly, waved to both of them, too, before turning back inside and hitting her hands hard on her forehead. When she had Rosie peek out later, they were all— Southampton and Norfolk, too—gone as if the gardens had swallowed them.

Late that afternoon in the Solent, the queen took the helm, gripping the big wheel with its spindles, fearing at first the ship would buck or veer. She felt the pull of the rudder, but it was not overwhelming, even as the *Judith* sailed into the wind.

"We'll put her on a larboard tack," Drake said, gesturing a zigzag path as he stood beside her. The helmsman had stepped away but had not gone far. Both men looked a bit nervous, but she didn't care one whit. For now, this ship was hers. In past dark days, when she was in exile in the countryside, when she was imprisoned in the Tower, even after she was queen, there were no moments when she would have chosen to be other than Elizabeth Tudor. Nor had she wished to be a man, though it would have made ruling easier and safer. But now—in this instant—she could almost have thrown it all away to go to sea. To be a captain, like Drake, to command not only a crew but a great vessel in the very teeth of the wind with the wild waves rolling . . .

"Turn the wheel again, Your Grace," Drake urged. "No, the other way, so by tacking, we can keep a steady course for the mouth of the Meon."

"I'm not ready to go back," she said, pouting, but she

shifted her weight to turn the wheel the way he indicated. "It's going to be dusk soon, and my day of freedom will be over. I can see the forested shore already, the woods just off the coast at Hill Head before the marshes begin. You don't need a cabin boy, do you?"

He laughed loudly, but the wind snatched the rich sound away. "You are that desperate to stay aboard, then?" he asked.

"Hardly that." She laughed, too, as he put a hand to the helm to help her get the tack of the ship just the way he evidently wanted. "If I should sign on with your crew, Drake, you would have to worry I would want your position."

He laughed again, more of a chuckle deep in his throat. She had seldom heard him laugh, not that there had been much to laugh about since they'd been together. Yes, this day at sea had done them both good. Even Jenks and Clifford seemed to be having the time of their lives, hanging about with the crew amidships, laughing at what she supposed were salty stories and jests.

"Actually, I mean," she said, "one of the Naseby lads might make a good cabin boy for you, if he really wants to go to sea."

"The older one, Sim," he said. "He looks at me as if I were king of the world—well, you know what I mean. If things work out so I can patch things over with my cousin and can keep this ship, I'll consider it, Your Grace. Otherwise, I'll be looking for another command."

"I'll find you one if Hawkins proves untrue—or foolish, and I believe he is not the latter, at least." She reluctantly gave up the wheel to the helmsman, who brought the ship about to swing into the mouth of the river. All too soon, they were headed up the Meon toward Fareham.

While Drake gave First Mate Haverhill orders about

trimming sails, which the older man yelled to the crew aloft in the shrouds, Elizabeth climbed back up on the halfdeck, where they'd spent an hour earlier before they'd dined on deck and she took the helm. She had not wanted to be inside one moment of her day at sea. To think people complained of *mal de mer*, getting so sick to their stomachs that they wanted to die! Every moment of this day, every minute with Francis Drake, she had loved.

Heading upriver was slower than going out, for they bucked both the land breeze and the current. This was not a strong tidal river to give them a good boost from behind. The sea slipped away; the forest closed in, clear to the eastern river shore. Too soon, they'd see the stretch of marshes and the town of Fareham, and that man of Drake's he'd demoted, formerly Hawkins's sailor, would be waiting with their land-bound horses. Meanwhile, the crew was balancing on the yards overhead to furl sail as if they could walk on the wind.

"Tops'ls down!" First Mate Haverhill bellowed on the deck just below her. "Just the lower foremast and mains'l!"

Back to reality, Elizabeth began to plan the rest of her day. She must return to Place House and sneak up those back stairs, and tomorrow mingle with her courtiers and hosts. She intended to interrogate Lady Mary, for if she knew anything about her husband's loyalty to the northern lords, the young woman might be forced—coerced—to tell. Elizabeth hated deceitful marriages, for she'd seen enough of those, but she was getting desperate to make Norfolk and his cronies play their hands. Then she'd find a way to trump them—and maybe accuse them of complicity in murder, too.

At first the queen could not believe her ears when a voice aloft shouted, "Fire!" She scanned the forest on the starboard side but saw no smoke in the trees. The summer woods were quite dry, though; even Hern the Hunter had mentioned that the shake shingles of his cottage roof were dry as tinder.

"Fire arrows!" another voice above her shrieked.

She heard a whoosh and a thud—and then she knew. Stooping behind the wooden bulwark of the ship, shading her eyes, she saw a streak of fire whiz by just above her head. That arrow pierced the lower mainmast sail and set it afire.

Then everything happened at once. With a scream, a sailor with an arrow in his back and his shirt aflame crashed from high above to the main deck with a sickening thud. Haverhill rushed to him, bent over him, then moved away. Dead? Another man dead with an arrow in him?

Jenks and Clifford bent low and zigzagged their way toward her, but Drake shouted at them to stay down and stay back. He yelled up at her, "You there, man! Down! Get down flat on the deck!" Elizabeth sprawled on the boards as Drake's voice cracked out, "Fire on deck! Haul water up the port side! Down from the shrouds! Fire on board!"

All the while, his voice got louder, louder. Perhaps he would panic as he had under Spanish attack. No, she realized he sounded louder because he was coming closer, up the short flight of stairs to where she lay. Hunched over against the next flaming arrow, which also slashed into the sail to ignite it, Drake half crawled, half rolled toward her and blocked her in with his own body. Smoke and heat began to belch out above them, but the air was a bit better here.

"Coming from the forest again?" she asked.

"Yes, but I don't think they can hit us from this angle. The ship's a sitting duck if we don't keep the sails unfurled to keep moving, yet that will make them burn faster. Then the masts and decks will ignite."

"It must be you the bowman is after," she said. "Only those I trust know I'm here."

"I shouldn't have left Giles holding the horses. But other than him, are you sure no one could have seen you leave or come aboard—and recognized you or your men?"

"I'm not sure of anything anymore."

"John Hawkins would never give orders to burn one of his own ships."

"Not even to discredit or disable you?"

"By my faith, if the Spanish are behind this, I will wring every one of their necks with my bare hands!"

"I'm going to peek to see if I can at least tell what part of the forest the arrows are coming from. We can have it searched later," she told him, breathing raggedly. The smoke and heat were getting worse. Her eyes stung, and she could scent the stench of burning canvas clear down into the pit of her stomach.

"Permission denied," he said, pressing her down, breathing hard, too. "Those arrows—from a longbow—are not coming from the forest fringe, but at least a ways in. They're powerful and perfectly placed to burn us to the waterline— or pick us off if we get up to shoot back or jump overboard."

"Shoot back at what? The enemy's invisible again. Just hidden, I mean, by the trees."

Men continued to scramble down from the rigging above them and take cover. The mainsail burned briskly, and the mainmast began to char. Blasts of heat slapped at them. The ship shuddered when it nosed into the riverbank and went slightly atilt.

Pinned down, aground, with flames crackling and spreading in the sails above them, they were not only sitting ducks but about to be cooked.

Chapter the Thirteenth

 "THE SMOKE AND FLAMES WILL COVER FOR US," Drake told her, starting to cough. "We've got to get you on shore." Jenks and Clifford must have realized they could safely move about also, for they appeared, eyes streaming tears from the smoke.

"Drake, you've got to get back to your men," she insisted, "to try to save the ship." They helped each other up; the three men clustered around her like a barrier. No more arrows came their way, though, if they had, their sound must surely be covered by their shouts of the crew and the roar of the mainsail burning.

"You come before the ship," Drake argued. "We'll go down a mooring rope together so I can get you back to town."

He took her hand and led her with Jenks and Clifford tight behind. Drake looked over the gunwales, then began to haul up a thick rope. "We're aground in the soft riverbank. The three of us will hail a smaller river craft and take you the short distance to the town wharf, where you can get your horses. Haverhill, to me!" he shouted, then started hacking again.

"Here, Cap'n!" the first mate cried, emerging bedraggled from the fog of smoke.

"Any more than one man hit?"

"Just Smythe, Cap'n—dead when he hit the deck."

"And the bucket brigade?"

"We'll keep it from spreading on deck, but the mains'l and mast are done for."

"I'm going to see that our guest gets safely back to town."

"Drake," she said, turning close into his shoulder so the others would not hear, "you regret you left the fleet at San Juan d'Ulua. Though we yet stand on your ship's decks where you are master and commander, I order you to stay."

She turned away from him. "Clifford, you go down the rope first to be sure it's secure, then I will follow, then Jenks."

No one argued, but she heard Drake say to Haverhill, "I want Hugh Mason brought forthwith to me, even if he's helping fight the fire."

"Didn't want to bother you with your guest here, Cap'n, but he never sailed with us."

"What?"

"He came aboard, all right, fuming at being told to stay below and in the galley. But he musta gone o'er the side soon after, when we was still in dock."

Even as Clifford seized the thick mooring rope and disappeared over the side of the ship, Elizabeth's stare met Drake's. "Hardly a sick stomach as he had in the forest," she said. "I'll wager that your Giles back in town isn't holding the horses, either."

Drake's face turned nearly as red as his beard, and a pulse pounded in his forehead. "I'll see to him—both of them. But now, at least let me send a company of armed men with you."

"And draw attention to me when I can slip back into

Place House better this way? Put the fire out, Captain, and save your ship, then hie yourself to me on the morrow so we can make plans to save ourselves."

She grasped the rope, which went loose when Clifford's weight left it; she stepped on an empty cannon platform to get over the side. She swung her leg up and over. Jenks helped lift her with a hand on her elbow; she felt Drake's firm touch on her waist.

Despite Jenks and Haverhill gaping at them, Drake told her, "Peace or war, garbed male or female, you are brave and bold, my queen!" He bowed smartly and kissed her dirty hand before he let her go.

The mooring rope was almost too thick to clench; the friction of it burned her hands. She started to slide too fast until she also gripped the rope with her legs. Soon Clifford helped her down, and Jenks followed.

"I'll flag a ship," Jenks said when they all stood on the stretch of grassy bank. She saw he had his pick of river craft, as several sloops and smaller trading vessels coming or going from Fareham had either stopped to watch the fire or to help with it.

He soon returned, and the three of them ignominiously took a small French merchantman piled with coal back into Fareham. Smoke- and soot-blackened, agonized and angry, the Queen of England noted well that Drake's man Giles and their horses were nowhere to be seen. At least that meant that John Hawkins and his lackeys were now the prime ones to be suspected, but England could no more afford to lose that man and his ships than she could Drake.

Pulling her cap down over her face in the growing dusk, afoot between her two big guards, the queen stretched her strides toward Place House.

Elizabeth felt sore all over; her feet hurt from the walk back from town in her new boots, and she was black and blue from throwing herself onto the deck. She'd scraped both hands on that big mooring rope when she'd abandoned ship.

Rosie Radcliffe helped her take a sponge bath and wrapped her in a robe, but Meg kept hanging about, even after she put some soothing marsh mallow salve on the queen's hands.

"Why aren't you running to see Ned and Piers?" Elizabeth asked. "I've told you all I know and why we must concentrate on John Hawkins now. I'll probably summon him here from London if he's still there. Yes, Cecil can send Keenan for him first thing in the morning. And I may call a Privy Plot Council at first light, so best you get some sleep, Meg, queen for a day. Well, whatever is it?"

Rather than looking at her, Meg's gaze met Rosie's as the lady-in-waiting combed the queen's long red hair.

"Your Majesty," Meg said, "I made a big mistake today. You see, Ned and Piers stopped under the windows there— just for a minute—to sing me a little song. Gracious, Rosie heard them first and called my attention to them."

"And reminded you of your duty to stay put," Rosie replied.

"Just tell me!" Elizabeth ordered. "I assured Captain Drake today that my closest servants always told me the truth, but you are hemming and hawing."

"Yes, Your Grace. I went to the window to watch—I mean, I was keeping back of the drapery but then stepped out for a second and—"

"'S blood!" Elizabeth said, rising so quickly the comb

caught in her hair. "Spit it out. Someone recognized you? I mean as yourself?"

"I don't know. Maybe not. Even if they did, they could just think your herb mistress was waving out the window."

"And think it's my herb mistress so finely dressed? And think if I'm supposedly resting that Ned and Piers would be singing me songs? I'm afraid to even ask, but who was it?"

Meg hesitated, then blurted, "The duke and the earl together. Then they hurried off."

Elizabeth pressed her hands to her head. "So you are telling me," she said, trying to keep calm, "that the Duke of Norfolk and the Earl of Southampton saw you gesturing and grinning down at Ned and the boy. That's what you're telling me when I expressly ordered you not to look out the windows?"

She was losing control. It was too much for one day. This meant that John Hawkins might not be the prime culprit. If Norfolk and Southampton had somehow realized she wasn't here, that changed everything again. If her enemies had somehow construed where she had gone, their orders to their hirelings—even to that missing Spanish archer—could have been to frighten or to fry her and Drake!

"When was this?" she demanded, as Meg cringed. "What time?"

"Ah—I'm not certain, Your Grace."

"Early afternoon," Rosie put in.

The queen began to pace. Yes, if those two had recognized Meg, especially since she was fussing over Ned and the boy, they would have had time to discover Meg was missing and put two and two together. She wished she could do the same. Her brain was spinning too fast. Another dead man, a rain of fire arrows, a half-burned ship, and she was no closer to being certain who was behind all this than—than if she'd spent all this time searching the forest for an invisible foe.

"Your Grace, I rue the moment but can't rue the reason. I just—Ned and Piers—I couldn't ignore them, not after—after losing my baby, then kind of losing Ned and myself, too."

"I know. And I did tell Ned it would buck you up to have him and Piers here today, but he still should have known better than to tempt you. You are both at fault. Hell's gates, Meg, don't look so morose. Besides, what you told me makes me realize that my first order of business tomorrow is not to call a Privy Plot Council meeting but to question Mary Wriothesley about her husband's actions. So it may be for the best, though if her lord and Norfolk have figured out that I had my herb mistress stand in for me while I went sailing in men's garb, he and his cohorts—and Mary, Queen of Scots, no doubt—will have a good laugh at my expense, damn them all."

"She'd best not try to look down her nose at you, Your Grace," Meg said, standing straighter and pulling her shoulders back. She lifted her chin and spoke decisively, which made Elizabeth recall why she'd ever thought she could pull this switch off in the first place. "After all," Meg went on, suddenly sounding like the best-tutored woman in the realm, "the Scots queen's the one who helped to kill her husband in that explosion in Edinburgh—everybody says so—and ran off with that blackguard Earl of Bothwell, even though her supporters claim he forced her. Lord Cecil said she's ruled by her female passions, and that's why she's doomed as a queen, while you are ruled by reason."

Yes, Elizabeth thought, her nemesis the Queen of Scots might be ruled by her female passions, those very passions that the Queen of England had almost let free today with Drake. She had smothered them before they could catch and flame like those lighted arrows in the sails, but it made her understand Mary Stuart the more, because she still felt the fire—not the one on the ship, but the one in her heart.

After the rather stilted Sabbath church service—given by the man who was possibly the only local Protestant cleric and one who had obviously never been invited to Southampton's home before—Elizabeth changed to a plainer gown for the rest of the day. As she was expecting Drake to show up sometime soon, she didn't plan to look *too* plain, yet she wanted to show him she was mourning the loss of his sailor and, almost, his ship. She was also awaiting her hostess, Lady Mary, who had been summoned to attend the queen alone in her privy chamber forthwith.

"So strange in a Protestant country," Rosie mused as she lifted Elizabeth's single-stranded pearl necklace over her carefully coiffed head, "that so many in the land are named Mary. They are too old to be named in honor of your royal sister, so it must be for your father's sister Mary, the Tudor Rose, or more likely for the Virgin herself."

"That reminds me of that so-called welcome pageant we had when we arrived here," Elizabeth told her, "with the Virgin Mary herself lecturing me. Yes, a thousand Marys, but these last years I've ruled, the name of another virgin is the very fashion, too."

"Indeed. At least near London, I hear not only of many newborn Elizabeths these days but also of Virginias in your honor."

"Listen to me—unlike Meg listened yesterday, my

friend," she told Rosie, as she stood and flicked her fan to cool her face and throat. It was a warm day already, and she expected her interview with Mary Wriothesley to be heated.

"Yes, Your Grace?"

"Sit at your embroidery in that back corner and do not panic or despair at what you hear. And what you hear, unless I give you leave to speak of it later, is to be held close to your chest—like a winning hand in a game of primero."

When Clifford came in to announce that Mary, Lady Southampton awaited in the hall outside, the queen had him move Rosie's embroidery frame for her. Once her friend was settled, sewing away as if her very life depended on it, Elizabeth told Clifford, "The Lady Mary may enter."

The young woman looked especially pretty this morning, the queen thought, perhaps still flushed with happiness over her tryst with her lover. Elizabeth had learned the name and the trade—Jamie Clewiston, son of the local goldsmith and apprenticed to his father—of the man who had played poor Actaeon, punished for gazing on the nakedness of the goddess Diana.

"I hope you enjoyed the Sabbath service, Lady Mary."

"Oh, yes, of course, Your Majesty."

After Mary curtsied, she sat carefully in the chair the queen indicated. Their toes and skirts nearly touched. Elizabeth took a fig from the dish on the side table and ate it slowly without offering her one. In the silence, the young woman squirmed slightly, but she knew better than to speak again until the queen did.

"Since you don't give a fig for me, I didn't think I'd give one to you. I brought these from London," Elizabeth said, her mouth half full.

The woman looked instantly appalled. "I—I don't understand, Your Majesty. My husband and I are honored to have you in our home."

"But your loyalty lies with another queen, is that not true?" She loved these figs, but they were turning to mud in her mouth.

"I—certainly not, Your Majesty. I'm sure you know that we have clung to the old faith, but you have given your people the right to follow their consciences if it is in private."

She spoke well. Her dander was up. It might take a lot to make her crumble.

"So you or your retainers would stand with me—fight with me—against Catholic, pro–Mary of Scots factions in the north, if it comes to that?"

"But—my husband should be here to tell you of our loyalty, and I beg you to send for him."

"If I do that, he would hear of your disloyalty to him, Lady Southampton. You see, how can I trust your profession of loyalty to me when I have seen more than once with my own eyes—and those of one of my servants yesterday behind the old burial mound—that you are not even true to your husband?"

The woman had gone stone still. Her eyes went wide; her pouted lower lip dropped open before she closed her mouth. She gripped the arms of her chair so hard her fingers went white.

"Well?" Elizabeth said. "I'm referring to the man who was turned to a very virile stag onstage, though I suppose the transposition from polite to passionate is part of his allure offstage, too."

"You—you mean that young man who played in the pageant?"

"Do not waste my time stammering about or playing innocent. Yes, the very same Jamie Clewiston to whom you pass notes, the man you met yesterday morning for a—well, a romance rather than a tragedy, at least so far," she added, and gestured with a fig.

Mary looked stunned, then sick. She pressed her hands to her stomach. Elizabeth ate the rest of the fig.

"You—do you mean to tell my husband?"

"Not if you and I can come to an agreement."

"That I never see Jamie again? I—we—"

Mary's eyes filled with tears. She began breathing so hard that the queen thought she might become hysterical, but, to her credit, she did not.

"I mean not to judge your situation or your heart, Lady Southampton, though, God knows, I detest unfaithful men, for the results are always bad, even bloody."

"But—"

"Listen carefully to me. I will keep your secret in exchange for a secret from you. I want to know what the Duke of Norfolk and your husband have been plotting. I realize you may not know much and may be a bystander in their plans, but you must give me something in return."

She hated herself for that. Granted, she could say she was helping to save a marriage, but she was also stooping to blackmail, which she detested in others. That hardly mattered right now. She had to protect herself, her power, her position. If these people were plotting, she must show them no mercy.

"But—if I tell you something, Your Majesty, it could mean more than the destruction of my marriage."

"I will settle for anything you know about Norfolk. As the premier noble in the land, he could, I realize, coerce your husband to stray from what is legal and divinely ordained. Norfolk is a much older man, a determined and convincing man, while your Henry is younger and impressionable. Well, of course," she said with an exaggerated shrug, "the choice is yours. If your lord learns of your covert activities and tosses you out, it will allow you to run off to the forest with your Actaeon instead of having to play mistress in this big place and your London home much nearer my seat of power."

"I can tell you one thing, Your Majesty—if it would be enough. I wager it would be, for it would be some sort of proof that Norfolk is in league with Mary of Scots—that he is yet hoping to wed himself to her against your wishes."

Elizabeth realized she'd misjudged this pretty young woman. She had not dissolved in tears but had seen that the best way to deal with this was indeed to deal and not fold.

"Say on," she said, trying to sound calm when her own heartbeat accelerated even more. If Mary had some sort of proof that Norfolk was secretly planning to wed the Queen of Scots, that was grounds for treason charges, for her cousin's clear purpose was then to seize the English throne for himself and his new wife. Elizabeth was certain Cecil could soon prove that.

"The Queen of Scots sent the duke a love token," Mary said. "It's a silk pillow for his bed, all embroidered with a scene and with words." She darted a look back at Rosie, embroidering, hardly looking up as if she had not heard a thing.

"What scene and words?"

"It's of a green vine in the shape of a scripted *E*, but one cut off at the top with a knife—like its head was chopped."

"Beheaded?" the queen said, her voice rising. She fought to keep from throwing her hands around her neck as she always did when she heard that dreadful word. Her father had ordered her mother beheaded; Tom Seymour, a man she had once thought she loved who had betrayed her, had gone to the block for sedition against her brother when he was king. Her cousin Jane Grey had been beheaded for claiming the throne when it by rights belonged to Elizabeth's sister Mary Tudor. Elizabeth, too, had come close to going to the block when her sister had her imprisoned in the Tower and wanted her life for a rebellious plot in which she was innocent.

"I suppose it could mean beheaded," the woman interrupted her silent agonizing. "The pillow's a pretty pale green, the vine and background both. He showed it to my husband, and I saw it."

Not a Tudor green, Elizabeth thought, for that hue was bold and dark, but a paler, more pallid green, like a faded tint. Was the color of it at all symbolic?

"And the words on it?" she asked.

"The pillow says—in her own fine stitches, I warrant— *My Norfolk,* and it's signed, *Your assured Mary.*"

"Assured Mary?" Elizabeth repeated. "Assured of what? My throne? My death after their revolt?"

"Oh, no, I'm sure it couldn't mean anything of the kind, Your Maj—"

"Do you know if there was anything secreted in that pillow?"

"I know not. I believe it was just a stuffed pillow for his bed."

"For his bed. Yes, that would fit the seductress. Anything she can do to string others along . . ."

"Please, Your Majesty, I beg you," Mary said, clasping her hands together as if in prayer, "please do not give my secret away, and I will mend my actions, I swear it. Norfolk and my husband talk much in private. My lord does not tell me of it, and I know better than to ask, but I just happened to see that pillow when Norfolk was boasting of its import to him."

"Yes, I believe that, the villain. Mary of Southampton, I believe you, and I offer you a bargain. I hold my silence on who told me about the pillow, and you hold your silence that you told me. Do I have your word on that?"

"You won't harm my husband?"

"Only if he harms himself first by deceit or insurrection. And do not of a sudden preach to him of loyalty to me, or he will know you are in league with me somehow. My court is departing on the morrow, and we shall leave things as they are—with both of us a bit sadder and wiser."

"Yes. Yes—I can't tell you how it's been here. My parents said I would grow to love him, and I tried. When children came, they said, I would change my mind, but there are none so far, and I can't abide bedding with—"

Elizabeth waved her hand to halt her confessions, then stood and reached out to clasp the woman's shoulder as she, too, rose. "The world of men is difficult to navigate, but you will only make things worse by being wed to one in the law and in God's eyes and to another in your heart, Mary."

The woman blinked back tears and bit her lower lip, but the queen could hear her unspoken question as if she had shouted it: *But how can you know this, unwed and untouched?*

The queen waited until the door closed quietly behind the woman, then turned to Rosie. "Do you think you could stitch me such a pillow, my friend?"

"It would not be quite like Norfolk's, of course, Your Grace, and the color of the silk might be a bit off, but men aren't judges of such, and it could be enough to startle the duke."

"And instead of a knife cutting off the top of an *E*-shaped vine, make an arrow slicing through one that is twined in the shape of an *M*—with an arrow stuck in it all aflame."

Chapter the Fourteenth

THE QUEEN HAD BEGUN TO WORRY ABOUT DRAKE, but he appeared the next morning as she walked between the house and the wilderness gardens. She told her ladies to continue their morning constitutional and went over by the fountain to greet him.

He bowed; she gestured him closer to the splashing water so their conversation wouldn't carry to her courtiers who strolled the grounds or chatted in groups around them.

"Your Majesty, I am relieved to see you are well, but I never doubted it."

"I walked home like a laborer from the fields, Captain, and I'm sore to the bone," she said with a tight smile. Indicating he should sit beside her, she perched on the lip of the fountain where the wind did not blow the spray. "As I suspected, your man holding the horses had also fled his post. Have you buried your sailor, Smythe?"

"He would be touched that you recalled his name, Your Grace. Yes, we buried him in a graveyard in town, though he was a seafarer at heart and would probably have preferred a sea burial. I don't know whether it was the arrow or the fall that killed him, but it's the third murder in this wretched business. Now it is not only your subjects' blood but my man's that cries out for justice."

"Yes, we now share that, too, and I swear their losses shall be paid for in full."

"I believe you," he said with a decisive nod, "and join you in that vow. Besides, I will avenge my ship being so attacked. Your Grace, word is all over town that the *Judith* has partly burned. I lightened it and hired two barges to tow us off the muddy shore and back to the wharf. Though my men have been told not to say *how* the ship burned, that has become known, too, and local folk are certain the Hooded Hawk was behind it all."

She hit her fist on her knee. "It infuriates me to think we're no closer to proving it is *not* a myth that threatens us both and stalks this entire royal progress!"

"And now my ship is maimed, though not destroyed. It will have to stay moored at the wharf until the mainmast can be rebuilt and another sail brought in."

"Must you remain with the ship, then?" she asked, turning more toward him and almost losing her balance on the smooth lip of fountain. He put out his hand to steady her elbow, then took it away again. "Drake, we are heading north at dawn on the morrow. I understand if you must stay with your damaged vessel, but I had hoped you could come along. I intend to send for John Hawkins, and I would like you with me when I question him."

"I forgot to tell you that I had four men search the woods before dark last night, and they found naught but a mish-mash of footprints near a brook—maybe the shooter's, maybe not, maybe one man, maybe two. But yes, Your Grace,

Haverhill can care for the vessel and crew until a new mast and canvas can be bought, so I can continue with you. I will find the men who have done all this!"

"That is settled, then. But your two sailors we suspect have not turned up at all?"

"No, and I'm half expecting I'll find them with my cousin."

"Which reminds me, *my* cousin may have been behind this latest attack instead of yours after all. It's highly possible Norfolk learned my herb mistress was, shall we say, sitting in for me, and I have pried out of our hostess, Lady Southampton, one particular piece of evidence that suggests Norfolk is indeed in league with Queen Mary of Scots. I am putting a plan in place to be certain of this before I move against him, since he is not only my kin but the greatest noble in the land. Of all the things this realm needs right now, stability is key—if I can manage it."

She blinked back sudden, foolish tears that it had come to this. She hated not only the fact that people in the same family could distrust and detest each other but that, as in her past, it could lead to the imprisonment or execution of a family member. Her father's brutal elimination of her mother, her own sister's attempts to get rid of her—she never wanted to face such horror, but here she was, confronting her cousins Norfolk and the Scottish queen.

She stood, for the breeze had shifted the fountain mist their way, making droplets dance in the sun in a shimmering rainbow. "Drake, I do not command you to come with me. It will be a three-day trip to Lord Sandys's home on the northern Hampshire border. If you wish to go back to Plymouth to see your wife or must stay with your vessel, I understand and will yield to your wishes."

Will yield to your wishes echoed in her brain. Perhaps she should not have said it that way. She gripped her fan so hard she felt its ivory ribs bend; despite the danger to them both, she didn't want him to go. Remembering her interview with Lady Mary this morning, she understood even more the allure of that which could never be, and not just because Drake was married. Elizabeth of England was ever, only and always, wed to her people and her kingdom.

"I have said I will go north with you. I must see this through—who is attacking us and why—and face down my cousin, as, I warrant, you must soon reckon with yours."

"Very well, then, though maybe it's best we do not travel so close together in the entourage. Cecil nearly had a paroxysm when he heard about the fire arrows, and I've vowed to him I'll not only wear the armor you have loaned me but keep my curtains closed with guards around me, unless we are in the midst of my people along the way. And Captain, come to my suite at dark tonight, for the Privy Plot Council will assemble for a final meeting before we set out."

Come to my suite at dark tonight—why did she always second-guess the way she talked to this man? Best she send him back to his ship and his home port, but she needed him . . . *needed him.*

Just as he bowed to take his leave, another gust of wind doused them both in spray. Despite their somber interview, he chuckled and she smiled back.

"Not quite sea spray," he said, "but, despite the fact disaster later struck, it reminds me of yesterday—one of the best times of my life."

As if she were a foolish maiden—or perhaps that silly, young mistress of this house when she saw her Actaeon—the queen's heart fluttered like a flag.

At the meeting of the Privy Plot Council that night, the queen faced a full contingent of her aides. "We are assuming," she began, "that the fact fire arrows were shot at Drake's ship, whether our foe knew I was aboard or not, could also implicate the skilled crossbowman whom Ambassador de Spes had imported. It's a Spanish trick—the Spaniards shot fire arrows and even used fire ships against our fleet in the New World."

"In a battle in which both Drake and Hawkins fought," Cecil added. "That means we have three main possible villains so far. First, Ambassador de Spes's skilled crossbowman, who may also shoot a longbow for all we know. Word is that King Philip himself selected and sent that man to our shores, and hardly, with his archery skills, simply as a spy. Second, Drake's two missing men, who could be in the employ of John Hawkins."

"Yes, and last, I hate to say it," the queen put in, "it could be a hireling of Norfolk or of the northern rebel lords with whom he is in league—or Queen Mary herself."

"A hireling?" Keenan echoed. "That sounds as if the Duke of Norfolk just snatched someone off the street, when the shooter himself must be skilled—clever, too."

"True," Elizabeth agreed. "The point is, we must not only find and stop the bowman but be able to link him to his master or masters—or to his royal mistress."

"Here we are," Meg said, "deep in the heart of Hampshire and possibly dealing with evils which reach to the rulers of two hostile nations. It does muddle the mind."

"I'm afraid," Elizabeth admitted, "it's come to exactly that in this little cat-and-mouse game someone is playing with me—and us. Someone wants to cause mental agony as well as physical fear."

Jenks, who had seemed to be hardly listening, asked, "Can flaming arrows be shot from a crossbow?"

"With great dexterity and deftness," Drake said, "and the attacking archer has that in spades. More likely the fire arrows came from a crossbow—one which may have scorch or char marks on it now, if we ever find the weapon, let alone its shooter."

"If it was a longbow which shot the fire arrows, it might be one of those taken from Hern the Hunter," Elizabeth said. "Despite all this drivel about the Hooded Hawk being resurrected in these parts, it's no more the Hooded Hawk than the man in the moon. I repeat, I think our enemy is playing with us, mocking us."

Meg, wide-eyed, leaned forward. "Are we completely discounting that it could be some sort of ghost? Your Grace, you admit that several ghosts stalk Hampton Court and a few other places, so why not the forests of Hampshire like they say?"

"Because," Elizabeth said, smacking her palms flat on the tabletop, making them all jump, "I'll not be affrighted by the supernatural, even in this shire, which seems to have one foot yet in the pagan world with its burial mounds and tales of Woden's wrath. Yes, I'll take precautions, but I will not cower. When my people gather to see their queen, they will see her. Thank the good Lord, our next host, after we spend two nights in village inns en route to his home, is Baron William Sandys, a man to be trusted, and I hear the forests are not so thick there. Now, enough for this night. We start out early on the morrow. Meg and Drake, you especially are to keep your heads down. All of you must be alert to keep your eyes open the rest of the way, so I bid you a good night's rest now."

Though she was relieved to put Southampton's manor and hunt park behind her, the queen hated the next day's ride. Much of it was through thick forests, so, unless crowds of curious or cheering people clustered along the way, she stayed shut in her curtained coach with Drake's armor on. She was still sore and felt stifled, hot, and beaten, even with Rosie's company as she stitched madly in the dim space on her version of the pale green pillow.

"I had to cut up a good summer gown for this satin," she said.

"And I shall see it is replaced with a lovely one, once we get through this endless journey and this dreadful mess!"

"I'm afraid all this bouncing quite ruins my usual even, tiny stitches, too."

"I would wager your sewing in a jolting coach is far superior to the Scots queen's any day. We shall see when we somehow get our hands on that pillow."

"Why did you not tell everyone in the privy meeting last night about that—and that your rival queen sent it to Norfolk, Your Grace?"

"I told Cecil, but—I'm not sure why I didn't share it with everyone. I will when we have your pillow completed. Perhaps we shall ask if they think I should simply confront Norfolk and force him to trade pillows with me as a dire warning to him—a last warning, I believe. But I am considering pilfering his pillow so I can get a good look at it, then decide what I must do. Lady Mary admitted she but glimpsed it, so there may be more to it, something else em-

broidered on it or something secreted inside. I guess, my
Rosie, either I couldn't admit, even to my friends, that I am
thinking of turning sneak thief—or I still can't bear to admit, even to myself, that I am probably going to be com-
pelled to take harsh measures against both Norfolk and
Mary Stuart."

"Maybe you would not have to play sneak thief yourself,
Your Grace, for any of us would do it for you."

"It's probably hidden in Norfolk's wagons far back behind us, or even in his saddle packs right under his bouncing bum!"

Rosie chuckled, then cried, "Ouch! Stuck myself, and
there's a drop of blood on the silk now."

"Somehow," Elizabeth said with a sigh, as she sank back
on her bolster, "that seems appropriate. But your suggestion's a good one, Rosie. Even before this pillow is done, it's
possible that Meg Milligrew should take more healing salve
to Norfolk's chamber at the inn. The point would be to go
when neither he nor his servants are there so she could search
for that pillow."

"I suspect you could occupy him easily enough, but his
servants, too?"

"I'm thinking. Rosie, take a respite from all that dim,
rocky sewing, for I think we've struck on a plan. That is, if
there is a safe place for the court to play fox and geese this
evening at the inn, where an arrow can't come flying at us.
Yes, fox and geese, I think, with Norfolk as the fox."

Their stopping place for the first night, Waltham Chase, was
a charming village, where everyone gave her a warm welcome.
It was obvious from their garb that farmers had come fresh

from their fields to cheer her arrival. Welcoming speeches were, thankfully, short. She was heartened even more to see that rooms awaited them in the obviously scrubbed and newly whitewashed wayside inn called the Bramble Bush. It boasted a tile roof, which could not catch fire, although many of the retinue had to scramble for beds in the village or pitch their tents on the town green.

Also, the queen was pleased to see, the Bramble Bush was built in a big square with a grassy central courtyard where tables of food were set out. Once those were cleared away, it would be the perfect place for a game of fox and geese. Though she was going to make Norfolk the fox, it was truly Elizabeth, with Meg's help, who would be the sly one tonight.

Her courtiers were so relieved to see their queen in such good spirits that they probably, she thought, would have agreed to play the game in a dirty barnyard. Though fox and geese was oft played as a board game, it was most fun when played life-sized in the snow or where the pattern of the chase could be laid out on a lawn. Here, Ned and Jenks drew chalk lines on the cobbles while the queen appointed the geese first. The courtyard now looked like a giant chessboard with added diagonal markings where persons would become the moving pieces.

Though she strove not to give away her nervousness, Elizabeth glanced up at the inner windows of the inn. Norfolk's room was directly across from hers. It meant that Meg could glance out to be certain the Duke of Norfolk and his servants were here in the courtyard and could not catch her upstairs where she shouldn't be.

"All right, now!" The queen clapped her hands to get everyone's attention. "Remember to beware of the fox."

"What fox?" Robin asked, annoyed at being chosen one of the geese. "You haven't named a fox, so I volunteer."

"You would be a good one," she said, forcing a smile, and keeping her voice light, "but I have another fox in mind. My dear coz, Thomas Howard, Duke of Norfolk!"

He looked as if he would protest at first, standing stiffly with his arms crossed over his chest and a sour look on his face, but the others pushed him into the center of the squares and X's along which he would pursue the geese.

"I haven't played this since I was ten," he muttered, but she could tell he liked being the center of attention. "Run the rules by me again," he said to her.

"Rules?" she told him. "How nice of you to want to play by the rules, my lord. All right, everyone! The geese can move only sideways, downward, or diagonally forward, but the fox can move in any direction. You can also jump over a goose and capture it, my lord, as in checkers, and multiple jumps are allowed in a single move. The geese only win if they pen you up so that you cannot move, and the fox wins by capturing all the geese. All right, now, Secretary Cecil is going to cast the dice and call out the numbers."

As she had recited the rules, Norfolk's long face had taken on an increasingly wary expression. He must have realized she was setting him up, perhaps even warning him as she had done both indirectly and directly before. She held her breath for a moment, praying he wouldn't take offense and stalk off to his room.

As she left the queen's quarters and headed down the crooked hall toward the Duke of Norfolk's chamber, Meg clasped the small stone jar of broad-leafed dock tincture to her stomach, hoping to still the fluttering there. The queen had invited all the servants to come down to watch the games tonight, and Meg could see with her own eyes from peeking out the queen's windows that Norfolk and the three servants he kept with him were below in the courtyard.

Still, she felt on pins and needles, like the ones the queen had said must have been used to embroider such an intricate message and puzzle on the pillow she sought.

A floorboard creaked underfoot; she hesitated. She'd never liked the Duke of Norfolk and was kind of afraid of him, too. If he caught her here, she knew well to say that she had a bit of the salve left and wanted him to have it lest his stinging nettle rash returned. But, ever since he'd jumped out at her in Southampton's wilderness gardens, she'd thought of him as the beast of the forest. Yes, she didn't put it past him to be behind the Hooded Hawk rumors, in league with the Earl of Southampton.

Of course, Norfolk was not the shooter of the lethal arrows, for he'd been in plain sight twice when they came flying in, but it could be one of his servants, she reckoned. She only hoped she could make it up to the queen for being seen by Norfolk and Southampton at the window the day the queen went sailing. This had to work.

After the next turn in the hall, she counted three doors on the left, just as Ned had told her. Once Norfolk went up to his chamber to bed, Ned and Jenks were going to keep an eye on him. Jenks would guard his horse in the stables, and Ned would sit at the top of the staircase to be sure the duke didn't sneak out for some mischief, especially once he saw his precious pillow was gone.

If she could find it and get it to the queen. Meg thought it would be best just to examine it, leave it there, and tell the queen what was on or in it, but Her Majesty wanted to see it herself. Wanted, she'd admitted, to see what Queen Mary had slaved over, to see her handiwork to know more the depths of her desperation.

The depths of her desperation. That was exactly what the queen had said, when Meg was so afraid her beloved mistress was mired in those depths herself of late.

She knocked lightly on the door, hoping that didn't draw anyone from a nearby room. Nothing. No sound, no movement. Perhaps the queen's invitation for food and fun had cleared out the entire inn.

"Now, you are not to take time to search overlong for the pillow if you cannot find it," the queen had said.

"But what if I spot a crossbow or longbow or more of those bolts or *quadrello* arrows?" Meg had asked.

"Then, if the coast is clear, bring those to my chamber immediately," she'd said, her voice excited. "But no heroics, that is my point, Meg, though if you do not spot the pillow at first—without disturbing his things—you might look around briefly. Briefly, for I do not know how long I can hold him."

Meg lifted the latch and pushed. With a creak, the door opened.

"Hello?" she said quietly. "Just brought a bit more healing salve for the duke's poison nettle rash."

Silence within, but cheers and laughter outside. She darted in and closed the door behind her.

The fox quickly gobbled up geese, including Drake and Robin. Elizabeth had been hoping Norfolk would get hemmed in so she could give him a cryptic warning, for the man had always loved intrigue. He was well suited for Mary of Scots in that respect, for she also planned and plotted, with her enigmatic *Your assured Mary* and the puzzle of the truncated vine on that pillow. Surely Lady Southampton had not made any of that up, for it was far too clever for her. That pillow existed, and Elizabeth must get her hands on it to read its implications clearly before she confronted or imprisoned Norfolk—or let him snare himself even more with the rebellious northern lords before she trapped and punished them all.

"I can't believe," Norfolk said to her, "you condescended to be a goose and let me possibly catch and devour you."

"It's just a game, Master Fox," she said, and forced a laugh. "Or, in your mind, is it more?"

He laughed. His teeth shone bright between his nut-brown mustache and beard.

"You see," she said, "you haven't caught me yet, and, with my friends and allies, I may yet surround you. Your move!"

She managed to evade him once again, though he captured Rosie. 'S blood, he was going to win this time, when he said he hadn't played in years.

Her next move, then, must be to keep him here after he'd won, and as a goose next time—though maybe she could make up a new rule that if the fox won, he played the fox yet again.

When he turned away, she glanced up at his chamber window. No sign of Meg, of course. Then she realized that where Norfolk's three servants had been, looking on and laughing off to the side, only one remained.

The pillow wasn't on his bed, where Meg had first looked. Nor was it in the tooled leather coffer at the foot of the bed. Men's garments there; she hoped she hadn't pushed them awry in her quick search. More coffers and boxes were stacked in a corner, seven of them, which must have been unloaded from his personal wagon. It would take her too long and more strength than she had to lift and go through them all.

Think! Think!

She opened the saddle packs she saw on the floor near the door and rifled through them. Nothing. At least she could hear the raucous game still going on full force outside.

When she moved away, she accidentally kicked the jar of salve where she'd put it on the floor beside her—hurt her toe, too. She was not to leave the salve, of course, unless she was caught and had to say that's why she'd come. Let him wonder who had taken his pillow.

She got on her belly to reach for the salve under the bed. His sword was here in its scabbard with his belt. How she wished she'd found a crossbow or longbow, even though Her Grace said not to spend extra time looking for such when they knew the pillow was a surer bet. But behind his sword was another saddle pack.

She stretched out to reach it and dragged it toward her and felt inside. Something soft, but not silk. Many courtiers on progress followed the queen's lead and brought their own bed bolsters or pillows, but in his saddle pack and under the bed?

When applause and cheers exploded from outside, she jumped so hard, she hit her head on the side of the bed.

She pulled out the pillow. Plain linen, that's all. No—no, this was a cover for another one within.

Her heart thudding in her chest, she opened the linen case.

Green! Pale green. But it wasn't what Lady Mary had told the queen was on it. Meg saw some sort of embroidered bird within a wreath. Could this be the wrong pillow? Another pillow, a mate to the one the queen wanted?

She turned it over. Yes, on this side was the very thing she was sent to get.

Meg thrust it back into its linen case. Then on second thought, she took three shirts out of the coffer at the bottom of the bed and stuffed those in the place of the pillow in the leather saddle pack before she shoved it back under the bed. Holding the pillow down at her side as if it were something unimportant in a sack, she hurried out the door.

She was just around the turn in the hall when two of Norfolk's three valets passed her. Her legs almost turned to butter as she merely nodded and went on her way. Their voices floated to her as she picked up her pace toward the queen's chamber.

"Don't see why he gave us the high sign we can't stay down wi' the others," one groused.

"Funny, though, to see his lordship playing the fox, eh? Good choice, I'd say."

Meg hesitated, thinking they might say something incriminating, but their voices faded and she heard a door slam. That was close! Wait 'til she told Her Grace she just missed getting caught.

She rushed into the queen's chamber, closed the door behind her, leaned against it, and finally exhaled. Then she recalled she'd left the jar of salve under the bed where it had rolled when she accidentally kicked it.

Chapter the Fifteenth

"LOOK HOW THE WOMAN SEWED HER SIGNATURE," Elizabeth muttered as she, Meg, and Rosie bent over the pilfered pillow. "Not elegant but grandiose, not bold but brazen."

She ran her fingertip over the stitches of *Your assured Mary,* but she did not touch the green vine or the knife cutting it. All the raised work was done in a slightly darker green than the pale silk background.

"How dare she be so intimate with a man she must have surely never met!" Elizabeth exploded. "She gives no title, no family name here, just *Mary,* as if it is a simple vow to give herself to him, body and—and conspiracy, for I swear, the woman has no soul!"

She jumped at the sharp rapping on the door. "The lord secretary awaits, Your Majesty," her yeoman's deep voice came through the old oaken door.

"Send him in!"

"Did you get it?" Cecil asked the moment he entered and Clifford shut the door behind him. "Ah, I see you did. Good work, Mistress Milligrew!"

"But one thing," Meg blurted, wringing her hands. "As I

told Her Grace, by chance, I kicked the stone jar with the curing tincture under his bed where I found this, then left it behind, the poison nettle tincture, I mean. If the duke figures out what it is, he'll know who was there."

"Yes, well," Cecil said, "let him fret that we are onto his machinations. It will either sober him up to behave, at least for a while, or push him over the edge, then we'll have him. Jenks and Ned are at their assigned positions?"

"Yes," Elizabeth said, as she turned the pillow so he could see it right side up. "I told them to man their posts as soon as darkness fell, and that is now. I wonder how long it will take Norfolk to miss this. If he sleeps with it every night, the blackguard, it may be soon. If he doesn't put it on his bed, Meg stuffed shirts in the saddle pack where he carries this, so he may set out with us on the road and believe he has it yet."

"The *E*-shaped vine is just as Lady Southampton said," Cecil observed, "cut off at the head. Yes, I read this as a personal threat against you, Your Grace. Leave it to wily Norfolk and an even wilier woman who has been twice wed—not counting her liaison with Bothwell—to be so clever at a seductive and subversive sport between them."

"Beyond that, do you think any of this is some sort of cipher they've developed? And look, here on the back . . ."

She turned the pillow over; she and Cecil moved closer to the lantern on the table. Rosie and Meg hovered on either side as Clifford's voice sounded through the outer door again, "Captain Drake here, Your Majesty."

"He may enter."

Clifford opened the door for Drake, then said, "Can't find the courier Keenan yet."

"Keep looking," she said, and, as the door closed, turned back to their study of the pillow again.

"Whatever is this?" Cecil asked, stooping closer to the small bird in flight embroidered on the back of the pillow in the lower right-hand corner. It's outline and eye were done in black thread, but its beak, legs, and feet were gold. Surrounding it was a wreath, seemingly attached to the beak as if the bird carried it or wore it as a halo. "Could it be a falcon—or a hawk?" Cecil inquired.

"And could that wreath be intended as a hood?" the queen mused. "I warrant this is as much of one as the sail surrounding the head of the hawk in the wax seal on John Hawkins's letter to you, Drake."

"It—it couldn't be a duck, could it?" Drake asked. "A male one, a drake, meaning I'm to be cut off, too? Could that weird-looking wreath be a sort of noose?"

"No one knew before ten days ago I would summon you to accompany me on this progress," Elizabeth reasoned aloud. "It seems highly unlikely that the Scots queen could have learned you would be with me, then had time to sew this and have it sneaked out past her hosts and delivered to Norfolk in that amount of time. Granted, the lethal archer seems to be taking aim at you also, but I cannot fathom how this could symbolize your name."

Rosie put in, "I rather think it's a dove, like the symbol of the Holy Ghost coming down from heaven. I realize she didn't embroider its body with white, but, you know," she went on when no one responded, "the dove descending on the Lord Jesus when he was baptized in the River Jordan."

"She's right," Elizabeth said. "And God spoke the words from heaven, *This is My beloved Son in whom I am well pleased.* But I can't see how any of that relates to the current situation with the Scots queen."

"Queen Mary has borne a son, in whom she is no doubt

well pleased," Drake put in. His gaze met Elizabeth's over the bent heads of the others. Did he recall their discussion of how much he wanted a child, when he knew she did, too?

"At any rate, that son is hardly hers now, as the Scots lords took the boy to rear when she fled with Bothwell," Elizabeth said. "This bird does resemble a dove more than anything, but maybe it's the dove Noah sent out from the ark after the flood to see if there was dry ground yet—if they could rebuild. That concept seems more on the mark with Queen Mary's current state and her hope to rebuild my kingdom with, as she believes, God's blessing."

"Yes," Drake said, "but a reference to the ark could be a covert reference to a ship—one under attack as ours have been by the Scots queen's Spanish allies. I'm trying to recall the rest of that Noah story. He sent the dove out twice from the ark, and the first time it returned with nothing."

"And the second time," Elizabeth said, "it came back with an olive branch to let him know the flood was receding. Since the times of the ancients, an olive wreath has meant not only peace but—"

"But victory," Cecil finished for her. *"Your assured Mary* and her next husband Norfolk may believe they are assured of victory in cutting off the green vine of Elizabeth."

Chills racked her. Again she felt that strange, icy circle between her breasts and her shoulder blades as if a ghostly shaft had sliced right through her. She imagined pain there; for a moment she could not catch her breath. She saw her dead falconer and felt his life bleed away as she held his hand. Poor Tom Naseby lay dead at her feet, and Drake's sailor crashed to the deck with a flaming arrow in his back. Warnings, all dire omens of worse to come?

Her voice shook as she said, "I believe you may be right, Cecil. But if my rival queen knows of the bowman sent to slice through the vine, why a knife instead of an arrow—or bolt or *quadrello*?"

"Worse, where and when will the next attack be made?" Drake asked, and stepped between her and the window as if to shield her from the outside. "You know, Your Grace, however warm the night, Norfolk's rooms are across the way, as is a slate roof where a bowman could look in here."

"I have guards both outside his room and on the roof, but you are right. I have no one inside Norfolk's chamber to know what is going on with him. But he's wily, a fox indeed, so he would not allow his archer to shoot from his room, where he could be traced. I may have set him up in that fox and geese game tonight, my friends, but he may well be playing hoodman's blind with me."

"The same game as blindman's buff?" Meg asked. "You mean he's put a hood of sorts over your head and amuses himself by dealing blows? You can't tell who's hitting you so it just goes on and on until you guess right?"

"Yes, but we must do more than guess! 'S blood, it has to stop here and now! If I can't control Norfolk, though he's daily underfoot, I will be forced to change my royal cousin Mary's status from guarded guest to prisoner. Once that's done, it's a slippery slope to worse things, and I can't abide the idea of a queen ever being executed again. My father may have done it to my mother and to my Howard cousin, Queen Catherine, but I can't stand the thought!"

Elizabeth lowered her voice, for it sounded nearly out of control. She could not believe she had blurted all that out, her deepest fears, when things had not yet come to such a pass.

"Maybe," Rosie said in the awkward silence, "the Duke of Norfolk is still seething over the fact the Tudors beheaded a Howard queen."

"I'm at the point where I don't care *why* but *what* he's doing. And I can hardly arrest the highest noble in the land over a pillow!"

A horrid headache suddenly clenched her forehead as if it were in a giant vise. She motioned them to leave her, and Rosie helped her into the adjoining bedchamber, where, once the door was shut, the queen burst into tears that splattered the beheaded vine like rain.

Elizabeth drank a soothing posset Meg sent in and slept the sleep of the dead, until a repeated knocking on a distant door roused her.

Her bedroom was pitch-black. For one moment she could not recall where she was. A low-burning lantern should be on the far table. Where was Rosie? At least her headache was gone, but she felt light-headed, disembodied.

Then she remembered everything—and that she had put Norfolk's precious pillow in its linen pillowcase under her own bed. She peered around the bedcurtain that, like the bed itself, she had hauled with her on her progress. Thank heavens, Rosie came back in with the lantern.

"What is it?"

"Justin Keenan's outside in the hall with an important message he will give only to you."

"Have him pass the note in."

"He had nothing written—something he's seen. About Norfolk, I believe."

" 'S blood. Is Cecil not with him? It must be the middle of the night."

"After two of the clock. I can tell by the new guard on the door. All Keenan will say is to tell you it's important."

"Let him in the outer chamber, and have a yeoman guard come in with him."

"Yes, Your Grace," Rosie said, shoving her bounteous hair from her face as she went back out.

Elizabeth realized she must look like one of the Furies, but Keenan was too disciplined and circumspect to come to her in the middle of the night without the sure knowledge of something dire.

She tied her long hair back and wrapped her robe around her. She felt a bit dizzy at first and thought she might lose her balance. Even this time of year, the slanted floorboards of the inn were cold where the mats did not reach. She tried to shove her feet into her woolen mules but kicked one away, just as Meg had said she'd kicked the stone jar under Norfolk's bed. Norfolk's bed, which the damned Queen of Scots wanted to share only so she could get the English throne and have a double claim to it through her own bloodline and Norfolk's, too.

Elizabeth found the other slipper and went into the outer chamber. Keenan bowed low. He looked distraught.

"Tell me."

"Both of my horses are gone. There wasn't room for them in the inn stables, crowded as it is tonight."

"You woke me for a horse theft, man? Are you dement—"

"I had them tethered out in back and was sleeping on the ground near them. They're the fastest courier mounts I've ever had, and they cost Lord Cecil a pretty penny."

"Then go to see Cecil!"

"The point is, Your Majesty, though I woke after the horses had been led off a ways, I glimpsed Norfolk on one, and two of his men shared the other. I think they're gone—horses and men."

She gaped at him. "You *think*? Did you not check? Norfolk gone?"

Six quick raps resounded on her door to the hall, four slow and two quick ones. Cecil—and Cecil never used that knock unless something suspicious was going on.

"Enter! But where's my guard?" she asked as Cecil, hastily dressed with his hose not even gartered, came in. He bowed jerkily to the queen and nodded to Keenan.

"When Keenan woke me, I sent one of my men and one of your guards to roust out Norfolk. Only one of his three servants is in his chamber. He's fled."

"How did he get past Ned? He's on the staircase. I can see how Jenks might have missed him if he took Keenan's mounts from out back instead of from the stables, where I had Jenks posted, but Ned? Hell's gates, if Norfolk or his men have hurt Ned, Meg will never recover. Keenan," she said turning to him, "I regret I was short with you. My brain is fogged, and I couldn't grasp at first how the theft of your horses was linked to Norfolk."

"I ask your pardon, but I was too overturned—about my mounts and the duke—to put things more carefully, Your Majesty."

"Cecil, send my other door guard to look for Ned Topside, then summon more guards here. If Norfolk has indeed fled, it could mean the onset of the revolt. Or he found that his pillow was gone, and that panicked him."

"His pillow?" Keenan said.

Another knock on the door. It was Ned and her guard with one of Norfolk's three men held fast between them.

"Where has your master gone, man?" she asked Norfolk's valet when her men hustled him before her. Keenan quickly stepped back into the corner to make room.

"Your M-Majesty, I didn't know he's gone 'til I was waked."

"This one sleeps just inside Norfolk's door to the hall, Your Grace," Ned put in.

"Then he should have known when Norfolk and the other two decamped—as should you, Ned!"

"The duke and the other two went out their window and down knotted bedsheets into the courtyard," he explained. "And I'd vouch for this one telling true, since I could hear his snores through the door to the hall where I sat. I'd moved closer off the back stairs to keep a better eye on the door, and here they slipped out another way. Maybe they knew I was there."

Elizabeth's knees buckled; she sat down hard on a stool. Her head spun with all this. Yes, she believed this bedraggled-looking servant of Norfolk's, too, for he was the one who had been left behind to watch the game of fox and geese last night when the other two knaves had disappeared, perhaps on some errand with a silent signal from Norfolk—perhaps to pack. Meg said she'd barely missed them in the hall. Did that mean Norfolk was intending to flee anyway? He could not have known his pillow was gone then.

"Ned, go back to Norfolk's bedchamber and look under his bed for a pair of saddle sacks. It's where Meg found the pillow. See if the three shirts in it have been disturbed, for then we'll know if it was the loss of his pillow that panicked Norfolk—and if so, how important it must be to him and his schemes."

"Yes, Your Grace," he said, and lit out.

"And this sorry barnacle?" Keenan said, stepping forward and gesturing at Norfolk's wide-eyed man. "I half believe his story, for he's not one of the duke's guards but the one who packs and loads his wagon."

"My guards are to hold him for further questioning. And, at first light, a search party is to set off to trace Norfolk's path. Granted he's gone north, but how far north? And to whom? Keenan and Cecil, stay with me a moment more. Rosie, you, too, though I doubt sleep will be back to visit any of us this night."

She was suddenly glad Drake wasn't here, because she knew she looked a fright. Yet she was grateful to Keenan for rousing her. She would see he had a fine mount to ride to-morrow, until someone could track down Norfolk, thief of horses and thrones.

Meg jerked awake when little Piers cried out in his sleep. She and Ned had laid a pallet in the small herbal distillery room at the back of the Bramble Bush's kitchens, hard by the flour-bolting room, which had made the boy sneeze. Ned had taken a nap between the two of them, but he was not back yet from his post outside Norfolk's bedchamber.

"Piers, my boy, I'm here," she said, as she rolled over beside him and touched him carefully. Sometimes he struck out if wakened too quickly from a bad dream.

"Oh, Mistress Meg," he said, and wrapped his skinny arms around her neck. "I had that nightmare again. Where's Sim?"

"Staying with Ursala and her little one, remember? They had to make do in the hayloft above the stables this night."

"Oh, aye," he said, pressing his face into her shoulder and not loosing her one bit. Rather than being pulled on top of him, she shifted her weight to lie beside him, holding him close.

"You were lost in the hedges again?" she asked. "Maybe if you tell the bad dream aloud, it will purge it. I heard once, if you bid it go away, it won't dare come back."

"It was all brambles and nettles catching at me again," he began, his high voice still shaky.

"Since this inn is called the Bramble Bush, mayhap that reminded you." From the large open-hearthed kitchen just outside their door, she could hear someone stirring where other servants from the queen's retinue slept on the floor. They were stuffed cheek by jowl in this inn tonight and would be at their next stop tomorrow night, too.

"Mayhap," Piers said, "but there's men on one side of the hedge, ones want to hurt my father. I can't see through who it is. I don't know where he went. I have to keep looking for him, but can't 'cause I needs stay hidden or the bad men will get me, too. 'A life-and-death matter . . . life and death,' they say. Does that mean they kilt him? I can hear them but not see them. And I can't run 'way, can't get my feet to move . . . and it's not the spell of the fairies done it this time to me . . ."

"There, there, my lad, it's all right. I'm here."

"Where's Ned, then?"

"Doing a service for the queen, that's all. Jenks, too, but they'll be back bright and early before we set out, so you'd better get some rest now."

"Don't let them—those bad men—find me and take me 'way, too," he said with a big sniffle.

"I won't," she said, her voice soothing. She finally let him go but continued to rub his bony back as he curled up in a little ball. "You just go to sleep now, and I won't let anything happen to you ever."

"Promise and cross your heart?"

"Cross my heart," she told him, and rubbed his back lightly until his breathing evened out and finally slowed.

Cross my heart, she thought, *for if I'd lose you, too, my heart would just break—break and—and stop, I'd see to that myself.*

"Keenan, Cecil, too—another word with both of you before we call this a night, and a dreadful one at that," Elizabeth said, and motioned them to sit at the small table in the outer chamber. They had just handed Norfolk's nervous servant out the door into the custody of her yeomen guards, who were increasing in number in the hall.

But again a rap on the door. Clifford admitted Ned, out of breath and wide-eyed.

"Yes, the shirts were out of the saddle sack under the bed—which sack wasn't there."

"He found the pillow," Cecil said.

"Which indicates," the queen noted, "he probably slept with it every night."

"And," Ned reported as Keenan's head went back and forth as if he watched a tennis match, "it looked indeed as if he hastily stripped the linens from his bed and knotted them, then went out the window with his other two men. The twisted sheets were still dangling partway to the ground."

"Then," she said, "Norfolk knows the pillow completely gives him away. What Ned has found is also another piece of evidence that clears the third servant of the duke's, for, if he were in league with them, he surely would have pulled up those bedsheets so they wouldn't be spotted at first light."

"The duke did leave this," Ned said, thrusting a square of parchment at her. "It doesn't have your name on it, Your Grace, but says *To Whom It May Concern.*"

"The wretch," she muttered, as she opened the letter. "That's his idea of a warped joke—and an insult to me. Well, if I cannot keep Norfolk under my thumb, I can stop him at the other end of his quest."

"To free and wed the Scots queen?" Cecil asked. "Earlier this very night, Your Grace, you were reluctant to move against her."

"We must stay nimble on our feet and adapt instantly to their maneuverings. Ah, how foolish of him to tell me this lie," she said, as she bent even closer to the lantern to read aloud the words:

"Written in haste to protect all of the queen's court and retinue—I fear that what I thought was a mere skin disturbance from poison nettle may be much more. Lest I have the red rash—"

"He's claiming to have measles?" Cecil said.

"Yes, though, of course, he implies it could even be the pox, because he knows I—everyone fears that above all things. *Lest I have the red rash, and not wanting any harm to come to the queen's precious person*—The lily-livered, churlish, ruttish maggot-pie!" she exploded. "I warrant he had this note carefully composed and did not just dash it off. He knew he might have to flee and tries to make it sound as if it is to help, not hurt me! And he dared to sign it *Her Majesty's loyal servant, Thomas Howard, Duke of Norfolk!*"

"And then," Keenan spoke at last, "to go down bedsheets, as if by merely walking the halls of the inn to depart, he might spread the pestilence to you—to all of us."

"Exactly. How dare he think I would believe such drivel!" she demanded, raking her fingers through her hair. "As soon as I arrive at Lord Sandys's house, I will write to Lord Huntingdon. I can surely trust him. I shall command him to ride north and be certain that Mary of Scots's guardian, Lord Shrewsbury, has her moved from his Chatsworth Castle, where she resides as my guest but continues to abuse my hospitality. Like it or not, she is going back to Tutbury Castle, where she will be much more closely watched!"

"Do you want Keenan to take that message to Huntingdon?" Cecil asked.

"If you can spare him. It must be someone we can trust, so yes. Indeed, I will even charge you, man," she said, turning to Keenan, who looked so alert it seemed he was ready to set out on the instant, "to ride along with Huntingdon to Shrewsbury to be certain my cousin is delivered safely to Tutbury and then report back to me."

"Being sent to Tutbury and under guard," Cecil said, "will send a clear message to her and to the rebels, Your Grace. She always did hate Tutbury."

"So she wrote me more than once. I've never seen the place, but have you, Keenan?"

"When she was there earlier this year, I rode in twice."

"Go on, man," she urged, wishing he weren't so close-mouthed. "Is it as godforsaken as she claims?"

"Even in the summer, the sight of it chills one's bones, Your Majesty. Though high up, it overlooks only the plain and the banks of the river there. You can see for miles, which surely grieves one closed in the tall tower. The castle is damp and noisome with a marsh under its walls, and the place is in ill repair."

"I see. I should say I'm sorry for that, but I am only heartsick—and deeply hurt and angry—at all this deception and treachery from my own kin. You may both leave me now. We set out just after dawn, probably riding north on that traitor's very heels—and, Keenan, on the hooves of your stolen horses."

Chapter the Sixteenth

 MARY STUART, THE FORMER QUEEN OF SCOTS, DE-posed by the Scots lords so that her son may rule under their care, the former queen now residing in the realm of England, is to be forthwith removed from Chatsworth Castle to Tutbury Castle by order of Elizabeth Regina, Queen of England . . .

Elizabeth sighed and crossed out the last few words. Since she would sign this order as *Elizabeth R*, why should she include her name and title in this letter to Shrewsbury, as if he didn't know who she was? Yet she wanted this missive Keenan would carry to Lord Huntingdon and then north to sound formal and formidable. She had rewritten it four times already and had a good mind to sign it *Your assured Elizabeth*, to see what Mary of Scots would make of that when they read it or showed it to her.

Still, this was only a draft of the letter. It had better be, since her hand shook and betrayed her impatience and ire. She did not feel safe, even as she sat at the table in this King's Oak Inn where her entourage would spend the night before arriving at William Sandys's mansion, the Vyne, in northern Hampshire on the morrow. She crumpled up the parchment and began again.

Elizabeth liked this inn even less than the one they'd stayed in last night. She wasn't certain but that she preferred being housed in comfort by courtiers she didn't trust, for it also made her nervous when her party had to pitch their own tents or hire rooms in nearby farmhouses.

Other things preyed on her poise. The roof of this inn was thatch, and a few well-placed fire arrows could mean disaster. She'd been in an inn that had gone up in flames once, and that memory haunted her. Fire, like flying arrows, was a fearsome thing. Then, too, she'd risked keeping only half of her guards here and sent the others ahead on the road to see if they could overtake Norfolk or at least learn if he and two men on two fine horses had passed through. Drake had begged to go out also, partly because he was searching for word of his crewmen, Giles Creighton and Hugh Mason. She had not wanted to let Drake go, but she did, and he took two others with him. All her men were to return by nightfall, but none were back yet, and she felt undermanned.

She sighed as her thoughts snagged again on her treacherous cousin Norfolk. He was no doubt either heading north, home to Kenningham, his stronghold in Norfolk, or going to meet with other malcontents who favored Catholicism and a Catholic queen. Either way, he could be the firebrand that could ignite a seething rebellion.

A sharp rapping rattled the door to the hall. Here she did not even have two rooms adjoined but ones side by side, this privy chamber and her bedroom next door. 'S blood, but she was coming to hate furtive knocking on the door!

"Enter."

She expected to see Clifford, but it was Jenks, whom she'd sent out at the head of one of the search parties. Her pulse pounded; she could read the excitement on his face.

"You have found word of our enemies!" she exulted, as he snatched off his cap and bowed.

"Yes, Your Grace, but not the ones you think. Far's I can tell, Norfolk and his men are long gone, but I do have news of men on two horses came through here ahead of us."

"Drake's men who deserted?"

"No, but at a farmhouse 'bout three miles from here, just off the main road, the Browne family took in two men on fine-looking, matched, blazed-forehead mounts four days ago. Heading north they were, too. And, Your Grace, one of them spoke mostly Spanish, but the other one turned it into English for him."

"De Spes's bowman and his interpreter!"

"They thought the foreign one was called Wan."

"Juan, no doubt. I believe Cecil was recently informed that the archer's name is Juan de Vila. Can it all be coincidence that Norfolk flees in the same direction at the same time as those Spanish hirelings? They could be hunkered down ahead, waiting to shoot at me again. But it might mean we are safer now with no more arrow attacks on the road. Did you question the farm family thoroughly?"

"Aye, and they didn't overhear anything useful, 'cause their guests mostly jabbered away in Spanish. And they didn't out and out see a longbow or a crossbow, but both men had long leather bags along the side of their mounts," he said, gesturing with outstretched arms. "You know, 'stead of saddle sacks 'cross the horses' croups."

"And those leather bags could have held bows. That is invaluable information, Jenks. Did you give the family a coin for their help?"

"Aye, Your Grace, and that reminds me of one more thing. When the master of the house put the coin away in a leather pouch, I saw he had a shiny sovereign—like the other two what's turned up."

"Damn the Spanish. Doing their dirty work on my mint's money with my face on the coins. Then they could be the ones who bribed Sheriff Barnstable to dispatch Tom Naseby, but I can't fathom what link they could have to Drake's cousin John Hawkins. Still, I wouldn't put it past anyone working for de Spes, and ultimately King Philip, to even use my image on that coin for target practice! Did farmer Browne say for certain those two gave him that coin?"

"He did. Oh, aye, he did overhear one thing. Seems this Juan is trying to learn a little English, and he asked the other one what time the meeting would be at the church."

"A meeting at the church? That's all they overheard?"

"I could fetch them in, Your Grace, if you want to talk to them yourselves, old man Browne and his wife."

"No, you've done very well, very well," she said, gesturing somewhat absently that he might take his leave. "A meeting at a church," she said to herself, as Jenks went out. It helped to reason aloud. She went on, "A beheaded vine, the sovereign's head on coins, a flying dove within a strange wreath . . . Hell's gates, I hate puzzles, but my life's become one—with too many opponents and the prize at stake my kingdom and my life."

For the second straight night, Elizabeth hardly slept one wink. Drake had not returned as had her other men, but he'd sent word with one of his companions that he was on the scent of his two men and would come straight to the Vyne to meet her.

Despite all her worries, her heart lifted the next afternoon to see the tall walls of the Vyne appear, just beyond the cheering crowds of the little town of Basingstoke. William Sandys and his wife, Catherine, met them with their family and retainers, as well as musicians and singers who broke into song as she alighted from her coach—her prison these last two days.

"Welcome to our home and hearth," Baron Sandys greeted her with a prideful smile. Like Henry Wriothesley, William Sandys was a young man, but she knew instantly he had more sense. After all, he was a staunch Protestant and supporter of his English queen.

"I'd settle for a cool breeze through the windows, my lord," she said, and dallied with each person, wishing all the while she could better stretch her cramped limbs with a brisk walk.

The Vyne was a grand home with a forecourt and a central gatehouse at the entrance. All structures were of rose-hued brick seemingly embroidered with black triangular patterns. But for the many tall, symmetrically set windows across the front façade, the place reminded her of Hampton Court. The Vyne could accommodate nearly four hundred guests in the bedrooms of its two long wings.

The queen had never seen the Vyne before, but years ago her father had visited here three times, twice with her mother. That made the Vyne instantly sweet and sentimental for her. The sites where her parents had spent time together as king and queen were few, and she treasured them.

"Those stands of oaks which surround the lawn are over a hundred years old, Your Grace," Sandys told her, pointing, as she surveyed the deep blue-green of the forest, now lightly gilded with autumn colors. At least those woods lay beyond a meadow and a marsh and didn't closely crowd the house, she thought. "A home on this site has welcomed travelers for centuries," her host went on.

"I can see this house is quite new, so there must have been one on this site earlier," she observed as he escorted her into the vast interior through the flower-bedecked central entrance.

"There are numerous Roman ruins in the gardens, Your Majesty. An important Roman villa or taverna stood here, hence the name the Vyne. Remains of the grape arbors are still visible if you dig round about. Since our little river, the Loddon, flows into the great Thames, we are nicely situated on a crossroads between east and west, south and north."

Yes, she thought, the Vyne was near major roads and the great watery highway of the Thames that could take one straight to London, but it also linked this southern part of England to the north. Could the church meeting the Spanish archer mentioned be near this crossroads? And was it mere coincidence that the name of her sanctuary for the next few days was the Vyne when the pillow Mary of Scots sent Norfolk sported a twisted vine?

After all, this great house boasted a small church within, albeit, she'd heard, it was more of a chapel. Off to the side she saw entrances to many rooms. As if he had read her mind, Sandys pointed out the entrance to the chapel. Perhaps she should examine every inch of that, she thought, trying to keep a pleasant look on her face as her host led her up the grand staircase toward her suite of rooms.

Drake traced the two men who had deserted his command not only by their descriptions but by those of their horses. The fools had taken the three mounts the queen and her men had ridden to the *Judith.* Such fine horseflesh as well as their trappings—especially in comparison with how ragged the two men looked despite their sailor's shirts—made them easy to follow. The only problem was, they had gotten a good head start, and he dare not go north of the Thames if he was to return to the queen at the Vyne yet today.

"Hey there, goodman," he'd called to more farmers and carters than he could count. "Have you seen two men in sky blue caps and shirts riding two fine mounts and pulling a third?"

"Oh, aye," the last man, a drover surrounded by cattle en route to London, had said. "Thought they was queen's men, couriers like the one come through these parts asking questions, but these lads looked kinda ragged and peaked, 'specially one slumped over his saddle."

That was when Drake realized they could actually be ill. That might have slowed them down or even made them halt, so he pressed on. Perhaps Giles and Hugh had told the truth about having the flux that day in the woods.

With Mountjoy, the queen's man he'd kept with him while he'd sent the other one back to her with a message, he finally saw the horses. They were unsaddled but tethered to a stone well behind an isolated cottage just off the road.

"Wonder why they didn't just ride on, Captain," the big, burly yeoman said. "And to leave those horses just tied there, where they could be taken—or seen."

"The two of them are skilled sailors but hardly strategists, Mountjoy, or they would never have taken the queen's property or disobeyed me in the first place. I'll ask you to wait here with our horses and those we must return to Her Majesty."

Drake dismounted and put his hand on his sword hilt.

He made certain his dagger was still sheathed in his belt. Since Hugh and Giles had deserted, he wasn't sure if they'd obey him now, either.

He intended to knock on the front door of the black-and-white-timbered and neatly thatched place, but the door stood slightly ajar, so he chanced a bold offensive. He pushed it open and walked in. A portly woman was bent over a table making piecrusts with a wooden rolling pin, her hands and gown all floury.

"Oh!" she cried. "Oh!"

"Pardon the intrusion, mistress, but I must inquire about the two men whose horses are tied in back. Friends of mine . . ."

"Oh," she said again, as if that were her entire vocabulary. Hoisting the rolling pin, evidently in case she needed to take him on, she said in a rush, "One took real sick, and my husband's gone for the leech, said don't go in, don't let no one near them. Took pity on them, he did, the one near falling off his horse."

Drake pondered if Giles and Hugh could be in league with the Duke of Norfolk, for he'd given out a story of being sick when he fled, too—but that meant Norfolk must have hired them just in the last few days, when Drake had feared they were working for his cousin Hawkins. No, he couldn't see someone as clever as Norfolk hiring those two.

"In here?" he asked the woman, edging toward the door she'd glanced at more than once. "Just a word with them . . ."

He lifted the latch, drew his dagger, so she could not see it, and shoved the door inward. Hugh lay either asleep or unconscious on a low trundle bed in the tiny, sparsely furnished chamber.

To his surprise, the door slammed into him, rattling his

teeth and his sword. When the door was ripped inward, he spun into the room. Giles lunged at him. Raising his dagger, Drake managed to sidestep, evading the first attack. He saw no weapon on Giles; the man meant to take him on with his fists.

"Halt!" he told Giles in his most strident captain's voice. "Halt and stand to!"

The man hesitated, frozen like a statue for a moment. Drake glared at him and sheathed his dagger. "I'm here for the truth, and I will have it, Seaman Mason! Are you two riding to report to Captain Hawkins in London?"

"Cap'n, your cousin's as like to string us up for this as you be."

"For what, man?" Drake demanded, still poised to take him on should he lunge at him again. "For deserting your duty—or for shooting fire arrows from the woods at the ship, burning her mainsail and mast?"

"What? The *Judith* burnt? We set out 'cause we was turned to no-'counts, and we was sick."

"Hugh perhaps, but you look hale and hearty to me."

"I've had it, too, the flux, but not as bad. And what else I've had up to here," he said, with a slashing motion of his hand across his forehead, "is being distrusted, then demoted to the scullery by my cap'n!"

"I'm no scullery maid napping!" came the woman's shrill voice through the door. She was obviously eavesdropping but had misheard. She rapped hard but didn't enter. "See here, now, is all well in there?"

"Is it well?" Drake asked Giles.

"Aye, Mistress Sarah! We're just talking!" Giles shouted to her through the door.

That must have satisfied the woman, at least enough to make her go back to merely eavesdropping instead of shouting.

"You were saying," Drake prompted, "that you felt demoted when I asked you to stay below for a few hours?"

"Aye, I did! The scullery, and when the queen's aboard, like I was some low, no-account jackanapes. No, Cap'n, we aren't going to Hawkins but out where we can start somewheres else—anywhere but on a ship."

"At the least, you've thieved the horses—royal horses. Damn your hide, man, you've ruined yourself."

"Pardon my say-so, Cap'n, but you should understand that. You know, in a split second, panic or pride makes you do something witless. Like flee a battle with a ship. Something you later got to eat crow for, if not worse."

Before Drake could stop himself, he slammed his fist into the man's jaw. He went down like a house of cards. Drake's fury ebbed as fast as he had struck out. The man was insubordinate and stupid but, on that last point, what Giles had accused him of was right. Did his entire crew see him as a man who had shirked his duty and besmirched his honor? Did they think that gave them the right not to stand and fight but to flee, at least until cornered? God willing, he would spend his entire life proving them all wrong!

Rueful now, Drake bent to sit the sailor up and lightly smacked his cheeks. To give up their trade, give up the sea, was a grievous penalty in itself and one, if he believed Giles, that would be self-imposed. He should have known he could trust them, but mistrust seemed to breed like flies on the queen's progress. In the years to come, as her captain, he must strive to protect not only his own honor but the honor of his men. Elizabeth relied on and trusted those loyal to her, even servants.

Giles opened his eyes. When they looked focused, Drake told him, "Here's the way it must be, man. You're going to answer all my questions—God's truth, straight out. Then I'm going to take the queen's horses back to her but leave you some coin to pay these people and get yourselves to—to wherever you're going, so you can start over as you said."

Wide-eyed, gingerly fingering his jaw, Giles gaped up at him. "You—you'd do that, Cap'n, and not take us back to hang from a yardarm?"

"By my faith, no one else—except the queen—will ever know. She's given me the chance to atone, and I'll pass that on—if you answer my questions, each and every one."

"I swear so, Cap'n. Don't fret 'bout us going near Cap'n Hawkins, neither. No way we would."

"I didn't mean to abase you in the kitchen that day," Drake added, for the Lord had taught him to forgive— forgive everyone except the Spanish, that is. "Nor did I mean to shame Hugh by demoting him to the status of groom, holding horses. But I didn't know if I could trust you after the two of you staggered out of the woods just after the queen—or I—was shot at. Prove to me I can trust you now before we part."

During the next ten minutes, Drake's nod and smile seemed to be enough to keep the mistress of the house at bay when, armed with a rolling pin, she pounded on the door and peeked in to ask if things were still all right. She evidently thought they were, for she gave Drake a hot partridge pie after he paid the old, stooped leech her husband fetched from the village to tend the sick man and dose the other, too.

"So you really *was* their friend," the woman said, as he departed her front door.

"I was their captain, mistress," Drake said, frowning, "and, sadly, that's a far different thing."

Elizabeth knew she surprised Baron Sandys when she asked him for a tour of the chapel even before the evening meal. With Cecil and Lady Rosie, she stepped into the exquisite little church from the back of it and said a silent prayer of thanks for her safety and deliverance—so far.

"Is this chapel ever used for aught besides holy services?" she asked. "Meetings or speeches or such?"

She felt she was dancing in the dark, but perhaps she could link the clues of the vine and a meeting in a church that Jenks had reported to her. How did the bird with the wreath-type hood around its head fit in? Was it another cryptic reference to a Hooded Hawk plot into which she must delve deeper?

The small Gothic chapel was exquisite with its crisply carved linen-fold paneling, Flemish stained glass her host proudly pointed out, and lovely choir stalls. Brightly colored tiles with flower designs were set in the backs of the seats.

"By an Italian artist," he told her, touching a bright blue tile with a red rose emblazoned on it. "A little-known technique called encausting. The paint pigment includes melted beeswax."

"How unique, but then this entire chapel is. Are your ancestors buried here beneath the floor stones?" she asked, walking slowly up the aisle with him toward the altar.

"No, though I would like to be someday—a long ways

off, I pray, since I am but twenty-four. My grandfather and father lie in the crypt of the old Catholic church in Basingstoke, the Church of the Holy Ghost."

Elizabeth heard Rosie's swift intake of breath behind her. Rosie had said the bird embroidered on the green pillow reminded her of the dove that represented the Holy Ghost, descending from heaven to bless the Lord Jesus. Elizabeth wondered if Queen Mary of Scots saw herself as the Lord's approved and anointed one.

"I should like to see that church on the morrow, too," she told Sandys.

"I had no idea you were so interested in church architecture, Your Grace."

"A current pursuit."

"Actually," he added, "since the new religion has come to the fore, the Church of the Holy Ghost is used as a meeting place sometimes, too, as you inquired of this chapel."

"How interesting. I shall thank you for not sharing our planned visit there with my courtiers. It rather ruins the sacred mood of a church tour to have a large entourage traipsing along. Ah, I see Captain Drake has returned, and I would like you to meet him," she told Baron Sandys when she saw her captain, cap in hand, awaiting her at the back of the chapel.

The queen steered Sandys to where Drake stood, but none too patiently, first on one foot and then the other. She was anxious to hear his report.

Taking Drake's arm, she preceded the others out into the Oak Gallery, which led toward the great hall, where supper awaited them.

"Any sort of success?" she asked Drake quietly.

"I found my men, but one was truly ill, and the other I

questioned—and believed. I would wager my future in the royal navy, Your Grace, that neither of them is our shooter or in league with my cousin Hawkins."

"Then you have done me a service. That leaves the Spanish hireling and my cousin Norfolk—and whomever he has made a devil's deal with to overthrow me. Likewise, I would wager my future that deal could include a Spanish king, a Scottish queen, and far too many knights and pawns."

"It sounds like a chess match, Your Grace."

"Precisely put, and I intend to win. You must tell me all the details, and we shall lay our plans after we smile our way through the feast. It's lovely to feel safe inside the walls of this grand house, but I'd almost rather be back dining out under God's great sky on the deck of your ship, Drake, fire arrows or not."

She forced a laugh, but the smile she summoned up for him was real. Too bad Robin's glowering countenance was the first thing she saw when she entered the great hall.

Chapter the Seventeenth

 THE CHURCH OF THE HOLY GHOST SAT ON THE EDGE of the little town of Basingstoke, a charming building, the queen thought at first glance. Its old stones wore a cloak of ivy, though it was turning reddish in the waning summer, as if the walls were bleeding.

'S bones, she scolded herself, everything she looked at now seemed somehow sinister. She was grateful she'd brought Drake and Rosie as well as Sandys and two guards, Jenks and Clifford. Ned and Meg had been left behind to complete their daily tasks and tend the Naseby boys.

Lord Sandys lifted a rusty iron bar from across the entry. The key grated in the lock; the wooden door screeched on its hinges.

"Sad to keep a house of worship locked and barred," Elizabeth observed as Sandys turned the key.

"There have been disputes in town about that very thing, Your Majesty. Though it's been converted to a Protestant church, most attend the one on the other side of town. But some die-hard, dissident Catholics on occasion come in to celebrate the Mass or perform some sort of rites after dark."

"Are those the kinds of meetings you mentioned?"

"I fear so. I'll not call whatever goes on here at night a holy service."

"If the church is secured like this," she said, sweeping her hand toward the door they passed through, "how do they get in?"

"I'll show you, but allow me to light a lantern or two first."

Though it was morning with the sun bright outside, two things darkened the stone interior of the church. The ivy had greatly overgrown the east-side stained glass window, dimming the splotches of multihued colors cast inside upon the raised stone lectern and baptismal font. Also, the church backed up to a thick stand of old oaks, with only the mounded, turfy headstones of a small burial ground separating the building from the wooded area.

The church had but few pews near the front, which was not unusual, for the common folk used to stand behind their seated betters in services. Elizabeth stared up again at the ivy-darkened stained glass window. Her mouth fell open; she jerked even more alert. She seized Rosie's arm and motioned for her to look upward but keep silent.

The window scene included a dove, the symbol of the Holy Ghost, descending on the Lord as he emerged from baptism in the waters of the River Jordan. The dove looked very like the one on the back of the green pillow, though its maker could never have seen this very church. Still, such a symbol was common enough that Rosie had recognized it earlier. And the glass bird had a halo around its head, so could that be what the wreath on the pillow was to suggest? The embroidered halo was dark green, though, and looked more like a tiny crown of thorns.

"Sorry, Your Grace." Her host's voice interrupted her agonizing. "This lantern does not want to catch—ah, there." He carried it over to light the second one, gesturing that they should join him across the narrow nave of the church. "The effigies before you," he explained, "are of my parents and my grandsire and his wife."

As he lifted both lanterns, the pairs of effigies on the two grand tombs leaped to life. The stone replicas seemed to shift and breathe.

"Their tombs are quite fine," she observed. Her voice echoed from the vaulted arches above, she noted, and Sandys's had carried clearly to her across the width of the nave as if this were a whispering gallery, as in great houses with rounded ceilings.

"My four ancestors share a common crypt below, though in separate caskets," he said, suddenly whispering as if a funeral service were being conducted even now. "Come and look behind my grandsire's monument, and you will see what I mean about how we believe Papists come in for their secret rites at night."

She followed him around the back of the effigies of two knights and their wives, staring blank-eyed straight up toward the stone canopy over their heads. It was, she thought, as if they yet shared a bed, though in attitudes of perpetual prayer.

Her thoughts skipped to how cruelly her mother's body had been interred under the stones of St. Peter in Chains Church in the Tower of London after she had been beheaded. No monument, no proper coffin, only an empty arrow box the body and head were stuffed in . . . an arrow box.

For a moment, Elizabeth thought she would be ill; she put her hand against the cold stone monument to steady herself. An arrow chest for a coffin . . . Again she felt that icy ache between her breasts and shoulder blades. Haunted, hunted, she was terrified by her memories and her present fears.

"See here, Your Grace?" Sandys was saying. The others in her little party crowded closer, leaning in to look where he pointed. Behind the effigy of the first Baron Sandys was a narrow set of stone stairs going down, perhaps to the crypt itself.

"Then this is the entrance to the burial vault?" Drake asked. "Your ancestors weren't just interred under the stones of the church floor?"

"There are some tombs like this in Westminster Abbey in London," Sandys declared almost defensively. More quietly, he added, "The thing is, my grandsire was afraid of being buried alive. He insisted an air duct and release latch be fashioned inside his casket and that there be two unlocked ways out of the crypt—even to fresh air."

"Then are you also saying," the queen questioned, "that the crypt below leads to an exit outside the church?"

Sandys nodded. "Strange, I know, but he would have it so and spent a great deal of money on a narrow escape tunnel, which exits just beyond the burial ground at the edge of the woods. I'll show you when we go outside, assuming you would not want to go down and through this way. It's dank and noisome in there."

Elizabeth recalled that was almost the way Keenan had described Tutbury Castle—damp and noisome. She'd ordered him to leave by noon after he met with Cecil. He was taking the order for Huntingdon and Shrewsbury to imprison the Queen of Scots. How Elizabeth had agonized over sending the command, for once she made her royal cousin her avowed prisoner, it was making her indeed her public enemy, abolishing all pretense that her rival queen was a guest in England. How she would like to understand Mary more so that she could read what her next move would be.

"You know, Sandys," she said, "if you can manage it, I would like a glimpse inside the crypt."

"Actually," he said, as he put both hands to the latch of the narrow wooden door at the bottom of the steps, "a single floor stone above does slide away to make an entrance also, but you have to put a little ladder down or take a jump. My father put that in, as embarrassed by his father's whims as I, but the old man said he heard once of a man buried alive."

"However did people know the man had accidentally been interred that way?" Drake asked. "Did they hear him shouting in his casket? How did he get out to tell his tale?"

"They opened his coffin about a year after his death to take a ring from his finger that his son decided he wanted and saw he'd clawed the inside of the coffin, trying to get out," Sandys muttered. "His fingernails were ripped back and his hands bloodied to the bone. And the expression on his face—well . . ."

If the door to the church creaked, this iron-grated and unlocked tiny one shrieked like a woman's scream. "Sandys," the queen said to him, "if *personae non gratae* are gaining access through this door and traipsing through your family's burial vault, why don't you or the caretakers put in locks?"

"It's in my grandsire's will not to seal the doorways out—ever. May I precede you with the lantern, then? It will be hard going to keep your skirts clean squeezing through here."

"I'll be fine," she said, holding her garments close and following him into the low-ceilinged vault. In a small, stale space lay four lead caskets, one of which had a little grate on top, no doubt for breathing, but she did not ask about that. Sandys was already opening the door that evidently led to a tunnel to the outside. Surely that underground exit didn't burrow through the graveyard but went deeper than those burials. Looking up at the low stone ceiling, she could see the very thin, faint outline of the paving stone that could evidently be moved away to access this vault, too.

"You're right," she told Sandys, "it's moldy and damp here—and dusty." As if to punctuate her words, Drake, the only other one who had stepped into the small space, sneezed behind her.

Surely, she thought, Mary of Scots's place of imprisonment at Tutbury Castle she so hated wasn't this chill and damp, but she must feel closed in like this. Perhaps the Queen of England would be plotting in secret, too, if she were so confined.

Elizabeth peered down the narrow, low tunnel Sandys lit with his lantern. "Even in these riding skirts, I'll not go farther, nor into the forest where you say the door comes out," she told him. Her gaze snagged with Drake's. That's all they needed, to be together in another forest when they weren't even safe in the open air in the middle of a river on a ship.

"I'll go," Drake said. "If you'll just let me take one of the lights from you, Baron Sandys, I'll be right back."

"That outer door at the edge of the woods is never locked, either," he told Drake, "though more than once I've been tempted to cover the entire exit over with a dirt mound. I must admit I have left a tree trunk close by that I'm always tempted to roll across it." He heaved a huge sigh.

"I'll just close the door behind myself and meet you all

outside, then," Drake said. Adventurer that he was, he nodded to her, then, bending over, plunged inside, where his form and light soon faded into darkness.

Sandys closed the door after him and ushered her out of the crypt and back upstairs into the nave. Before they went outside, the queen again studied the dove in the stained glass window, then gazed up at the altar with the priest's lectern on one side and the baptismal font on the other. Above and behind the altar she could see a vaguely lighter area where a large cross of Christ crucified must have hung for many years. During the Reformation, many of those had been replaced by a bare cross, for was not the Savior's redeeming work done and he long out of his torment?

Yet in this Church of the Holy Ghost, she felt frightened that her work and pain had just begun.

"Is this room as pretty as the ones at the queen's palace?" Piers asked Meg.

"Now you just sit where I said with your cup-and-ball game," she told him. "No, hardly as pretty as those in her palaces, though she brings many of her favorite things along on progress with her. I'll be done with these fresh strewing herbs in just a moment, so you are to stay right where I put you on that Turkey carpet, my boy."

She bustled about the spacious guest bedchamber, relieved, as the queen had been, that they weren't stuck in another tiny room at an old inn. This was Meg's favorite place so far on this entire trip, because she felt safe here, and she thought Her Majesty did, too.

She kept an eye on Piers as she rubbed dried lavender into the bed curtains. He was quite adept at tossing the little leather ball in the air from the cup, then catching it again. It was a game Ned had bought him as reward for learning his lines so well. If they could only keep the boy as their own! If only—

"Oops!" he said, as the ball went skittering past her feet under the big bed. "Guess that was a clumsy miss, eh, Mistress Meg?" he said with a laugh, as if he had made some sort of jest.

"Mayhap it runs in the family," she muttered, remembering how she'd managed to leave her stone jar of healing salve under Norfolk's bed. "Crawl under, then, and fetch it back," she said, and kept working. She'd overslept and had to finish this before the queen came back from Basingstoke, but what she was thinking of now was that she'd blurted out that she felt as if the boy were family. Yes, she could imagine that, and it warmed her heart.

"There's a real pretty pillow in a cloth sack under here," came muffled from under the bed.

"Now you leave that alone, you little knave!" she scolded, and dropped to her knees to peer under. "Piers, that's not to be touched, so put that back—no, I'll do it," she added, and scooted farther under.

"But the thing is, I seen it afore," he told her.

"Stuff and nonsense. Not this one, for it's special. It came from far to the north and belonged to—"

"To that grand Duke of Norfolk, didn't it?"

Meg, stretched out on her stomach, reaching for the pillow he had partly uncovered, gaped at him in the dim light under the bed.

"How'd you know that, then, Piers?"

"I was just across the hedge, the one Sim and me heard was broke with a stile and all. You know, back home. We were going to climb over when a man gave that pillow to the duke. Didn't know 'twas the duke 'til later when the queen took us in."

"The other man who gave it to him—what did he look like?"

"Don't rightly know. Mostly he was looking the other way, but had big shoulders and a fancy leather quiver of arrows on his back."

"Why didn't you tell me this before?"

"Sorry! Didn't know it was of any account."

"I don't mean to scold. Of course you didn't. And when you hid back behind the hedge, you and Sim overheard what the two men said?" she asked, frozen in anticipation.

"Sure, but can't remember too much. Like, 'She sends it to you with love and hope and trust'—real fancy talk. And the duke, he says something like 'This will seal my part with her,' or 'my pact with her,' I guess it was. Did the queen send the pillow to Norfolk, but now he gave it back?"

"Wrong queen," Meg muttered. "Leave that pillow there, get your ball, and come with me."

"I thought you weren't done. Are you going to punish me?"

"Come with me, I said. No, I'm not going to punish you, but we must find Ned and wait for the queen to come back."

They scooted back out from under the bed. Meg left her strewing herbs, took the boy's hand, and pulled him out of the queen's suite and down the long second-floor corridor that overlooked the forecourt through which they had arrived yesterday. Glancing outside, she saw the queen returning with Lord Sandys and the others she'd taken riding to see the church in town.

"Piers," she said, pulling him close and pointing out the window, "you run down to wherever the queen dismounts.

You stand there quiet til she sees you, hear? When she motions you to her or says you can speak, you tell her that Mistress Meg sent you to tell her something important and then—for her ears only—tell her exactly what you told me about the duke receiving the pillow."

"But won't she be angry I trifled with her pillow? And under her bed?"

"She'll understand. And you tell her I've gone to fetch Secretary Cecil and Ned, because I wager she'll think we need to talk about all that. You understand me, now? And don't forget to bow real low to her, like Ned taught you. And let me hold your cup-and-ball game. Now, go!"

He was off at a run, skidding around the corner toward the staircase. Meg looked out the window as the queen's party rode so close to the building she could no longer see them, then she rushed to find Ned and Lord Cecil.

Chapter the Eighteenth

ELIZABETH WAS SURPRISED TO SEE CECIL, NED, AND Meg waiting in her privy chamber when she and Rosie came in from their ride to Basingstoke. Perhaps they had guessed she'd find something at the church that needed discussion, as indeed she had. She was risking the assumption that the Church of the Holy Ghost, with its descending dove in the stained glass, was the place that some of Mary of Scots's supporters—perhaps Norfolk included— intended to meet. It was on a crossroads, it had a secret way in, and the place was obviously sacred to Catholics. The entire thing stank of sedition and insurrection.

"But—did you not bring Piers with you?" Meg blurted before the queen could say a word.

"Piers?"

"Yes—yes, I sent him to you just a little while ago, when you rode in."

"Meg, what is it? Why are you all assembled? I have not seen Piers."

"Did you ride around in back and dismount there? Oh, gracious, he may be lost in this big place!" she cried, and started for the door without being given leave or offering a curtsy.

"Meg, stop!" Elizabeth ordered, though for a moment she thought the woman might defy and ignore her.

"Your Grace," Cecil said, "Mistress Milligrew sent the boy down to tell you that both Naseby lads saw the green pillow delivered directly to the Duke of Norfolk and overheard their conversation, too. With further questioning, we may be able to get more out of them than—"

"But I've got to find him!" Meg cried, interrupting Cecil.

She was coming unhinged, Elizabeth thought. "Meg, we'll find him. He's probably with his brother, is that right, Ned? Ned!"

"I don't know. May I help Meg search, Your Grace, and we'll bring both boys to you straightaway?"

"Yes, go—and bring Jenks back with you!" she called after them. Ned remembered to bow and back toward the door before he turned to rush away, but Meg just ran out as if her very life depended on it.

If the queen wanted to dissolve into tears and tantrums, poor Meg seemed to be acting those frustrations out for her. In a two-hour search of the Vyne and its grounds, they had not found Piers or his brother. Meg and Ned had just come back in, the first time Elizabeth had seen them since they went to look for the boy.

"He can't—can't have just disappeared!" Meg wailed, as Ned tried to comfort her. "And Sim gone, too? It's foul play!"

"But you know how boys are," Cecil said. "Perhaps Piers

became distracted by Sim or someone else, and off they went for an adventure in the woods or town."

"No!" Meg insisted, pushing Ned away. "No, they wouldn't—Piers wouldn't."

"No, my lord," Ned put in, as Meg rushed to the window to look out, "Piers wouldn't. And they wouldn't just head back toward Guildford as Captain Drake suggested when he helped us search, even if Sim did once want to take over his father's place as hedger."

"I just thought," Drake put in, "they might have been homesick, and now we are closer to Guildford than we have been in days."

"Meg," the queen said quietly, calmly, going to stand by her at the window, "to help us find them, you are going to have to tell us what Piers did say. Exactly what message did you send him to recount to me about Norfolk receiving the pillow? What can you recall? Meg!" she said, taking her by her upper arms to give her a slight shake.

The woman's eyes seemed to finally focus from far away, and yet she seemed to stare right through Elizabeth. Pray God, the queen thought, she wasn't going back into her dark abyss, thinking of her infant son again.

"I can't lose him, Your Grace," she whispered. "Just—can't."

"You won't. Now listen to me. Even if someone has taken the boys, we will find them, but you must recall clearly whatever he did tell you."

"He—he said they were looking through the hedge, you know, back near Loseley House, the very place from which we later learned the fatal arrow had been shot. They went to see where the hedge had been broken through with the new stile."

"Good. Say on."

"He has nightmares of that spot, Your Grace," she cried, pressing her palms over her eyes. "He dreams that men there want to kill his father, and he hears them saying that something is a life-and-death matter."

Elizabeth shuddered. "Then maybe Norfolk ordered the man with the pillow to silence their father, especially if they had stolen his arrows to try to cast the blame on him. Or maybe Piers overheard their plans to shoot at me but didn't quite grasp it—except later, in the depths of his dreams."

"I don't know. I don't know!"

"What else did the boys overhear?"

"That the man giving the duke the pillow said something like 'She sends you this with love and hope and trust.' And 'This will seal their bargain' or some such."

"I swear I will have Norfolk arrested and imprisoned the moment I can find him!" Elizabeth announced to them all. She did not let go of Meg's arms. She felt as if she were propping her up, as if the woman would crumple to the floor otherwise. "I don't give a fig," she went on, "if our evidence is just a pillow and the testimony of eavesdropping boys, I will have him put away at the very least! Meg," she said, lowering her voice, "did Piers describe the man delivering the pillow?"

"He had broad shoulders and a leather quiver full of arrows. I figured we'd get more out of Piers later, when you questioned him, too, but he didn't see his face clear. Oh, what if that's the same one's been killing men that took my Piers?" she wailed, and burst into tears.

Though Elizabeth longed to comfort her, she motioned for Ned to tend to his wife and stepped away. On the far side of the room, the queen huddled with Cecil and Drake, speaking over Meg's loud sobs.

"I would wager a kingdom—which indeed I am doing—that the man who brought the pillow is the lethal archer who has dogged our steps since Loseley House, and he, as well as that pillow, links Mary, Queen of Scots to Norfolk in complicity of treason."

"It's all starting to come together," Cecil agreed, nodding, "and, I fear, it leads straight to the launching of the insurrection."

"This messenger, who may also be the murderer," she went on, "probably stole Tom Naseby's bolts, with which he hit Fenton, and he may be the one who pilfered two longbows from Hern the Hunter, so that he could plant evidence against him if he needed to throw us off again. It's me he's been toying with, but the key is that the boys will be able to link that murderer to Norfolk. And since Piers must have overheard the words clearly, it cannot be that Spanish archer—unless it was his interpreter speaking for him, but then why would he have a quiver full of arrows?"

"I'd guess that the interpreter could be the archer," Cecil said, "except we know the approximate date that Juan de Vila entered England with the interpreter. That would not have given either of them time to head north to see Queen Mary and receive and then deliver that pillow. Besides, her so-called host Shrewsbury cannot be so dimwitted that he'd allow a Spanish-speaking man access to her, however much 'tis rumored the woman is skilled at wrapping men around her little finger."

"You're right about the timing," Elizabeth agreed. "As for who is allowed to see her and who is not, she hasn't been a strictly held prisoner—so far. Who knows who has had access to her? The point is, what we must do is learn for certain who the messenger is." Her gaze met Cecil's frown. "What?" she prompted. "What are you thinking?"

"That, if he's a courier, Keenan might know the man."

"It can't be, can it," she said, gripping her hands tightly together and lowering her voice, "that Keenan could *be* that man?"

"No, impossible," he insisted, frowning. "He hasn't been sent north for months and knows naught of archery, not that I've ever heard. I keep him busy. Before this progress began, he was in and out of Hampshire, helping to arrange things for us, but was not ordered north."

Detesting herself for even bringing up that possibility, she sighed with relief. All she needed was for someone she trusted—someone she'd included in her Privy Plot Council meetings who knew entirely too much—to turn traitor. Keenan had been busy working his way up with Cecil and could not have had time to deliver something on the side to Norfolk even if pretty, flirty Mary of Scots had begged him to. Could he? The man could ride like the very devil.

"You're right," she said, "but we shall question Keenan about couriers he's seen in the north or en route there. And here we just sent him away again—and to our enemy."

"He'll be our eyes and ears there as well as our hands," Cecil assured her. "I can vouch for what a fine job he's done with that."

"And I can vouch for you, so there you are. That means we're back to closely examining Captain John Hawkins, when I can ill afford to find him guilty, either."

She sank into a chair. "But first," she went on, looking from Cecil to Drake, "I believe the better, quicker way to find someone to question is to observe the next secret meeting in the Church of the Holy Ghost. Wait here. I'll be right back and explain. I think the answer to the who and when is still encoded in that green pillow, if we can but learn to read the signs and symbols."

She went into her bedroom, got down on her knees—as she never would to another person—and pulled out the pillow. She carried it into her outer privy chamber and over to the bright window light where Ned had been comforting Meg, though he'd now taken her from the room.

Flipping the pillow over, Elizabeth studied the embroidered bird—the dove of the Holy Ghost, as she now believed. "Cecil," she said, "if you still have that magnifying glass John Dee gave you, please fetch it."

"What is it, Your Grace?" he asked, squinting down where she looked. "Jenks, you always had hawk's eyes. Come over here and try to read it in the sun while I fetch the glass. It could be some sort of spy's code."

Spy's code? the queen thought as Cecil hurried out and she, Drake, and Jenks squinted at the bird in the sunlight streaming through the window. Those people meeting at night in that church could well be spies for the lords who were planning to coordinate a rebellion in the north. Surely, if it caught fire there, they would need help from the south, too—and two of her hosts here in the south, Sir William More and the Earl of Southampton, could be in league with them, sending their own spies or agents to meet in the church at the crossroads of north and south.

"That wreath looks like a bunch of scratchings 'til you read them all sideways by turning the pillow," Jenks said, doing exactly that.

The queen gasped as he slowly rotated it. "Numbers?" she said. "Are those tiny numbers attached to each other? Some sort of secret code, indeed, maybe matching numbers to letters of the alphabet to give people's names or key places? Read them to me as best you can," she ordered, rushing to the table for parchment and ink.

"Looks like they just repeat over and over, Your Grace. It's a wonder the Scots queen could make them so fine and small."

"Can you read them, man?"

Cecil rushed back in with his glass, even as Jenks read out, "Starting at the place the bird's beak touches the wreath, it reads eight, two, six, six, nine, one, two. Then it starts over, eight, two, six, six, nine, one, two."

"Yes," Cecil said, huddled with Jenks, holding his glass over the pillow. "We should have tried magnification before, but it just looked like a thorny wreath."

Elizabeth ignored them now, quickly transposing numbers to letters and words. "*H-b-f-f-i-a-b*?" she cried. "It doesn't spell anything, though with the three vowels, I supposed it could be made to form several words as a sort of anagram. I had thought it might be a word like *r-e-v-o-l-t-s*, but there's no such pattern. How I wish you had brought one of your cryptographers along, Cecil."

"Could the numbers stand for people's names?" Drake asked, as he and Cecil came over to sit across the table from her.

"Or the names of houses or shires the conspirators dwell in?" Cecil said. "The *H* could surely stand for Hampshire and the *F* for Farnham, or Fareham, for that matter."

"Your Grace," Jenks put in, bringing the pillow to the table, "I know this is important, but I would ask permission to go help search for the boys—and be with Ursala. I don't think she'll come apart like Meg, but—"

"Yes, of course. But Jenks, I do believe we might find the boys another way than random, panicked searching. Tell both Meg and Ursala I will do my very best."

"I fear someone thinks they know too much," Jenks said, as he bowed, went out, and closed the door behind him.

"Your Grace," Cecil said, keeping his voice low, "if someone involved in all this snatched those lads right out of this house—"

"Or Piers ran into his brother, they went outside, and the wrong person overheard them talking about what they'd seen," Drake put in.

"Neither of you has to tell me that someone in my household is not to be trusted, even with Norfolk gone," she said, frowning and steepling her fingers before her nose.

Please, dear Lord, she prayed, *don't let it be Robin who's betrayed me from within. Don't let him be another of those who want to give my power and people to Mary of Scots.* Years before, Elizabeth had considered having him wed Mary to control her, but the Scots queen had haughtily rejected him as the English queen's rejected suitor—and as only her master of the horse. Surely he didn't have his hand in all this now, just to frighten her—or even to scare Drake away. No, not him, for there were numbers of others who—

Then it hit her.

"Drake, Cecil, what if these are just numbers?"

"What?" Drake said. "They are numbers."

"But what if they signify a date on which something occurs? Mary knew of it, was looking forward to it, maybe the beginning of the rebellion."

"Read out the numbers again, Your Grace," Cecil prompted.

"Eight, two, six, six, nine, one, two."

"The eighth month—August," Cecil intoned. "Two, six could mean the second, the sixth, or—"

"Or the twenty-sixth," Drake said, "which is today."

"And the year, sixty-nine," she said, "this year. Today—if we are correct, that signifies today! What about the one and the two?"

"The time the rebellion commences?" Cecil asked. "One or two of the clock—or twelve, as she may have combined those earlier numbers."

Elizabeth stood. "Lord Sandys says the forbidden Catholic meetings sometimes start around midnight, ones held in the Church of the Holy Ghost on the edge of town. It may be all wrong—a long shot—but I'm getting desperate. I believe we should visit the church at midnight tonight."

"You can remain here while Drake and I go with a full contingent of guards to arrest everyone in sight," Cecil said, as he and Drake scrambled to their feet.

"But what if it is just envoys or representatives they send?" she demanded. "I want not the ones left holding the bag but the ones who made the bags—and the pillow. So here's what we are going to do, and neither of you will gainsay me on this."

Chapter the Nineteenth

THE QUEEN DONNED MEN'S GARB AGAIN THAT NIGHT, but when he saw her, Cecil reacted as if she were a mere lad.

"Just send the troops, Your Grace, and wait here with me. I insist you stay safely here, or at least that I go with you."

"We've argued this before, and I have said that I must go in person and you must stay here to oversee things. Desperate doings demand desperate measures. Just be grateful I have not decided to lead the army I may soon be sending north to stem a full-fledged rebellion. Besides, troops are noisy and could scatter and alert whoever appears—if anyone appears. We still are not certain we have read that pillow aright, so this, like all else we've tried lately, may be an exercise in futility."

"If your purpose is to merely gather information, let Ned and Jenks go."

"I am taking them with me. Dear Cecil, I shall be careful. I do not intend to go into the church to wait for the arrival of the plotters, for I could be trapped there. I shall stay outside by the woods until they are inside, then hide behind the effigies to eavesdrop."

"But the woods have been so dangerous that—"

"All right. Another compromise. Wearing Drake's armor, I shall not go into the woods but hide myself behind the stones in the old graveyard until our enemies enter. Then I shall go into the church via the tunnel," she rushed on, perhaps now trying to convince herself as well as him. "Drake will lead me in, since he knows where its entrance is. If the Naseby lads can pull off eavesdropping, the queen can, too."

"So you could send Ned ahead of the conspirators into the church but stay behind yourself with Drake and two guards."

"I'll stay behind with Drake and Ned and send Clifford and Jenks inside. All will be armed. If I deem those assembled worth trapping rather than just following after we hear them speak their piece, we can simply seal their secret escape and have them caught like rats in a trap in that barred and locked church—and then I'll send for a full troop of guards. All will be well, you'll see."

Elizabeth used the servants' stairs and plunged out into the dark night. She met her men beyond the gatehouse where Jenks held the horses.

"How are Ursala and Meg?" she asked them.

"Ursala is trying to keep up Meg's spirits," Ned reported, "but she's just staring off into vacancy again."

"We'll find the boys," Elizabeth promised, as Jenks gave her a boost up to ride astride. "If we don't learn where they are from listening, we will seize one of the conspirators and force him to tell us."

That's if anyone comes tonight, *her inner voice taunted her, and if* the plotters know where the Naseby lads are and haven't dispatched them *one way or the other already.* Talk about playing fox and geese—this indeed might be a wild goose chase.

She had not reckoned on the full moon rising, but it suddenly rolled over the horizon like a ripe peach, bathing the scene with an eerie, pale red-gold light. At least her party was all in black. The armor of Drake's she wore could catch the glint of moonshine, but she kept her inky cloak wrapped close about her.

It was somewhere near ten of the clock when they arrived and Jenks hid their horses, tethered far back in the thick stand of oaks. No lights emanated from the church, but she wasn't certain they would show anyway with the thick ivy over the window. Still, somehow Lord Sandys and others in town must have known when outsiders were meeting here at night.

"Jenks and Clifford, time for you two to get inside," she ordered. "Go quietly and carefully, lest someone else has gone in before you, and remember, I said the wooden door leading up from the crypt into the church shrieks like the very devil."

"Yes, Your Grace," Jenks said. "I have the kitchen grease right here for the hinges so's you won't make a sound when you open it later to hear what's going on."

"Good. Though we can use no lights, perhaps the full moon will help. Conceal yourselves behind Sandys's parents' effigies, the ones in the corner. Should our visitors hold some sort of service, it's conceivable that they might use the lectern or baptismal font, however good listening posts those would be. Remember, voices echo in there, so you must keep silent, but I warrant their words will carry to you."

Clifford and Jenks nodded. She had instructed them in all this before, but she wanted to make certain nothing could go wrong. She, Drake, and Ned watched the two of them disappear down the pitch-black tunnel, where they would have to feel their way along. Drake closed the door behind them.

"At least they won't get lost in there," he whispered in her ear. "It's a straight shot."

"I wish you hadn't put it that way," she countered, hoping her voice sounded brave, for her heart was thudding so that she kept thinking she heard hoof beats already. She almost tripped over the dead tree trunk that Sandys had mentioned he was oft tempted to roll across the entryway. It would be useful if they did need to trap the conspirators inside.

The three of them hid in the graveyard behind the tallest, straightest headstones they could find. Drake was quite close, Ned a bit farther away. Elizabeth knelt so she could peer over, but her left calf muscle threatened to cramp, so instead she sat on the ground with her back against the stone.

She glanced at Ned, huddled with his arms around his bent knees and his head down. She knew he balanced on the edge of despair. How much he had meant to her over the years she'd been queen. Loquacious but loyal, too full of himself, but finally able to admit he loved Meg so that he found domestic joy as well as accolades for court drama— and then to lose so much, his son, and for a time his wife. She prayed all would go well to recover Piers for them and Sim for Jenks. Jenks, too, had been with her from the first, her bodyguard once in bitter exile and now—

She jumped and strained to hear each time a new noise came to her ears. The hoot of an owl, the breeze in the branches, even the cry of a cuckoo in the oak trees. Four headstones away, Drake jolted at what sounded like the scream of a hawk, which sent shivers up her spine.

Time went by. Why didn't someone come? If this plan

went for naught, at least she was soon heading back toward her own protected palaces, but she could not bear to leave all of this unsolved and unpunished. And with that rebellion brewing . . .

A horse whinnied nearby. Could the sounds of their own mounts carry this far?

She twisted around and got back on her knees. Mounted men—she couldn't tell how many—reined in near the woods. Just two of them? Then she heard more hoofbeats, coming from the direction of the town. Yes, at least three more. How long had she and her men been here waiting? It could indeed be just before midnight, for, as the moon had risen in the sable sky, it had shrunk and faded to palest, coldest silver.

She accidentally clunked the chest piece of her armor against the gravestone. She froze, but the men didn't seem to hear it. The sibilant sounds of their whispers floated to her on the night breeze, but she could not pick out distinct words. Another man arrived, a lone rider in a cape and hood, who seemed to emerge from the woods.

"Ah, our hawk's here, too," someone said, as the lone man dismounted. Elizabeth sucked in a sharp breath; her eyes widened, trying to pierce the darkness. She saw he did not wear a cape but rather a doublet with padded shoulders and flowing sleeves so that it seemed he had wings—and he sported a hood, one that, like the ones her own stable of falcons wore, completely covered his head but must surely have slits or holes for his eyes and mouth. He was about Robin's height and build and, as he dismounted gracefully, his moon-silvered silhouette showed he carried some sort of bow and bore a quiver of arrows on his back.

The group of men—six of them—lit candles and quickly

vanished into the mouth of the tunnel as if the graveyard had swallowed them.

Meg couldn't bear the waiting. Ned had said the men they went to find tonight could know something about Piers, like who had taken him, where he was held.

If that was so, why had she been left behind again? This time, not even to stand in the queen's stead but to be shuffled aside when the one who needed her most in the entire world was out there, missing her—or, if worse had come to worse, she would be missing Piers, like her little baby Ned, forever.

She glanced across the small room at Jenks's wife, Ursala. Holding her little Bessie on her lap, she'd fallen asleep from exhaustion, slumped over on the stool with her back against the wall. Meg could see her friend had been crying, but what good did that do? Meg had cried herself sick when little Ned died, but that did not help. Only action was worthwhile, even if that action was to follow her boy—her boys—in death.

After all, the queen always acted. She might fume and fuss, rant and rave, but she always acted. Nor did she do what men advised her. Despite the danger, she did not stay here when Cecil told her to. Though she was queen and Meg just an herb mistress, Elizabeth of England set the tone for all women, if they only heeded her ways. Yes, discretion could be good, but decisions and deeds were what got results, that was the lesson Meg had learned.

It wasn't a long walk into town, she thought, trying to buck herself up even more, and she knew that the Church of the Holy Ghost was on this side of little Basingstoke.

Meg stood in one slow motion and took a step to see if

Ursala would awaken. She and Bessie did not stir. Meg walked toward the door. Lifting her cloak off the hook on the wall, as a last thought, she took with her the bow and quiver of arrows by the door that Ned had used in his Robin Hood play. They were no doubt just for the stage and show, and she'd never shot such a thing, but if she had to, she would.

Elizabeth waited only a few minutes, lest someone else should come who could trap her between him and the others. She was anxious to go inside, to hear what was being said. Motioning to Drake and Ned to follow her, she stood and moved toward the mouth of the tunnel.

She was prepared for it to be absolutely black inside, but she was surprised to see that a candle had been wedged in the clay floor just inside the door and another farther on. Did that mean someone else was coming, or just that the men inside were used to lighting their way out? Should she leave Ned behind as a watchman? No, she wanted both Ned and Drake with her. Everyone had been so prompt here, she decided they were all inside.

Bending to avoid scraping the low, earthen ceiling—some of it with tree roots sticking through like gnarled fingers—they hurried down the length of the tunnel. Their good luck held! The men inside had not closed the door to the Sandys crypt but had left it wide open, as well as the door to the stairs. They were not whispering inside, either, but evidently talking full voice.

Were they speaking Spanish? she wondered, and stopped so quickly in her tracks at the bottom of the narrow steps up that Drake hit into her, then steadied her with his hands.

"*Ave Maria, gratia plena*," everyone was chanting in a dissonant, singsong melody she had not heard since her royal sister had forced her to attend Mass years ago. Not Spanish but Latin. Were they only here to have a Catholic service? They kept repeating that single phrase over and over.

Then a voice cut in, "Hail Mary, the next queen of England, too!"

Drake's hands tightened on her shoulders before he evidently realized he should let go. She was regretful he did, because she was tempted to charge up the stairs, shouting at the traitors that *she* was their God-given queen, not their beloved Mary.

"Best we get down to business," another man said.

Their voices carried well, though they echoed strangely. She knew she'd have trouble recognizing them with the reverberations in here, so she was going to creep up the stairs to look through the effigies to catch a glimpse of the men, especially that one garbed like a hooded hawk. She'd known he was no phantom, but who was he? Four candles flickered on the altar, but that hardly helped.

"Everything is set to go within a fortnight," the same man continued. "High and low will rise to fight under her banner as we sweep south toward London. Unless, that is, the Hawk and his—ah, his owner can swoop in for the kill soon, to save us all the trouble."

Several men laughed briefly, gruffly. She picked out one distinct snicker. How dare they jest about regicide—murdering their rightful queen!

She peered between the head of the male effigy and the stone pillow on which he stiffly lay. The conspirators stood in a circle before the altar, all dressed in black, like a coven of warlocks. From here, by glancing along the wall, she could also see Jenks and Clifford, crouched behind the next pair of effigies, ready to spring. Yet she could not see the speaker's face. If she could, the few candles they'd brought in with them would do little to illumine his features, anyway. It had been dim during the day in here, but it was all deep shadows upon shadows now.

What she could see if she shifted slightly to the right was the Hooded Hawk figure, at least his mask, if that's what it was. Could that be Norfolk himself, and he did not want to be identified even among these men? Surely—surely it was not Robin. If he would but speak, perhaps she could tell, or Drake could recognize his cousin Hawkins's voice if that were he.

As if the very stones in here breathed out chill breath, she began to tremble. Could the man wear the hood because his visage was as ruined as old Hern the Hunter had said? A stag had gored his face, so he always wore the hood. However the man's face under there looked, he was the murderer, she was sure of it.

"We shall ride to free Her Majesty from whatever castle in which they hold her," a new voice said. "Then she will be well protected behind our vanguard as we move south, picking up new recruits for the cause as we go, those who will rise to throw off what the so-called new religion has spawned. We shall forge an alliance with the Spanish and return this land to its rightful faith and ruler . . ."

It was almost too much for Elizabeth. She longed to scream at them, to seize from Drake the sword she had insisted he muffle with a cloth in its scabbard and attack them on her own, hacking them apart.

"But you let me speak for zee Spanish, no?" came another

voice, one heavily accented. "I give—ah, how you say—zee word of zee *magnifico rey* Phil-eep-ay *Segundo* to give sheeps."

"Juan means ships," another voice put in. "We have here signed pledges of aid from the Spanish King Philip."

"Then all we need," the first voice said, "is to hear how the current queen is holding up under the barrage of the Hooded Hawk to ruin her bold attempt to defy us on this summer progress to stir the hearts of the people, so—"

It was the last thing that made sense. Behind her a strange voice bellowed, "Look out, men! You're being watched from behind this tomb!"

Chaos crashed around her. Another plotter must have come in through the tunnel. He scraped out his sword as Drake drew his to fight him off. Metal clanged; men shouted. As the traitors before the altar rushed to help their comrade, Jenks and Clifford, swords raised, leaped from behind the other effigies to take them on.

In the resulting clash, the man who had shouted grabbed at Elizabeth. He missed as Drake shoved him away, but the stranger had her cap in his hand; her hair spilled free.

"A woman!" he shouted. "A woman here!"

In but a moment's swordplay, Drake ran him through, then grabbed her wrist and shoved her down the steps behind him as he took the next man on.

"Go!" Drake shouted in the clamor. "I'll hold them on the stairs. Go!"

She half ran, half fell down the staircase to the crypt and dashed in, only to hit her hip on the corner of the first lead casket. In the return of darkness after the candlelight above, she blindly felt her way along, past the other caskets, smack into the tunnel door she was certain had been left open. That man who gave them away must have closed it behind him. Where was the latch to it? Sandys had had trouble with it yesterday, and he'd had a lit lantern in his hand.

At first when the paving stone over the top of the crypt shuddered and began to roll aside, she felt relief. Clifford and Jenks must have prevailed above, however badly they were outmanned, and they were opening the ceiling crypt to help her.

In the dimmest of candle glow from above, which seemed so bright at first it almost dazzled her, stood two men. One went back to the fight, so only a huge, broad-shouldered, hooded figure loomed overhead, holding a crossbow and drawing a bolt from his quiver.

The noise of a sword fight and the grunts and cries of men still sounded above her. Should she scream for Drake and give herself and him away, or would the others all charge him and her then? Besides, she could hear him still fighting on the stairs. Surely someone would see and stop this demon who bent his knees to peer down at her.

He cranked the bowstring taut with his foot in the rachet stirrup, fitted a bolt, and aimed at her. She leaped aside, crouching behind the closest casket, pressing to the wall next to the escape door as he shifted his position above and let the arrow fly.

It zinged at her, glanced sideways off the casket, then her chest armor, hit the wall somewhere, and skittered beneath her feet.

"Like a hawk diving at a pretty little dove," he said in a guttural, unearthly but taunting voice. "Or like fish in a barrel instead of a queen in a coach."

He knew it was she! Was he supernatural?

As she heard him crank the crossbow again, she felt madly

for the latch, found it, and lifted it as the second arrow pinged into the crypt with a clatter against a lead casket. Elizabeth yanked open the door and tore down the tunnel, praying not only that she would be safe but that her men and her dear Drake would somehow escape the overwhelming onslaught.

Six of them to their four, Drake thought, now that he'd killed the one who had touched the queen. Not good odds, but he knew the queen's men would be skilled with a sword, except perhaps that actor of hers, and if he ended up dead, poor Meg would be bound for Bedlam at best.

He parried, thrust, moved, putting everything into it. Despite the fact the enemy had left four candles burning on the distant altar, it was so damned dim in here. Worse, he had to fight up the steps while his opponent leaned down to hack at him.

He was quite sure this was the Spanish-speaking man he battled, and that fed his fury. He imagined he fought hand-to-hand combat on the *Judith,* that he had stayed to fight in the battle with the Spanish dogs, but he knew he had to get to the queen, escape with her to protect her. When their swords met and held for one moment, Drake heaved the Spaniard away, shoving him up the steps, where he tripped him and ran him through. He'd half expected it to be someone he'd recognize, but it wasn't.

"Jenks, Clifford!" he shouted. "Lights out! To the tunnel!"

The two big men took his meaning. Jenks ran his weapon through the altar candles. When one rolled to the stone floor, still lit, Clifford, swinging his sword in a wide arc to hold off his attackers, stomped it out.

Just before he fled, Drake thought that the full moon through the ivy-laced stained glass window looked like an evil eye glaring at him. In the dark, from memory, the queen's men raced toward the tunnel to follow her out and, perhaps, to seal the others in here.

Drake tripped over his opponent's body and twisted his ankle on the steps, then bumped into someone on his way into the crypt below. "Jenks?"

"Aye, Captain. Lead on. Clifford?" he bellowed.

"Here!" the yeoman called, and evidently swung his way down into the crypt through its open roof stone to join them. Now how had that got open? Drake wondered.

Their luck held, Drake rejoiced as they started down the tunnel, though it was now pitch-black. Had the queen snuffed the lights, or had the man who'd given them away done that?

Drake hit into the closed door at the other end so hard he bit his tongue. "Ugh!" he woofed out. "I know she wouldn't have closed it on us. Someone must have either followed her out or been waiting out there for her. Here, reach around me, one of you, to see if we can budge it."

He and Jenks tried. Again. Again, to no avail. *By my faith,* Drake thought, *since it doesn't have a lock, someone must have rolled that tree trunk in front of it, and the queen could not have managed that.*

He spoke again, though he tasted bitter blood in his mouth. "We'll have to hope we don't get sealed in here from the other end, that we can fight our way back into the church, then find a way out to reach her, and fast—for someone must have followed her outside."

"We're good as trapped here if those men be waiting for us when we go back," came Clifford's voice.

"We have no choice, no choice at all. If it weren't for her

safety, I'd have stayed to fight, not fled. Back, men. Swords raised, back."

Her brain going as fast as her feet, Elizabeth ran deeper into the woods. She wanted to flee toward the town, but who could she rouse to let her in at this late hour? The road to the Vyne was too open, and her horses tethered far into the woods.

Her first impulse had been to take one of the conspirators' horses, but they had shied away from her. No time. The Hawk pursued her. She pictured the hunting scene she'd witnessed many times: With talons outstretched, a hawk dove toward its hapless prey to rend it apart.

She ran headlong into the thick, dark woods, the last place she wanted to be chased, but if she could reach her own horses or at least hide here until help came . . .

Footsteps behind her, spitting leaves under boots. The Hooded Hawk was flesh and blood, hired by . . . By Norfolk? Her cousin Mary? King Philip or the Spanish ambassador? Someone even closer? She had no illusions now that the killer had ever pursued Drake. The murderous missiles had not come from John Hawkins or one of his men. She had always been the target, first to be terrified and now to be slain.

A cramp seized her side. She'd never outrun him. Like a great bird of prey, could he see in the dark? Closer—she was certain he was coming closer, flapping his wings.

Trying not to gasp aloud for breath, she stopped and pressed herself to the far side of a huge tree. Evidently, when he heard her steps cease he stopped, too, nearby.

The breeze rustled through the leaves above. She heard the owl cry and the cuckoo she'd noted before—and, she thought, the distant sobs of a woman, or was she just going mad in her fear?

"Here, here, here," she heard whispered, as if the forest were giving her position away. That was what old Hern the Hunter had said he heard when the Hooded Hawk passed through the woods at night before he struck: "Here, here, here."

As she sucked in shallow breaths to prepare to run again, she heard the distinctive sound of the crossbow string being stretched taut by the foot stirrup crank. She could not see him, but did he have her in his sight?

Panicked, thinking he'd be delayed by his foot in the crank, she ran.

He came after her, even as a vine snagged her steps and she went down. She hit her head on a tree root in a spot the moon shone through. Her cape splayed out; her armor not only clanked but gleamed dully.

"Here, here, here," the man whispered as he stopped and stood over her. "Here lies the present and former queen, for this must be done."

His voice was still disguised, yet did she know it?

"Get away from me. My men will catch you."

"They're trapped, just waiting to be picked off with my bow when I'm done here. Ah, if only I had one of old Hern's fine longbows I took from him at night. My grandfather taught me to shoot it well—the crossbow, too. Sadly, both are dying arts."

He laughed low in his throat at his demented pun. The demon was enjoying all this. Could someone kill simply for pleasure? Perhaps she could keep him talking until help came or she found a way out of this trap.

"You don't mean your grandfather was old Hern?" she asked.

"He knew Hern years ago and told me of the Hooded Hawk, so, off and on, I brought him back to life this summer." He began to crank his crossbow again. "I would have shot you in the heart to make it faster, but your armor is in my way. A head shot will have to do. I do regret that part of all this—such a close and easy shot."

"But why are you doing this? Did the Scots queen send you?"

"Hawks don't explain themselves. They are simply trained when young, follow their master's orders, and want their rewards."

"You—are you just a hired man, then? If so, you know I can pay you more than anyone else."

"You once called me a hireling. I didn't like that. Besides, first you'd bribe me, then take off my hood and hang me high."

"Keenan!" she cried.

"Always clever, always sly. They told me that. Then I saw it at such close range—even this close to you. Oh, I was well paid, but best of all, my skill with the bows was finally appreciated—feared. I'd rather send my own messages instead of carry them for someone else, and this is what I say: The true Catholic Church must rule not only France and Spain but England and Scotland, too . . ."

He raved on as if a dam had been loosed, but he also lifted the crossbow at such close range and aimed it straight for her head. She raised a hand to ward off the bolt, but she knew she was doomed.

Strange how pictures truly did flash through her mind. Her father's face, angry, fearsome. Her brother, so dear, and how they used to laugh together. Her beloved Kat Ashley, who had reared her in place of her lost mother. Robin. Dear

Cecil, who had been a father to her. She'd meant to honor him with a title but now never would. She had lived through so much to be queen. In this last moment of her life, she was yet queen.

"Stand back!" she ordered him, but he only leaned closer. As he moved to release the bolt, she jerked aside, he straddled her hips with his feet to hold her still, she heard a thud-twang, and . . .

As his own shot went wild, into the tree behind her, he crumpled over, writhing and gasping atop her with an arrow through his throat.

Elizabeth kicked and shoved him away and scrambled free as Meg and Piers burst from the dark thicket. Sim was with them, too, a small bow and arrow in his hands. Shaking, the lad fitted another short arrow in the painted bow.

"Wait," the queen cried. "He's down, and I want him alive."

"Din't know if I could hit him with this Robin Hood bow of Master Topside's," Sim cried. "He's lots bigger than the birds I usually hit with just a stonebow."

Elizabeth hugged him and Piers to her sides.

"Did you hear my cuckoo call, Majesty?" Piers asked. "That's how Mistress Meg found us where this Hawk tied us in the woods. When she freed us and we heard your voice, we come arunning hard as we could, but she's just been crying—can't hardly talk."

Meg's face was streaming tears, but she managed a smile through them, now on her knees, pulling Piers tight to her.

"We've got to let my men out of the tunnel or the church where they may be trapped," Elizabeth said, amazed to hear her own voice so steady. "But first, I have to know who this is for certain."

She bent over the thrashing man and tugged off his hood. Keenan indeed, his face contorted in agony. Keenan, gasping for air with a crimson throat and the boy's arrow still stuck there.

"Meg, stay here with the lads and this prisoner. I don't put it past him to fly away!"

The queen sprinted through the woods toward the tunnel entry, only to find that Keenan must have rolled the tree trunk against it. Yes, longbowmen had huge shoulders. He and someone else had rolled that paving stone off the ceiling of the crypt.

She tried to shove the trunk away, but she'd need a horse to dislodge it. She almost shouted to see if her men were on the other side, but what if her enemies had been victorious and were looking for her?

Then Elizabeth saw that the conspirators' horses were gone. Had the traitors overcome her captain and her guards and fled? She must get to her horses, ride for help on her own.

She wanted to dissolve in tears and tear her hair, but that was the weak woman in her, that part of her she must always control and conquer. Going at a good clip, she started toward the woods again. She'd tell Meg that she and the boys must stay with the man who must have worked so hard to use the legend of the Hawk to frighten her. That had surely not been Keenan's idea. No, he'd admitted he had a master. Norfolk was surely behind all this. But now Keenan had a torn throat, so could he tell her all the things she was desperate to know?

Hard hands seized her and spun her around. Before she could scream, a voice said, "I didn't know it was you, Your Grace, but I can tell by the feel of you."

She hugged him hard. "Drake! My men?"

"By my faith, beat up, cut up, but well enough. We killed two, but while we were in the tunnel trying to follow you, the rest broke out the stained glass window and fled. We escaped the same way and fanned out to look for you. We're to meet at our horses."

"We have the Hawk," she said. "It was Cecil's man Keenan, working either for Norfolk or Queen Mary, and I fear that is one and the same. Come with me."

She took his hand and led him back into the woods, realizing too late that he limped badly. "Meg?" she cried, when she realized they were lost. "Meg, call out your location!"

For one moment, she and Drake stood holding hands in the dark woods like lost children. "Lean on me," she said. "I know they are out this way." He did as she said, with his arm across her shoulders. In the unknown future, they would rely on each other, she thought, even if he were halfway across the world.

"Here, Your Grace!" Jenks said, emerging from the trees, his sword still drawn as if there were other dragons to fight. "We're over here, Meg and the lads, too, but that traitor Keenan—the Hawk—has bled out and died."

"Then I have no one to question, but I know for certain what they are planning," she said, as Jenks bent to help Drake walk and she stepped away, on her own again. "Soon I must fight for my throne, and will again and again if I must, far in the future—forever!"

Elizabeth the queen began to walk briskly, but she could have soared.

Afterword

 "ARISE, SIR FRANCIS DRAKE," THE QUEEN COMmanded, and smiled at her friend as he rose from his knees.

Cheers swelled from his crew, her courtiers, and the townfolk of Deptford, into which Drake had sailed his ship, the *Golden Hind.* Over the years, he'd fought the Spanish and returned to England with booty from their great galleons and exotic gifts from afar. They called him *El Draco* now, the Dragon. He had just returned from a three-year voyage, far beyond the Indian Ocean, for he'd circumnavigated the globe, which announced to allies and enemies alike that Elizabeth's England was a power to be reckoned with.

"You may keep the sword," she told Drake with a smile, "for you may yet need a supply of them in your queen's service."

"I have never run from a fight since you took me on, Your Grace, and never shall, even if King Philip sends that armada as he's been threatening. We shall put it down just as you did that Northern Rebellion years ago—and the threat of the Hooded Hawk."

"Sometimes I yet regret signing Norfolk's death warrant, but he never ceased plotting as often as I pardoned him."

"Some say if you could be convinced to have one cousin executed, the warrant for Queen Mary could also—"

"No! However much she yet tries to connive against me, I cannot have her beheaded. A woman beheaded—after my mother was—Do not speak of it if we are to be friends."

"I would be your friend forever, Your Grace."

"We shall survive and thrive together," she promised, looking into his eyes, then turning away toward the others. Drake's proud but shy wife, Mary, was here, beaming. They had no children, either, something else he and the queen shared.

Sim Naseby, Drake's cabin boy for nearly ten years and now a full-fledged sailor, stood amidships with his brother. Piers was going out soon from Ned's troupe with his own company, the Queen's Countryside Players. Meg was sad for that, though her eleven-year-old twin daughters, somehow conceived on that perilous summer progress to Hampshire, kept her busy.

"You've done a fine job chasing our enemies at sea, Drake," William Cecil, elevated earlier in the year to the peerage as Baron Burghley, said, and clapped the captain on the shoulder.

"Chasing and catching, but not yet conquering, my lord. By my faith, I have dedicated myself to that cause, just as Her Majesty has devoted herself to her people."

"Well said!" Elizabeth told him. Then she added more quietly, "But on clear days like this, Sir Francis, I'd almost rather go sailing."

Since her beloved England was becoming such a seagoing nation, she oft thought of her work as sailing through the good days and the bad, the serene seas and the brutal ones, onward and outward, standing like a figurehead at the very prow of her beloved ship of state.

AUTHOR'S NOTE

THE GREEN PILLOW THAT MARY QUEEN OF SCOTS SENT TO THE Duke of Norfolk actually existed, with its cutoff vine and the *Your assured Mary* signature. Also, I found in my research that "Drake's movements during 1569 are unknown" (from *Sir Francis Drake* by John Dugden, p. 42). As explained below, the queen actually did take a summer progress to the exact places used in the story. Putting together those historic facts and embroidering them with my imagination got me going on the plot for this ninth novel in the Queen Elizabeth I mystery series.

I believe that Drake's debacle at the Battle of San Juan d'Ulau was actually the making of him. Just as George Washington's ignominious defeat at Fort Necessity early in his career made him a stronger, better leader, so did Drake's first big failure. This battle, by the way, has the dubious distinction of being the first fought between Europeans in the New World.

It is recorded that Queen Elizabeth always bid her ships' captains farewell with the following words, so no doubt her friend Drake heard these more than once: "Serve God daily, love one another, preserve your victuals, beware of fire, and keep good company."

Some notes about the key historic events, characters, and places mentioned in the novel:

—The Northern Rebellion the queen had feared for years began shortly after this story ends. It was put down by her by troops led by a cousin she could trust, Henry Carey, first Lord Hunsdon, who was a key character in the first book in this series, *The Poyson Garden*.

—Thomas Howard, Duke of Norfolk, was not put on trial for treason until January of 1572 and not executed until six months later, because Elizabeth so hesitated to have a relative beheaded. Cecil finally pushed her into signing the death warrant.

—Henry Wriothesley, second Earl of Southampton, was arrested in 1570, and again in 1571 and sent to the Tower in 1573. However, he died a natural death at age thirty-seven. His line lives on royally in that he was an ancestor of Prince William, grandson of the current Queen Elizabeth.

—The places the queen visited during her 1569 summer progress can still be seen today. Loseley House can be toured, though Place House near Titchfield is in ruins. The Church of the Holy Ghost in Basingstoke has recently been refurbished. The Vyne can be visited, and information about all these places is available on the Web. Farnham Castle is now the International Briefing and Conference Centre with guided tours.

Special thanks to Chris Hellier, curatorial assistant of Farnham Castle, for information on Bishop Robert Horne.

And as always, my gratitude to my husband, Don, for proofreading and for living for so long with the queen—Elizabeth, I mean.

In each of the books in this series, I focus on one particular aspect of Elizabethan life, and, of course, this time it is the sports and games of the day. Many books have excellent information on this, but one of the earliest and most complete is Joseph Strutt's *The Sports and Pastimes of the People of England*, published first in 1801.

In 1595, Queen Elizabeth I decreed that bows should be converted to calivers and muskets, "because they are of more use than bows." So, as ever, time marches on.